Eden Falls

by Richard Mindell

Richard Mindell

The Reginald vanFenwick Press
Stoughton, MA

The names, characters, places and events in this book are the product of the author's imagination and are purely fictitious. Any resemblance to actual persons, living or dead, or to places or events, is purely coincidental.

Library of Congress Control Number: 2003106805

ISBN: 0-9728169-0-9

First Edition

published by

The Reginald vanFenwick Press

Stoughton, Mass

The Reginald vanFenwick Press is a division of
The Reginald vanFenwick Publishing Co.

Manufactured in the United States of America

"If I am not for me, who will be? If I am
only for me, what am I"

__ Rabbi Hillel

Other books by

Richard Mindell

The Borschenschaft

Wind Circle Drive

The Reginald vanFenwick Press
Stoughton, MA

Chapter One

The Incident

Eden Falls, Vermont, May, 1965

They dragged him from the ball field into the woods behind the school. His face was swollen and his body was covered with bruises. His new shirt, the one his mother had given him the day before, was torn and stained with his own blood.

He was eleven years old. He had been tormented, beaten, and humiliated. He was nearly unconscious, but he still felt the heavy rope being tied around his neck. The coarse fibers gripped his skin.

The older boys hooted and shouted their approval. They were all sixteen except one, who was older. His face was concealed by a black hood. He grabbed the free end of the rope and threw it up and over a thick tree limb. He held the rope and stared up at the limb.

The young boy lay on the ground. He was exhausted. He didn't protest the thick rope around his neck.

Suddenly the hooded boy put all of his weight into a mighty pull. The young boy's head jerked back and he was yanked to his knees. His neck was on fire and the pain in his throat consumed him. His hands gripped the noose and his fingers dug into his skin trying to get between his neck and the rope.

The other boys fell silent. The hooded boy gripped the rope high above his head and pulled down again, lifting his own feet off the ground for extra leverage.

The pain shot through the young boy's spine. His head felt as if it would explode. He kicked out to find the ground, but only the tips of his toes made contact. His lungs burned for oxygen. He kicked hard and he kicked again, and again.

One of the sixteen-year-old boys took a step backward, then another boy did the same.

The hooded boy looked at them, but he held his grip firmly on the rope. Then he turned to the young boy, leaned back and pulled down on the rope as hard as he could, drawing it into his abdomen as he pulled. He worked his hands up the rope and repeated this action three more times, each time more determined than before, until the young boy's feet were nearly five feet off the ground. The oldest boy looked at his friends who stared back in disbelief. The hood concealed his smile.

The young boy's protests became weaker as he fell into a semi-conscious state. His hands lingered on the noose around his neck until they gradually let go and fell to his side. His neck bled from the noose and the damage inflicted by his fingernails.

The young boy swayed from the tree limb as the older boys watched. His head stopped pounding and his neck no longer burned. He pictured his mother's face and he was sorry he had ruined his new shirt. He saw her smiling at him. He knew she'd forgive him, but he still felt bad. He remembered she had said he looked so handsome in the shirt, that the colors brought out the color in his eyes. He wanted to say something to her but he didn't want her to see his new shirt. He wanted her to put her arms around him, just one last time. He wanted her to hold him, and make the pain go away.

His eyes stared straight ahead, wide open. He was dead.

Chapter Two

The First

Eden Falls, Vermont, March, 1997

A heavy fog settled hard in the small Vermont town of Eden Falls. It wasn't an unusual morning, as far as Vermont weather was concerned. Vermont valleys are often shrouded in a thick, opaque fog in the early morning hours of March and April. Mud season. The woods outside Eden Falls were like a northern rain forest. The air was heavy with moisture and a near-impenetrable mist hung between the trees, yet the temperature was a brisk thirty-two degrees.

Thomas Downey had lain in bed the previous evening watching the weather forecast on the eleven o'clock news. He'd watched with great interest, even though he knew Vermont weather was too fickle to rely on a Gary Pearl forecast.

Gary Pearl was the WVTV weather anchor. He had what was generally regarded as the worst job in Vermont, predicting the Champlain Valley and Green Mountain weather. Pearl traced a huge, slow-moving front as it moved eastward across New York State. He stood in front of a large computer-generated map of the northeast and pointed to a large band of unsettled weather moving eastward across the Great Lakes and headed directly for New England. The front contained a lot of moisture and promised to deliver a saturating rain for all who were in its path. The heaviest rains were expected to fall in northern New York State and northern Vermont, then the storm's worst punch would move up the St. Lawrence River into eastern Quebec and the Maritimes.

"We're gonna get wet!" Pearl said. "No two ways about it, folks." He described how the storm had dumped nearly two inches of rain on Messina earlier in the evening and had caused locally severe flooding on the New York side of Lake Champlain. Pearl said he thought it was some sort of a record but he wasn't sure. "The full force of the front is expected to hit us before dawn. Steady, hard rain is your official Gary Pearl forecast for Thursday." Pearl said the chance of precipitation was one hundred percent. He was right.

Downey eased himself out of bed early the following morning. He was a tall man, about six-three, and rail thin. His dark, deep-set, Mediterranean eyes were the first feature you noticed when you looked at him. They were the eyes of a much older man who had seen too much of life. His black, short-cropped hair always looked neat, even when he slept. It was a rich black that glistened in the daylight. He was clean-shaven, average looking, and, except for his eyes, he was able to blend in. That was the object, to be left alone.

Thomas Downey didn't want to wake his wife who didn't have to get up for another hour and a half. He looked over at her, then shifted his eyes to the clock radio on the night stand next to the bed. Five forty-five. Good, he said to himself. He didn't use an alarm clock. He never did. An alarm clock would wake Leah. Besides, so strong was his self-discipline that he could awaken at whatever hour he desired without artificial stimuli.

He slipped out from under the covers and stood next to the bed. He quietly opened the window and inhaled the saturated air, the white air, Vermont air, filled with the smell of rain and the sweet scents of early spring. He turned away from the window, sidled his way to the edge of the bed and counted to eleven as he walked across the room toward the closet door. The faint light of pre-sunrise lit his way. In the middle of winter, when the days were short, he had taken the same eleven steps, each morning, in total darkness. He had taken them a thousand times on mornings just like this so Leah could sleep. He could take them with his eyes closed, stopping just a few inches from the closet door every time. He never stubbed his toes. Eleven. He had rehearsed them over and over again in his mind during the past few days, measuring every movement. There was no room for error.

Eleven. His toes stopped about an inch from the closet door. He reached for the light switch to the left of the door and flicked it on. Light escaped through the space between the door and the floor. Downey looked at his wife who was still sound asleep. He opened the door, being careful not to let more light into the bedroom than necessary. He moved around the door and entered the large walk-in closet, quickly closing the door behind him. He dressed in a pair of insulated long johns, wool hunter's pants, two wool sweaters and two pairs of wool socks, then he opened the closet door to go back into the bedroom.

The door hinges were silent. Downey had applied a drop of household oil to each one the day before for good measure. He shadowed the light with his body and flicked off the light switch, then he moved carefully past the bed and Leah and into the hallway. He slipped past his son's bedroom and walked quietly down the stairs. His thick wool socks muffled the sound of his footsteps.

At the bottom of the stairs, Downey turned left and felt his way down the hallway into the kitchen. A small fluorescent light over the stove partially illuminated the kitchen and mudroom. The old floorboards squeaked terribly, but Downey knew where to step to avoid hitting the noisy spots. He stopped and bent over to put on his shoes.

At once he was greeted by a large dog, breed unknown, who knew it was too early for a family member to be up. Like all dogs, however, he was curious and would never pass up an opportunity to see what was going on. With Downey bent over to lace up his shoes, the dog licked him on the side of the face. It was a loving kiss, the soft pink tongue cutting a wide, moist swath up the left side of Downey's cheek, past his nose, over his tightly closed left eye and all the way to his hairline.

Downey fought his desire to acknowledge the animal. The dog sniffed Downey and licked him again, a less enthusiastic peck on the forehead. Once again, Downey refused to look at the beast who lingered for a moment as if he were unsure about what to do next. Then, as Downey hoped, the large animal gave up and ambled back to his blanket without making a fuss to await the usual coincidence of light and human noises that signaled the right time of day to arise.

Downey looked at the dog and wondered what would happen if dogs could talk. *Yes, officer.* Downey imagined the words coming out of the dog's mouth. *He sneaked down the stairs just before dawn, put on his hat and coveralls and left.... Oh, about six o'clock.*

Downey was amused by the image, but only for a moment. Surely there would have to be a different plan if the dog could talk. He knew it would be the only cause for levity for many hours. He looked up and stared at the dog who had already fallen back to sleep. His face became sullen. "But dogs can't talk."

Chapter Three

The Law

Wojo was short for Wojohowski, Stanley T. Wojohowski, Eden Falls, Vermont, sheriff. Wojo was a giant of a man by anyone's standards. He was six feet, two inches tall and, while nobody was sure what he weighed, it was generally assumed it was in the mid-three-century range. His arms were like tree limbs and his hands were thick and weathered. He posed an awesome sight. His face looked as if it was stuffed into too little skin and his sheriff's uniform bulged at every seam, particularly the collar. He wasn't fat. He was just huge. He was as wide as two men, and locals liked to say he had the strength of a dozen farm hands.

Sheer size wasn't his only intimidating characteristic. When Wojo looked at people he looked directly into their eyes and held his focus until the others looked away. It wasn't a game, a stare-down. It wasn't contrived. It was his innate being. This was his turf. In Eden Falls, Vermont, Sheriff Stanley T. Wojohowski was the alpha male. There was no doubt about that.

Wojo was born and raised in Eden Falls, was damn proud of it and not afraid to say so. "Sixth generation Vermonter," he liked to say. "My father was born in Eden Falls in 1915, my grandfather was born here in 1893, my great grandfather born here in 1869. My great, great grandfather fought in the Civil War, was a captain in the Union army at the age of nineteen."

His wife Muriel, a smaller and slightly better-looking version of her husband, drove a school bus for the regional high school. The two grew up just a few miles from each other, "just down the road a ways," which, in Eden Falls, was like being next door neighbors. Wojo and Muriel went to grammar, middle and high school together and married shortly after graduation. It was what everyone had expected.

Muriel Wojohowski was up each morning at five-thirty and out of the house by six. She and the other bus drivers gathered in the parking lot of the new high school around six thirty and were on the road by six forty-five, sharp. Muriel was never late.

Wojo usually got up with Muriel, but he didn't this morning because he wasn't feeling well. His sinuses throbbed as he lay in bed. His head ached and he had that cottony, sick taste in his mouth. When he finally arose at the sound of her leaving, he was in a surly mood. He sat up and heard the rain beating against the window and it made him angrier. He summoned whatever energy he could muster and dragged his enormous body out of bed, stood up and looked out the window. "Shit!" He put his hand on the cold window pane and he knew the rain would be freezing on the roads. This was going to be a lousy day. He sucked a large wad of mucus up into his sinuses and swallowed it. "Shit!" He needed a handful of aspirin.

Wojo showered, put on his sheriff's uniform, strapped a leather holster and a .357 magnum revolver around his waist and went downstairs to make coffee. A large tom cat walked across the counter and was about to step onto the stove, but Wojo made a sharp hissing sound and stamped his boot on the floor and the cat shot back across the counter, jumped onto the floor and disappeared down the basement steps. Wojo filled a small pot with tap water and put it on the stove to boil. His head continued to throb. Even though the water was barely warm, he took the pot off the stove and poured its contents into a mug. Then he dumped in two tablespoons of instant coffee crystals and stirred. The mixture was so concentrated that it was beyond black; it was a muddy, swamp-like brown. A froth grew around the edges as he stirred. He looked at the coffee and put his nose up to the mug so the steam would reach his sinuses, but there was no steam. He put the mug on the counter and examined his creation. It looked and smelled frightening, but it didn't seem to bother him. It wasn't the worst coffee he had ever made. He wanted a jolt, something to wake him up. Both nostrils had closed up on him and his head felt as if it were under water. He hoped the coffee would shock his system.

He took the coffee mug with him as he walked through the pantry into the garage. He opened the door to his sheriff's cruiser, got in, and started it up. As he pulled out of the garage he heard the sound of huge raindrops landing by the thousands on the roof. They made a horrendous noise. The windshield wipers couldn't keep up with the deluge, even on high speed.

"Shit!"

Chapter Four

The First (continued)

Sunrise broke over the horizon but couldn't penetrate the heavy rainclouds. Downey finished tying his shoes and stood up. He looked over to the window above the kitchen sink. The window was black, and reflected back toward Downey what little light there was in the room. He looked at his watch, which said ten after six. He was right on schedule. He was a meticulous planner and that's the way it had to be: Thomas Downey, man of details, inevitably, on schedule.

Stepping gingerly between the squeaks, Downey went into the mudroom and put on his insulated coveralls and wool cap, which he pulled down over his ears. He reached into the far corner of the closet, behind the winter coats, and pulled out a rifle with a hunter's scope. He ran his hand along the back of the top shelf and grabbed a box of shells that he put in the left breast pocket of his coveralls. He closed the zipper on the pocket knowing the shells would remain perfectly dry.

The rifle was deadly from three hundred yards. He would be within thirty yards. How could he miss? He couldn't imagine the possibility, but the possibility still existed. There was always the chance he could flinch. He wasn't trained for this. He was a man of great intellectual capacity, not a man of action. He was a "brain" as the intelligence community might say. But this was a test of nerves as well as preparation.

How would he feel when it was over? He had asked

himself that question more times than he cared to admit. Would he become overwhelmed with remorse? Would there be a shocking realization the moment the gun went off that his life would never be the same? He closed his eyes. You can't have the bullet back once it's been fired, he said to himself. In an instant, a flash, a loud BANG, the hot metal is on its way. He wondered if he would experience an overwhelming sense of revulsion? Or worse, would he feel wonderful, euphoric? What if it feels good? he wondered. That prospect terrified him more than anything.

Downey had pondered this event for years. He had always known that it would happen, eventually, someday. He had convinced himself over and over again it was right. There would be no room for fear or guilt, of that he was certain. The more he thought about it, the more his resolve became his obsession.

He thought about his plan. He was confident he had considered every variable, everything one could possibly imagine. Details were his specialty, something he could control, unlike emotions. Fear and remorse were emotions, and emotions were things he could neither control nor comprehend. Emotions had always betrayed him and they certainly would betray him this morning if given the chance. They were not to be trusted. The timing of their intrusion was unpredictable and their path was uncertain.

Downey put a pair of knee-high rubber boots under his free arm, opened the door to the garage and walked out of the house. He closed the door slowly, gently letting the striker slip into the strike plate. They interlocked without a sound.

Downey could see well enough in the muted light to navigate his way through the garage. He had gotten up at the same time the previous morning for a dry run so he knew what to expect. He had gone through the whole routine to test his plan, and especially his mettle. Measuring his route he had noticed all the features of the woods behind his house more than ever before, especially the ones that afforded him an advantage. He had timed himself, from the bedroom to the garage, to his destination, and back. He knew precisely what to expect.

He stood at the top of the driveway, which veered off almost immediately to the right and continued for two hundred feet downhill through the woods towards the road. An S-turn near the bottom of the driveway made the house unnoticeable from the road and relatively isolated from the rest of the neighborhood. From where Downey stood at the top of the driveway, the gravel surface opened up into a flat area about forty feet by forty feet. Like most of the driveways and town roads in Eden Falls, the Downey's driveway was unpaved.

A small stream passed through the property at the top of the driveway. A sturdy footbridge built of hemlock logs and tamarack decking allowed one to cross the stream from the driveway to the horse paddock and the woods behind the house.

On the other side of the paddock there was a gate and through the gate there was a path that led back into the woods. It followed the remains of an old logging road over which skidders dragged whole trees out of the woods to a clearing down by the road. The path continued uphill for several hundred yards under a canopy of large pasture pines. Aggressive white birch, clustered like subway commuters at rush hour, flourished along the edges of the path. Deeper into the woods the pasture pines and white birch gave way to sugar maple, oak, black cherry, elm, ash, gray birch, ironwood, hemlock and cedar trees. Wild apple trees and patches of wild raspberries full of thorns grew in clearings that Downey intended to avoid. Despite the seemingly haphazard collection of species and patterns of growth, the woods behind Downey's house were nature's way of reclaiming the land once tilled by hard-working farm families who, much like Vermont's old-growth forests, were becoming extinct.

Just outside the garage Downey surveyed his clothing, his weapon and his determination. He found all to be in proper order. He retraced the morning's activities in his mind, from the moment he got out of bed to the moment he stepped out of the house. Did he shut off the closet light? Did his wife stir and look at the clock? Would she tell the police that her husband had awakened unusually early, dressed in the closet and snuck out of the house before dawn?

He had considered turning her clock an hour ahead, just in case she woke up, but that would have caused other problems and wouldn't have fooled her. He had to believe she hadn't awakened. She was a deep sleeper. But what would happen when she reached for him lying next to her and he wasn't there? He loved to snuggle up against her in the morning before he got out of bed. They would lie together, neither one saying a word, she in the fetal position and he wrapped around her. It wasn't a sexual embrace. It was physical, tactile. She filled all of his senses.

Downey trusted Leah, but she was the only one. People, like emotions, could never be trusted. They caused him pain, but not Leah. Their morning embraces sustained him until the end of the day, when the two would rendezvous in their secret chamber. He thought about Leah and the scent of her skin and how much he needed her, but only for a second. There was no time.

He paused for a minute to let his eyes adjust to the light, then headed across the driveway, over the footbridge and up past the horse paddock. It didn't take long for the cold, dank air to cause him some discomfort, but he was undaunted by the conditions. He knew he'd feel better once he started moving. He hiked across the paddock to the far gate where he stopped to put on his rubber boots. The boots were over-sized so they could fit over his shoes and the legs of his thick coveralls. Details. They were common boots worn by many who work outdoors or walk in the woods during mud season. The footprints could belong to anyone wearing a similar pair. More details. He had purchased the boots a year ago for this very occasion, so the chance of someone remembering him, like the checkout clerk at Ames, was almost zero.

The boots felt uncomfortable at first. Downey wiggled his toes and shifted his feet until they felt better. He took a few steps and made a minor adjustment. Then he looked up.

The heavy rain was an omen, a good omen, a comfort. Now well into the woods, he picked up a game trail and continued along the trail up a steady grade through second-growth woods for about a quarter of a mile. He stopped and sat for a few moments to contemplate his surroundings. He looked around, three hundred and sixty degrees, and was satisfied no one was out for an early-morning walk in the woods at this hour and in this weather, not that that was likely. Still, he couldn't be sure. He looked around again and listened carefully for a sound, any sound, other than the rain and his own heavy breathing.

With the rain increasing in intensity, Downey got up and broke off the trail and headed down a steep grade through old growth trees, some as large as any that can be found in Vermont. The spaces between these old trees were larger than in the younger woods and the forest floor was softer. The ground was covered in a foot-thick carpet created by hundreds of years of organic matter piling up in layers upon layers of soft decomposition. The carpet smelled sweet like rich organic soil, especially in the rain.

Downey remembered how much he used to love to run through the old-growth woods when he was a child, particularly in the fall when the forest floor was covered with freshly fallen leaves. He would run aimlessly until he was exhausted. Then he would fall down into the leaves and listen to his heart pound and he would smile.

At the bottom of the slope, Downey picked up a small gravel-bottomed stream that was swollen with the melting snow and early spring runoff of the Green Mountains. Little vegetation grew in the stream beds. The water was too cold and it ran too fast, especially in the spring.

Noting his exact location and marking it by aligning

three small rocks in the stream bank, Downey entered the stream and started walking with the current. He could feel the ice cold water against his feet through the rubber boots. He understood how sailors perished in the North Atlantic during World War II, set adrift in the freezing water after their ships were blown from under them by Nazi submarines. As long as he stayed away from deep pools in the stream he'd be okay. He had to keep his feet dry or risk hypothermia.

As he walked he had trouble finding smooth footing. The rocks were slippery and he had to move slowly to keep from falling. Yesterday on his practice run he had avoided the stream and now he was sorry. "Stupid!" he said. He had to keep up a certain pace or he'd run the risk of falling behind schedule and that would mean he'd have to abort.

It was a moment of self-doubt. Was he capable of doing this, or was what he was about to do reserved for other people, people who were different than he, people who were made to do this deed? Surely he was as capable as any of these people. It's such a natural thing, like birth, he reasoned. It was there, the feral side of man's nature. It existed in all of us, lying in wait for the right moment to rear its ugly face.

Downey continued downstream for several hundred yards, then stopped. He looked around. The woods were alive but still. Noting and marking his position, he took a single step out of the stream onto the gravel bank, then another. His feet didn't make an impression in the gravel so he picked up a small stick and stuck it in the ground at the precise locations of his first two steps. He made a mental note of his coordinates. He took two more steps and marked them with sticks, like the first two, then headed in a straight line at ninety degrees from the stream for several hundred yards. He continued in this direction, counting his steps until they numbered three hundred. He calculated his new position at nine hundred feet from the stream. He knew in this terrain he would cover roughly three feet for every stride. If he walked in a straight line, and kept the disruptions to his prescribed stride to a minimum by avoiding downed tree limbs, dead trunks, patches of thorny wild raspberry bushes and carpets of baby maples, which he hated to disturb, then he would be within fifty feet of where he wanted to be at three hundred paces. This was critical because he didn't want to over- or under-shoot his destination.

At the three-hundredth step he knew his calculations had been accurate. He was well within the fifty-foot margin of error he had allowed himself. All of the careful planning and the dry run the previous morning had paid off. He was still on schedule, ahead, perhaps, having picked up a few minutes once he got out of the stream. Had he wound up at the wrong spot after three-hundred paces he would have been in trouble. It would have been too risky. Someone might have seen him, or heard a dog barking, a dog that had heard him coming through the woods. But that didn't happen.

Downey paused for a moment, then started walking easterly until, at about forty paces, the peak of a house became visible through the trees. During the summer months, when the hardwoods were filled with leaves, the house would be nearly invisible from this spot. Downey slowed his pace and became keenly aware of the structure and the clearing in which the house sat. The house was a large split-level built on the side of a slope. Its owners had just repainted it a dark, chocolate brown with deep, forest-green trim. It was an unusual combination of colors but it blended in with its surroundings.

The house was unpretentious. A detached two-car garage sat at an angle off to the right. The owners had built a flagstone patio in the rear of the house. A gas barbecue, several chairs and a table were arranged on the patio. Beyond the patio was a swing set that was so rusty Downey figured it hadn't been used for many years. There was a small shed and a large pile of cut and split cordwood stacked neatly next to the shed. The wood was partially covered with a blue tarp.

The front yard was tidy except for the mud. Another pile of carefully stacked firewood grew off the side of the garage. The woodpile, like most woodpiles in Vermont, defied the laws of physics. Downey studied it and wondered why it didn't come toppling down, much like balancing forty to fifty bales of hay in the back of a pickup, he thought. A farmer might drive for miles with such a load and not a bale would shift, let alone fall off.

Chapter Five

A Wolf in Sheep's Clothing

Wojo was taking a sip of the slurry in his coffee mug when a 1987 Olds Cutlass pulled out in front of his cruiser on Route 14 about two miles north of town. The car headed in the direction of Eden Falls. The car was badly rusted and a collage of Bondo and duct tape decorated all four fenders. The Bondo remained unpainted. The car was dark red except for the driver's door, which had been replaced with a green door scavenged from a similar year and model at the local salvage yard.

Wojo followed the car into Eden Falls. It stopped in front of Toot's General Store and the driver and passenger got out.

Wojo didn't recognize either man. The driver was in his early thirties, about five feet, ten inches tall, one hundred eighty pounds, dressed in blue jeans and several layers of flannel shirts. He was soaked from the pouring rain. The other man was younger. He wore a camouflage jacket and a ratty-looking John Deere cap that was so streaked with grease and dirt that its logo was nearly unidentifiable. Both men wore unlaced Sorrell boots that were covered with mud. The two men ran between the gas pumps, up the wooden steps onto the porch in front of the building and into the store. The rain was steady and hard.

Wojo pulled up as the two men disappeared in the doorway. He stopped just a few feet behind their car, got out of his cruiser, and stood by the trunk. He reached down and picked something off the rear bumper. He studied it for a moment then got back into his cruiser and pulled off to the side of the parking area away from the Olds sedan.

The two men came out of the store a few minutes later with a couple of coffees in Styrofoam cups and a bag of doughnuts. They got back into their car and pulled out onto Route 14. Neither man noticed Wojo or his cruiser until the driver looked in his rear view mirror a mile or so out of town.

"Fuck me!" he said.

The man in the passenger seat saw his buddy's eyes looking in the mirror. He looked back to see what the problem was, then turned back to the driver. "What the fuck, it's thirty-five here," he said. "You're doing fifty. What the fuck d'y'expect?"

The cruiser's lights came on and the driver pulled off the road and stopped. Wojo didn't get out at first. He radioed the license plate into the state police barracks in Williston to check for ownership and outstanding warrants. State came back with owner: Brad Hurteau, thirty-one years old, a DUI in 1989, two speeders, one in 1991 and one in 1996, no outstanding warrants, one unpaid parking ticket issued in Burlington in 1991. Wojo also got a physical description of Hurteau which matched the driver of the Olds.

Wojo put on his sheriff's hat and finally got out of the cruiser. Suddenly his cold symptoms and pounding headache were gone. The heavy rain didn't seem to bother him. He walked up to the driver's door, slowly, purposefully, giving the car a thorough perusal as he walked. The driver had already rolled down the window.

"Good morning," Wojo said in a friendly voice. He tipped his wide-brimmed sheriff's hat. The driver looked up and smiled.

"Morning, officer."

"Can I see your driver's license and registration?"

The driver handed both to Wojo. He had removed them from his wallet while Wojo was sitting in the cruiser.

"Mr. Hurteau?" Wojo asked, looking at the driver.

"Yes, sir."

"You know how fast you were going, Mr. Hurteau?"

"I guess I was going a little too fast, Sheriff."

"Step out of the car, please." Wojo stepped back to give Hurteau room, then bent over and looked at the passenger who was about to open the glove box.

"You touch that glove box and I'll blow your fucking head off." Wojo put his hand on his gun.

Hurteau glanced into the car. He and his buddy exchanged bewildered looks. His buddy stopped instantly.

"Get the fuck out of that car!" Wojo yelled to the passenger. "And put your God-damned hands on the roof." He turned to Hurteau. "You too!" Both men complied.

"What's the problem, Sheriff?" Hurteau asked.

"Both of you slide down to the trunk, real slow. Place your hands on the trunk and spread your legs real wide."

"Why're you doing this, Sheriff?" Hurteau complained. "We're on our way t'work. What'd we do?"

"Mister, if you open your mouth one more time I'm gonna close it for you permanently." Wojo gritted his teeth. "Now get your God-damned asses back there, NOW!"

The two men slid around to the rear of the car and bent over the trunk, spreading their feet wide apart. Wojo moved directly behind them. Suddenly he balled-up his right hand in a tight fist and swung it viciously into the lower rib cage of Hurteau's buddy, putting all of his enormous weight and great strength into the blow. The sound of ribs cracking was muffled by the sickening noise of the man's breath rushing out of his lungs which had collapsed behind the broken ribs. The air carried blood and spit with it. The man slumped to the ground behind the car.

Hurteau spun around toward Wojo but he was too late. Wojo had already recoiled from the punch and grabbed Hurteau by the throat, lifting him off the ground. Hurteau grabbed Wojo's hand but Wojo's hand was like a vise. Wojo held his grip until, strong as he was, his arm could no longer support Hurteau's weight. He finally let go, dropping Hurteau to the ground next to the other man. Hurteau was conscious but having trouble breathing. Wojo stepped back and measured Hurteau. With another vicious move, he pivoted off his left foot and drove his right boot directly into Hurteau's midsection with tremendous force.

The kick drove Hurteau back against the rear bumper. His head hit the trunk hard. He slowly slid down the trunk and landed face down in the road where he blacked out.

Wojo walked around to the driver's side and reached into the car for the keys. He came around back, stepped over the two men lying on the ground and opened the trunk. Inside were two dead deer, both does, one about a year old and no more than sixty pounds. Wojo was furious. Hunting season wouldn't start until late fall. Just as he had suspected from the hair and blood on the rear bumper, the two men had been jacking deer up on Jasper Hill Road.

Both men began to stir. Wojo bent over and grabbed Hurteau by the collar and stood him up. The other man lay in pain by Wojo's feet, but he was conscious.

"Been jackin' deer this morning, boys?" Wojo asked.

Neither man responded. There was no need to. The evidence was in the trunk.

Wojo put his face up to Hurteau's. "I ain't gonna turn you boys in because if I do you'll be back out here jackin' deer next week." Wojo looked at the other man, then back at Hurteau. "Right, asshole?" He looked at the other man again. "So I'm gonna take care of you boys myself." Wojo grabbed Hurteau's right hand and found his trigger finger. With a sharp snap he ripped it back and around until all three knuckles were badly broken.

Hurteau shouted in pain and fell to his knees. Wojo held on to what was left of the finger and didn't flinch. He shifted his glance back and forth between the other man and Hurteau. The other man's face was filled with disbelief. Wojo looked down at Hurteau.

"Catch you jackin deer around here just one more time and I'll blow your fuckin' brains out," Wojo said. He held onto Hurteau's finger as he spoke.

Hurteau's face turned white but Wojo didn't let go. Instead, he tightened his grip on the finger, which was nothing more than a bag of bone fragments.

"Do you understand me?" Wojo asked.

Hurteau couldn't speak but he shook his head to indicate he understood.

Wojo let go of the finger and looked at the other man. "The same applies to you, shit-for-brains. If I see you in this town again I'll break every other rib in your body."

The man didn't respond. He was having trouble breathing and he was bleeding hard from the mouth and nose. One of his broken ribs had obviously punctured a lung.

Wojo walked back to his cruiser and reached inside for the radio. He called his assistant, Deputy Cain, and told him to come to where he had stopped the two men. "Send up an ambulance," Wojo said. "Car hit a couple of deer. Two men hurt pretty bad. Better hurry it up."

Chapter Six

The First (continued)

The driveway widened out in front of the house. Two small patches of lawn framed a walkway made of paver bricks that led to the front door. The rest of the area around the driveway was mowed once or twice a year, but it would hardly be considered a lawn by most people's standards.

Downey wanted to come out of the woods facing the gable end of the house with the front of the house to his right and the back of the house to his left. His goal was to have a clear view of the driveway.

As he approached the edge of the woods he stopped and knelt down. He took a quick but thorough survey of the house, the yard and the driveway. A light was on downstairs in what he assumed was the kitchen. That's a good sign, he said to himself. The pickup was still parked in front of the house in the turnaround. The driver's side of the truck faced Downey. That was also good.

He looked up at the sky which, despite the hour, was ominously dark. He looked at his hands. They were blue with cold even though he felt little discomfort. The pain was masked by the intensity of his concentration.

Dropping into a crouched position, Downey moved slowly, cat-like, through the smaller trees and sumac bushes at the edge of the woods, until he caught an unobstructed view of the stone wall that ran along the gravel driveway between the driveway and the woods.

The stone wall had been built a century ago by some sheep farmer and his family to separate one pasture from another. It had been repaired every spring by successive generations of farm families who had survived Abenaki Indian raids, the north country's harsh weather and all sorts of adversity, but weren't able to survive the political climate of the New Vermont.

Downey stared at the wall. He remembered the first time he had seen a stone wall strangely juxtaposed in the middle of the woods, seeming to separate nothing from nothing. Native Vermonters knew it wasn't that strange to see such things in the woods: an old car; an old washing machine; parts of an old horse-drawn farm implement thoroughly oxidized, covered in rotted leaves and barely recognizable; a milk can; a tire; an old steel toy to which some farm kid awoke one Christmas morning, or an old stone wall.

From the moment he conceived his plan he had worried about leaving a trail, something the police with their sophisticated forensic equipment might find: a piece of thread from his coveralls, a shell casing, a broken fingernail, a foot print, a drop of sweat. But he would pick up the shell casings and the rain would surely wash away everything else, and he knew the forest floor, with its soft carpet of leaves and fir needles, thick, moist and very forgiving, would return to its original form minutes after he stepped on it. Only a fool could leave a trail in this deluge, and Thomas Downey was no fool. He firmly believed he would be impossible to track.

Downey knelt behind an enormous pine tree a short distance from the stone wall. It concealed his whole body. The tree was surrounded by small sugar maples and thick clumps of young white birch trees. Several large, rotten tree limbs lay on the ground like dead warriors slain in the last ice storm, their bodies abandoned by their comrades.

Downey knew he couldn't be seen from the house. He looked down at his hands again and balled them up into a fist. He opened and closed each hand several times to increase the circulation in his fingers, switching the rifle from one hand to the other. He suffered no serious ill effects from the cold rain and thirty-five degree air temperature other than discomfort.

Despite the cold, his clothes were soaked with sweat from the extreme physical effort and the many layers of wool clothing that insulated his body. His heart pounded, a slow, deep pounding, not like the beat of exhaustive exercise, but more like the pounding of fear, or anticipation. He looked at his watch. It had taken him a few minutes less to complete the route than what he had allowed. He was, indeed, ahead of schedule.

The rain continued, steady and hard. Raindrops mixed with Downey's sweat, ran along his brow and raced down the bridge of his nose and around his nostrils. He could taste the salty mixture on his lips.

He studied the landscape in front of him and calculated the distance between the woods and the stone wall at about fifty feet. It was too far and too open to traverse. No one would see him on his way to the stone wall, but his retreat across the open area back to the woods might be compromised.

Downey looked to his left. The stone wall veered away from the driveway and headed toward the tree line. It entered the woods not far from where he crouched. There, the distance from the stone wall to the pickup truck was no more than thirty yards and the view to the truck was unobstructed. This was the spot to which Downey had been drawn during his trial run the previous morning. This would indeed be the place.

Downey duck-walked along the edge of the woods toward the new spot. He kept the thick sumac and wild raspberry bushes between himself and the house until he reached the spot where the stone wall entered the woods. A clump of paper birch saplings growing on the other side of the wall provided the perfect cover. He looked at the house and the green pickup.

His thoughts turned to Leah. She would be reaching for him in bed right now. He looked at his watch, again. He could feel the warmth of her body pressed up against his back. He closed his eyes. He felt her breath on the nape of his neck and her hand moving gently up his abdomen and resting on his chest. For a brief moment there was no rain, no cold, no soaking wet clothes, no stone wall, no house and no pickup. There was only Leah.

Suddenly a squirrel let out a harsh scream that startled Downey. The animal took an aggressive stance on a rock about fifteen feet away. It screamed again and jerked its body toward Downey as if to intimidate the larger mammal. Downey looked at the squirrel but didn't react. Instead of returning the "eeeep" he turned his back on the squirrel and the house and leaned his buttocks against a flat stone that took some of the weight off his legs. Hidden from view, he decided to rest for a few minutes.

He unzipped the left breast pocket of his coveralls and removed three shells from the cardboard box without removing the box itself from his pocket. He loaded the shells into the magazine, turned around to face the pickup and arranged himself in a comfortable position to aim and fire at his target. He placed the barrel of the gun in a crotch between two rocks on top of the wall at just the right height and pressed the butt end of the rifle firmly against his right shoulder. He wiped the sweat off his brow with the coarse cotton sleeve of his coveralls and looked through the scope.

The sweat that still dripped from his brow quickly covered the eyepiece and mixed with the steam emanating from his face to cloud the lens. He pulled his eye away and tried to wipe the moisture off the end of the scope with his sleeve, but the fabric had lost its absorbency and instead of wiping the lens clean it smeared his sweat all over the glass. Downey rubbed harder and harder and finally managed to dry the lens enough so he could almost see through the eyepiece. He put his right eye to the scope again but again it clouded up before he could focus on an image.

How could he have missed such an obvious detail?

"Stupid!" he murmured under his breath. "A stupid mistake." He had decided not to bring the rifle on his practice run the day before for obvious reasons, but he could have brought the scope. But how could he have known? Surely there had been no way of knowing or anticipating such a thing. But that was no excuse. There are never any excuses. It was a careless mistake and there was simply no room for that type of mistake. That's why some people fail and some people succeed, he said to himself in a harsh tone. Failure. Total failure.

The scope was worthless and without the scope he wouldn't dare try. He wasn't much of a marksman and he knew the odds against success without the scope were unacceptable.

For a split second he thought he might panic. It was a feeling he rarely felt anymore. The memory of a previous time in his life when he had experienced this feeling flashed before him and it upset him greatly. It was a memory he had tried to forget for years and he had been successful, mostly, until now. Suddenly it came rushing back. Panic! It was a feeling he detested, a total lack of control. He rarely took risks. He was a master planner, a master of details, and people who rarely took risks and planned everything in advance were supposed to have things under control. Only those who lacked self-control would panic, but not those who were prepared, nor those who detested emotion.

Panic was an emotion, the enemy, and there was no contingency plan for that. There was no contingency plan for a foggy lens, either. For this, there was no excuse except incompetence. His error made him angry. It would have been so easy to bring a towel to wipe the sweat off his face and clean the lens.

If his prey appeared at this moment he would not fire the rifle. His aim had to be true, deadly accurate, or he would not pull the trigger. He needed time to think.

As he sat in the rain by the wall contemplating his next move, he noticed the steam rising from his body was beginning to subside. He was cooling down. Perhaps if he tried to relax he could hasten the process. He felt relieved and began to focus on a way to dry the lens. There was still time to come up with a solution, and time to regain his composure.

He racked his brain to think of every possibility, anything with enough absorbency to dry the lens. He retraced every step he had taken from the moment he had gotten out of bed to the moment he had reached his perch. There was nothing. Every inch of his clothing was soaked with rain, except his long johns, which were soaked with sweat.

Then he remembered the box of rifle shells he had taken from the top shelf in the mudroom closet. Surely the small cardboard box would be dry. He unzipped the left breast pocket of his coveralls and reached in with his right hand. With the dexterity of a surgeon he separated the rest of the shells from the cardboard box without removing the box from the pocket. Then, careful not to let it get wet, he removed the empty box from his pocket cupping it in his palms to protect it from the rain.

Now, in a strange twist of irony, the rain was his enemy, for he needed to keep the porous cardboard dry enough to soak up the moisture from the scope when he rubbed it against the glass. He tore off a small piece of the cardboard box and placed it on the lens. Then he turned it on its side and rubbed its edge against the sweat-streaked glass, up and down, until the glass was perfectly dry and clear. It worked. He knew he had been given a reprieve.

Downey felt relieved but he realized he would only have a few seconds once he put his eye back to the lens before it would cloud up again. In such conditions that's all anyone had the right to expect. But that would do. His plan would still work. He knew he had come close to the edge, but there was no time to ponder his mistake or his own weaknesses. There was only time to sit and wait.

Moss covered most of the stone wall. Downey sat motionless and studied the irregularly shaped rocks, thinking about who had put them there and how the forest had adapted to this man-made scar. The wall was once four feet high, or higher, but frost and time having their will, the wall was now as wide at its base as it was tall, and the rocks that once lay on top of the wall now lay strewn around the ground on either side, as if rearranged there by Mother Nature to prove to the farmers that certain things were just inevitable.

"Something there is that doesn't love a wall." Downey muttered. "That sends the frozen ground swell under it, and spills its upper boulders in the sun..."

Downey had become a part of the wall. It was as if he had been placed there like the stones by the farmer years ago to hold up an adjoining stone, each dependent on the other, wedged and balanced according to their unique shape in near-perfect harmony. Downey watched as raindrops worked their way down the stone wall through the moss and lichens and tiny fissures and formed little rivulets to find their way earthward, where they might join forces with others to combine their strength and seek their way to their destiny; like the sweat that filled the pores of Downey's skin and ran down his face, following the lines that age and worry had put there.

As he waited, rifle positioned, eyes focused, Downey finally felt the cold in his hands and feet and the drenched clothing against his skin. A chill ran up his spine. Was it the cold or his conscience? Had he suddenly lost his will? The rifle felt like it weighed a thousand pounds and the cold steel began to burn his hands. His arms began to wilt, but he was determined to remain single-minded of purpose and not allow the elements to distract him. His plan did not allow for human frailty.

He closed his left eye and aimed the rifle at the driver's door. He aligned the door carefully at the intersection of the cross-hairs inside the scope. The lens on the scope didn't fog up. He took in a deep breath and let it out slowly, imagining the sensation he thought he would feel when he pulled the trigger. The scope brought his target so close that Downey could see the writing on the glass in the lower right corner of the side-view mirror. "Objects in mirror are closer than they appear."

The wind picked up and changed direction. Thousands of tiny droplets danced around the light that illuminated the front door and part of the yard. It was light enough to see clearly now, but the mist in the air and the heavy rain made it difficult to focus. Images seemed more like apparitions.

In another four minutes the sun would rise above the horizon, Downey thought, but he would already be back in the woods where daylight would appear a few minutes later than in the open. It was the perfect moment. Downey looked at his watch. "Now," he said.

As if on cue, the side door of the house opened and a heavy-set man of average height walked out holding a small brown leather notebook in his right hand. With his left hand the man closed the door behind him.

The man had a full head of thick, bushy hair, neatly groomed and graying slightly around the edges. He was wearing a light brown rain coat, a dress shirt with an open collar, no tie and a pair of dark brown slacks. A pair of rubber boots with felt liners covered his feet.

The green pickup was about fifty feet from the house. The man looked up at the dark clouds and heavy rain, pulled up his collar, retracted his head slightly into his coat like a turtle and started for the truck. He hurried, head down, following a muddy path to the driveway.

He has no clue I'm here, Downey said to himself. He doesn't have a clue. He wondered what the man was thinking at that very moment. Did he know he had kissed his wife for the last time? Was it a special kiss? Forever. Did he enjoy his last meal and was it his most favorite food? Did he say goodbye to his son? And the people he worked with? And his dog and cat? Did he put on his favorite clothes that his wife washed for him the night before. This was, after all, his special day.

The man reached the pickup and took his key chain out of his pocket. He reached for the keyhole just below the door handle. His head was square in the cross hairs of Downey's scope. He inserted the key into the slot and started to turn it, expecting the lock inside the door panel to go "click" and the door to open. Instead of a click, there was a loud bang.

His shirt collar turned bright red a split second after the first bullet pierced his neck just under his jaw. It burst open the carotid arteries, spewing shots of rich, oxygen-laden blood in rhythmic pulses out of the side of his neck. Blood poured down his collar in between the powerful spurts as his heart rested between thrusts.

The second bullet entered the man's face through his cheekbone and exited through the other side of his head, just behind his left ear. It took large fragments of bone and brain tissue with it. What remained of the man's head flew backwards. He went limp but his body seemed suspended in air as if everything had turned to slow motion. Then he crumbled to the ground, notebook still in hand. The keys hung from the keyhole in the lock in the door. Shots of blood no longer spit from the man's neck. His heart had stopped pumping.

The woods were deadly silent. Somehow they knew, the trees, the rain, all of the creatures that were within earshot. Downey methodically picked up both shell casings and eased away from his temporary home among the stones. He studied the area to see if he had left anything, a fragment of clothing, a button, a piece of cardboard from the box of shell casings, anything that could tie him to this thing they call murder. His head was clear. He couldn't remember the last time he had been able to focus on one task, to be so aware of everything around him. It was as if someone or something had granted him the senses of a cat, sounds, objects, magnified a thousand times.

Satisfied he had left no clues, Downey turned and began his retreat into the woods. The woods were his womb and the rain had become his ally once again. His movements were stealth-like, one eye and one ear focused in front of him and one eye and one ear tuned to the driveway and the house.

The deed completed, he had only to concentrate on his escape. There was no time to assess how he felt. That was a luxury he could afford later. For now, he had to put all of his thoughts into the second phase of his plan.

Instead of taking the same path back to the stream, Downey headed off to the right, down slope for about five hundred yards through another part of the woods. He came upon the stream about a quarter of a mile from the spot where he had stepped out of it coming in the other direction earlier in the morning. Once he reached the stream, he entered the water and worked his way back upstream until he came to the spot where he had carefully stepped out of the water before. He stepped out of the stream, trying to step in the same footsteps he had made the first time.

He followed these steps for about fifteen feet away from the stream, then carefully retraced them back into the stream. He had completed a triangle. He removed the sticks from the ground and tossed them into the stream, then he continued up the stream back toward the point where he had originally entered it before dawn. There, he exited the stream for the last time, kicking loose the three rocks he had aligned earlier to mark this spot. He followed the path back through the woods behind his house, through the horse paddock into his own yard. He removed the rubber boots from his feet before walking across the footbridge toward the garage.

His heart pumped again, but not like this morning. Now it pumped like the heart of an athlete. He thought about his victim, and how the blood from the first bullet had spurted out of his neck. He put his hand to his own neck as if he had suffered a similar injury. As he did he felt the elation, the thrill of what he had just done. He had anguished about how he would react. He had heard of men being unable to control themselves, of violent nausea and an overwhelming sense of remorse.

Downey felt nothing. Instead he was filled with energy and life. It was over, finally, at least for now.

Chapter Seven

Facing Leah

Downey picked up his copy of the *Burlington Free Press,* which was lying in the driveway wrapped in a thin yellow polyethylene bag. He went into the garage, set the rifle down and started to peel off his rain-soaked coveralls. His arms came out easily but his wet blue jeans stuck to the legs of his coveralls. He pulled at the right leg and nothing happened, then the left with similar results. The harder he pulled the more the garment clung to his legs and the more frustrated he became until he was ready to burst. He felt trapped and he got a sudden urge to kick out wildly and rip the coveralls off his legs.

When he realized the futility of his actions, he stopped. Beads of sweat had formed on his face and he panted for air. Was this a delayed reaction? Am I going to lose it now? He took several deep breaths and released them slowly to calm himself. Then he began to separate the coveralls from his legs by methodically rolling the thick, saturated, quilted cotton outer garment down each leg, inch by inch, until both legs were free. He opened a large wooden trunk and put his rifle and his coveralls inside.

It was the first time since pre-dawn that Downey hadn't been attached to the rifle. He looked at his hands, which had regained their normal color. He thought about the wall and the pickup and the man. Then he looked at the door that led from the garage to the house and tried to anticipate what he would encounter when he walked inside.

Leah would be up, just getting into her morning routine. She'd probably be making coffee and wondering where he was. She'd have questions.

He went over the answers in his mind. He stood in the garage, motionless, knowing this would be the most difficult part. He rehearsed his lines again. They had to sound natural. When he felt everything was just right, he put the newspaper under his arm, took a deep breath, opened the door to the mudroom, put his head down, and rushed in.

"Don't pay them," he yelled as he burst inside the house. "Don't pay them," he shouted again as he slammed the door and walked, his head still down, into the kitchen. He shook his head and picked at his clothing, which was stuck to his skin. "I had to walk down to the end of the driveway for this thing." He held up the paper and continued to pick at his clothing. "Boy, it's raining hard."

His wife glanced at him with a smirk on her face that said he looked like a clown. The meaning of his woeful appearance didn't seem to register.

"Why don't you get out of those things?" Leah suggested. She was petite, about five feet, two inches tall and one hundred ten pounds and very attractive, even in a terry cloth robe. She was six years younger than Thomas Downey, but in some ways, she was far more worldly than he. She was an assertive woman who was more than a match for her moody husband. She leveled him out, taught him how to come out of his shell.

It was her ability to reach inside of people and touch them emotionally that made her so desirable to Downey. She helped him deal with feelings he had buried deep inside and she forced him to do things for himself for the sheer joy of it. She breathed life into their relationship.

Leah worried Downey the most. Could he tell her about what he had done? Could he trust her not to turn him in? Of course he could, he reassured himself. But Leah was so honest. How would she react? Would she leave him and take Tommy with her? After all, who would want her child raised by a murderer, even if the murderer was the child's father?

These thoughts had lingered in Downey's mind for days. The uncertainty of how Leah would react tormented him. Leah and Tommy were the most important things in his life. He wondered if she would be supportive or if she would retreat from him in a state of revulsion. That possibility scared him to death. He had to conceal everything from her, everything that had happened that morning. He knew this would not be an easy task. He knew his wife had learned to read his nonverbal signals, the unintentional ways in which he communicated his feelings to her when he was upset, or angry, or tired, or when he was in need of affection, or when he was trying to hide something from her, a little white lie perhaps, or something major, like he had just killed a man.

Leah's intuitiveness was what worried Downey the most. Could he control his body language so he wouldn't be an open book? He knew he could be sufficiently dispassionate to fool others, but could he fool Leah? For how long? A month? Six months? He worried that lying to her would create a barrier between them. He knew what he had done had changed him, forever. He was a different man, now. He couldn't go back to being just Thomas Downey, husband, father, store owner. He was something else, a killer. How would he telegraph it to Leah? Would he slip and say something? Would she catch him looking out of the window on a rainy day, his mind obviously in some other place and time? Would she insist he tell her and would he consent in a moment of weakness or self-doubt?

He knew what he had done that morning would have an extraordinary effect on Leah as well. It was important for her to know, he had reasoned before that morning. But not yet.

"I mean it," Downey continued. He tried to sound annoyed. "Don't pay this guy."

"It was probably a substitute driver, Thomas. Do you

want coffee?" A small puddle was beginning to form around her husband's feet. Leah turned away from the coffee maker that seemed excruciatingly slow and focused for the first time on her husband's dreadful condition.

"What happened to you?" she asked trying to hide her laughter. "Where were you?" She walked over to him and started to pick at his clothing.

He raised his arms as if to embrace her but she backed away quickly, laughing, her hands cupped together over her mouth.

"No you don't!" she screamed and took another step back. "Get out of those things...look at the mess you're making. Thomas! Go into the mudroom and take those things off." She laughed.

He loved the sound of her laughter.

"You look ridiculous," she continued as she took another step back. "I know you, you were probably out there playing in the rain like a four-year-old." She looked at him and laughed again. The image of this serious man frivolously splashing around in a puddle of rainwater in their driveway obviously amused her. "Weren't you? You are a child, indeed, Thomas Downey. I'm going up to get Tommy." She slipped past her husband and ran upstairs to wake their son.

Downey went back into the mudroom and stripped. He put on a clean pair of briefs and a terry cloth robe that was hanging from a hook on the back of the door. He wiped his hair vigorously with a clean towel. Then he stepped in front of the mirror. He looked at himself and wondered if he would look different to other people. Is it like losing your virginity? Some say you can tell when a man loses his virginity. It's a special look, a glow, like the look women reportedly acquire when they fall in love, or become pregnant.

Downey wondered if it was the same with other people who did what he had just done. He didn't want to say the word, *murder. MURDER!* It was a death, but it wasn't murder. Thomas Downey was not a murderer. He continued to look into the mirror. He looked older, he thought, like his father. But his father would never have killed a man, no matter what. He turned away from the mirror. He noticed that his heart no longer pounded. The stone wall, the stream, the fogged lens, his father, all seemed like a million miles and a lifetime away. Surely he could cope.

Chapter Eight

Sirens

"I think there's a fire, Daddy," young Tommy Downey yelled excitedly to his father. "I hear sirens."

Seven-year-old Thomas Downey Jr. couldn't get down the stairs fast enough. His mother gasped as she watched him from the top of the stairs. When he hit the bottom step he flew around the banister into the kitchen to find his father.

"There's a fire, Daddy!" he yelped, as he ran to his father.

Downey grabbed his son and lifted him up for a big hug. "Probably just a chimney fire," he said, more for Leah's ears than his son's. Leah agreed.

"Can we chase it?" his son asked. His eyes were opened wide and bright and the whites were as pure as can be. He looked directly into his father's eyes.

The two often got in the car and chased the sound of sirens. Sometimes it was hard to pinpoint their origin because sounds play funny tricks off the hills. Still, more often than not, the two found the source of the alarm. It was usually nothing but a small brush fire or a burn pile that got out of hand, a few volunteer firemen gathered around the chief's car talking while a couple of their comrades sprayed water from the tank truck on the remaining embers. The toughest fires were the small grass fires that occasionally spread to a dry cow pasture. Once the petrified cow patties caught fire they burned forever and were nearly impossible to extinguish.

"It could be an accident, Daddy," Tommy interjected. "Maybe it's an amulance."

"That's am-BU-lance," his mother said. "BU, BU, am-BU-lance." She laughed and turned to her husband. "Tommy's probably right about the ambulance, Honey." "Besides, maybe you should wait until the rain dies down." Her tone became more serious. "A car went off the shoulder and hit a pole on Route 14 last night. The shoulder was completely washed out. I heard it on the news this morning. Maybe you should go in later, Thomas." She paused. "Burt's supposed to open. He'll be fine without you."

She looked directly into her husband's eyes. She stared at him. "I reached for you in bed this morning, Thomas." She moved toward him and put her arms around his waist. "But you weren't there? Are you all right?"

"I had a pretty good case of diarrhea," Downey said without hesitation. "I used the bathroom downstairs so I wouldn't wake you." He turned and grabbed up his son again in one quick playful motion. He kissed Tommy, set him down and went upstairs to shower. On the way up he yelled to Leah. "Call Burt and let him know I'll be here if he needs me. Please? I love you!"

Chapter Nine

The Investigation

Like most Vermont farm communities, Eden Falls hadn't changed much from the late 1800's to the 1970's, except the obvious technological advances from which even the remotest communities in the Northeast Kingdom couldn't hide. In the late 1960's, however, an influx of people from out of state began settling in northwestern Vermont. Most were employed by the new IBM plant in Essex Junction. An equal number were University of Vermont students from Boston and New York and Hartford, Connecticut, who had graduated and remained in Vermont because of the lifestyle, but the main draw was IBM. The newcomers were educated, professional people; engineers, manufacturing specialists, research and development people and the support professionals necessary to keep a plant with ten thousand employees running efficiently.

So expansive was the IBM facility that it had its own phone exchange, zip code, fire and police departments. It was, without question, the largest employer in the state, and its opening a few years earlier had had a dramatic effect on life in Chittenden County and the surrounding communities, including Eden Falls.

Until the IBM plant was built, everybody in Eden Falls knew everybody else. A change in the makeup of the community of any sort like a birth, a death or a new family moving into town was a major event. Family farms, handed down from generation to generation, dotted the landscape. There were no supermarkets in Eden Falls. There were few, in fact, in the whole state. Everybody shopped at the local store which usually anchored the town center.

Toot's General Store, in Eden Falls, had been in operation since 1928. It carried everything from meat and groceries to hardware, guns and ammo, clothing, gifts, beer and wine, magazines and books, auto supplies, school supplies, camping supplies, household supplies, canning supplies, sugaring supplies, pet food, fencing, over-the-counter pharmaceuticals and beauty aids and just about everything else anybody could ever want or need. Toot's General Store was also the local post office. Mildred Toot was the town notary. Alfred Toot was the town fire warden. If you needed something after hours, you could call Mildred and she'd put it out for you. You could always pay her the next day. Gas pumps, air, propane and kerosene and a creamy stand during the summer months completed the package.

Stores just like Toot's could be found in every town center throughout Vermont. Once inside, one would be hard-pressed to tell one old Vermont general store from another. The wide pine floorboards had dips and rises and creaked under every step. Dust covered much of the old glass and wood display cases that had been installed decades earlier. Old-timers knew if you dug far enough back on the shelves you could find merchandise that had been priced years before and had never been repriced, and you could buy it for a fraction of what it would cost today. The Toots had a policy of letting their customers buy things at the original ticketed price. If the customers found a bargain, more power to them.

Toot's General Store was also the place where people went to network. In the early morning hours, members of the Eden Falls road crew gathered inside to drink the first of many pots of coffee that were consumed every day by customers and friends. They ate a few doughnuts, spun a yarn or two, talked about the weather and looked at the new shipment of work gloves, while the diesels in the town trucks idled outside. If you wanted to know who got a new snowmobile in town, you went to Toot's General Store. If you wanted to let people know you were putting up forty or fifty cord of oak and maple this summer and were looking to sell some for next winter, you went to Toot's, or "up to Toot's," as the locals would say. If you wanted one of Mrs. Grace's luscious apple pies with the thick, doughy crust, you went up to Toot's, but you'd better hurry because they went fast and Adeline Grace only baked four pies a day. Eden Falls didn't have a town newspaper. It didn't need one. If you spent ten minutes at the general store every other day, you'd get all the news you'd ever need to know about what was going on in Eden Falls, and then some.

But times had changed in Eden Falls and in many towns like it throughout the state. Flatlanders, as the locals called them, were coming in and they brought with them new demands on town services, larger schools, paved roads and ideas about preserving the land and the rural character of the community that ran afoul of the Vermont spirit of independence and tolerance. They also brought a faster-paced, more impersonal way of life. Flatlanders were better educated than most native Vermonters and they acquired far more material things than what most locals thought to be one's normal share. They drove new cars, took exotic vacations and had snippy tongues. They wanted everything in writing, handshakes wouldn't do, and they were quick to call a lawyer to work out misunderstandings rather than work things out directly with a neighbor or business associate. There was even talk of putting up a stoplight at the corner of Martin's Hill Road and Route 14, it being impossible to make a left from the former onto the latter most of the day because of the increase in the number of cars using Route 14. The flatlanders wanted to fit in but they couldn't, no matter how hard they tried. They were just a different breed. Worse, Eden Falls now had strangers, and that made many local folks uncomfortable and angry.

The local kids also resented the new kids. Problems

surfaced immediately at school where children of IBMers and children of fifth-generation dairy farmers were thrown together. The new kids with funny accents were teased, tormented and in some cases physically assaulted. This was especially true in the mid-sixties when the first wave of flatlanders hit town, including James Downey, his wife, and their son, Thomas.

As the population grew and the number of flatlanders living in Eden Falls's new residential developments increased, the teasing and tormenting stopped. The local kids slipped into the minority and faded to the back of the classroom as the teachers focussed on the college-bound kids from the IBM families. Special classes were created for non-college-bound students. They became known as the "dumb" classes.

Flatlanders and locals butted heads in other arenas as well. The demand for housing created a building frenzy that threatened the very nature of Eden Falls's idyllic landscape. In response, newly arrived residents flocked to join local planning commissions to slow the rapid growth. Many flatlanders wanted to close the town to new residents fearing it would someday remind them of suburban New Jersey. They passed tight zoning laws that discouraged further building.

This hurt natives who were reaching retirement age and whose children had moved off the farms. The only asset these people had was their land, and now the newcomers were telling them they couldn't develop it. Their land had become nothing but a property tax liability. To some it meant financial ruin. Even the time-honored tradition of breaking off small plots from the family farm to build houses for your kids was dead. Everything required a permit and permits were hard to get. Tensions in the community reflected these changes.

Thomas, Leah and little Tommy lived in a house on Beaver Creek Road, a gravel road that connected Route 14, the paved state road that ran through the center of town, to Burley Road, named after Revolutionary War hero Joseph Burley. Burley and his family were the first recorded settlers of Eden

Falls. They built a modest homestead in 1762 near what is now the center of town.

The Downeys owned eleven acres of mostly wooded land which abutted an eight hundred-acre state-owned wildlife preserve. Thomas Downey's victim that cold spring morning lived on the other side of the preserve. The police figured the killer had come from, and disappeared into, the preserve.

"Bet on it," Wojo said. "He went off that way." Wojo pointed past the stone wall into the woods. "Had to. Best way out. Knew the rain would hide him. Smart." None of the law-enforcement personnel hovering over the body was sure to whom Wojo was speaking, but nobody interrupted. When Wojo spoke, everyone listened. That was the way things worked.

"He knew exactly where to be," Wojo continued. "He knew what time Adrian'd be leaving for work, knew his routine." Wojo turned to his right to get some sort of acknowledgment from Deputy Cain, Sheriff's Deputy of the Town of Eden Falls, a mute who was always with Wojo except when he was out with the volunteer rescue unit or at home in bed.

"Better have someone call state and have 'em send someone over," Wojo said to Deputy Cain. "That's the way they want us to do it." Wojo looked at Cain. "They don't think we can handle it ourselves." He waited for a reaction from Cain who was standing a few feet behind him.

Cain nodded and put his thumb up, his way of telling Wojo it was done, and state, as the Vermont State Police Special Investigations Unit was called, was already on its way.

The SIU was the unit local cops were supposed to call to investigate serious felonies, especially homicides. The assumption was, local cops couldn't handle it.

Sheriffs like Stanley T. Wojohowski, however, were an unusual breed. They knew everything that happened in their town. Men like Wojo believed they didn't need the help of forensic science to solve crimes in their town. They relied more on personal contacts, gut feelings and brute force, and they were very effective. But state would run the investigation nonetheless.

Within a few minutes a dark green 1997 Chevy Caprice with blackwall tires and a two-way radio antenna mounted on the trunk pulled into the yard behind Sheriff Wojohowski's squad car. A casually dressed man in his late thirties stepped out of the unmarked cruiser. He was very tall, over six-four, and had trouble unraveling his long legs from the vehicle. His medium length hair looked wind-blown, but it always looked that way, even when he was indoors. His mustache covered his upper lip and he had a nervous habit of biting at the longest hairs, trying to trap them between his bottom front teeth and his upper lip. The man's name was Simeon Cotter, lead detective with the SIU.

Two uniformed state troopers and the medical examiner were already at the scene. The rain was heavy and dripped from the brims of everyone's hats.

"Didn't touch it, Detective," Wojo said, as Cotter approached. The others turned around and looked at Cotter. "Left it exactly the way we found it. Left the good part for you, Detective." A couple of the rescue workers snickered and stepped away from the body. "This is a messy one," Wojo added. "Hope you got a good stomach."

"How are you, Wojo?" Cotter asked as he put out his hand.

Wojo took it and gave it a hearty shake, putting a little extra mustard into the squeeze to let Cotter know how he felt about the intrusion. The two men had met several years ago under similar circumstances. Wojo had arrested a carload of Canadians he pulled over for speeding and found two ounces of cocaine in their car. When word of the collar got out, Cotter showed up to take the Canadians into custody. Two of them had been wanted on an aggravated assault charge in Whitingham and were on state's hot list. Wojo released them only after Cotter threatened to arrest him for obstruction of justice.

Cotter looked at the other men standing around the body. "What do we have here, Sheriff?"

"Adrian Bessette." Wojo paused and looked down at the dead man. "Wife heard the shots a little after seven. She's inside with her son. Looks like two shots. Looks like one of 'em hit him in the neck, caught the bleeder. The other one hit him in the face, took out the back of his head." He looked up from the body. "Brains all over the yard."

"Did you know him?" Cotter asked.

Wojo looked down at the dead man. "Adrian Bessette, age forty-seven, lived in Eden Falls his whole life, family man, worked as a production manager for Harraday's Printing in Burlington. Been there as long as I can remember." He turned to Cotter. "He was a good friend of mine, Detective."

"Has anybody touched the body?"

"I told you, Detective, we haven't touched a damn thing." Wojo shook his head. "I told Deputy Cain here, looks to me like the shooter came in from the woods. Must've fired from the stone wall. He probably took off the same way he came in. Adrian's wife didn't see anything and she didn't hear anything except the shots. Just two. Both hit home. You probably want to question her, and have a look in the woods too." He looked at Cotter. "Gonna bring in the dogs, Detective? Better do it right away before this rain washes away the scent."

"Absolutely," Cotter responded. "We'll get him, don't worry, Sheriff."

"I ain't worried, Detective," Wojo snapped. The two men looked at each other. Nobody else spoke. "I'm thinking we ought to talk to some of the neighbors around here," Wojo added, breaking the silence. "See if anybody saw anything. We might get lucky. Maybe somebody saw a strange car parked somewhere or saw somebody coming or going on foot. Maybe somebody saw something in the woods." He pointed toward the woods in the direction of Thomas Downey's house. "That's where the answers are, Detective." He looked toward the Bessette house. "Not in there."

"Maybe so, Sheriff, but I'd like to see Mrs. Bessette first."

The others began combing the scene looking for anything from a shell casing to a shred of clothing to a button fragment. A team of dogs was brought in from the Williston barracks and was about to go off into the woods to look for a possible escape route. The dogs had already picked up the spot where Downey had crouched and fired his lethal shots and they were barking excitedly, ready to tear off into the woods after their prey.

It had become painfully obvious to those at the scene that there would be little physical evidence to recover. They had found no murder weapon, no shell casings, nothing useful left behind by the killer, and there were no tracks. The odds of recovering usable fingerprints were also remote, given the weather and the killer's apparent proficiency. Cotter hoped the dogs would turn up something his men couldn't find.

Once the dogs were ready, they were led into the woods along the trail Downey had blazed back toward the stream. Corporal Lister had trouble controlling the enthusiastic animals who seemed confident they could stay with the scent they had picked up at the wall. They followed Downey's progress with little difficulty until they came to the stream. They paused for a few seconds sniffing and scratching the gravel bank at the spot where Downey had entered the stream on his way home. They seemed confused. Lister suspected the killer used the stream to mask his scent and he knew the killer had but two options, upstream or downstream. The dogs seemed to favor upstream so Lister let them have their way.

They headed upstream to the spot where Downey had entered the stream earlier that morning. At first they looked like they had lost the scent but one of the Labs, named Mike, suddenly found it on the bank and yelped to his mates. He sprang against his leash, trying to follow the scent where it led, footstep by careful footstep out of the stream and back towards the stone wall and the crime scene.

At first Lister resisted. He knew the direction Mike wanted to go would lead them back to Bessette's house, full circle. But Mike insisted. Lister relented and he and two troopers followed the dogs. They rumbled through the woods until the roof of the Bessette house came back into view.

Lister knew he and his dogs had been duped. The killer had anticipated the dogs' inability to distinguish direction and had led them into a circle from which they could never extricate themselves. No matter how hard they tried to find a new scent, they continued to run around in a giant loop. The dogs were limited by their own great skill and the cunning of their prey.

While Lister was in the woods with the dogs, Wojo and Cotter entered the Bessette house. Mae Bessette was inconsolable as Wojo and Cotter walked into the kitchen. Before anyone spoke, Adrian Bessette's son rose from a chair next to his mother and came forward. The young man had been crying.

"I know this is hard for you and your mother, son, but we'd like to ask her a few questions," Cotter said.

The young man looked past Cotter through the large picture window as he tried to compose himself. He watched the medical examiner who had just finished his crime scene exam and was driving away with the body. Several detectives continued to pore over the scene trying to find something, anything, to go on. The youth turned away from the window and looked at Wojo.

"Mother's not up to talking yet."

"I know, son," Wojo said. "How about me and you talk for a few minutes till your mother feels up to it." He nodded in Cotter's direction. "This is Detective Cotter from the State Police."

"Do you know anyone who may have wanted to hurt your father?" Cotter asked.

"I don't know." He burried his head in the crotch of his

elbow and wiped his tears on his sleeve.

"What about a business associate," Cotter asked after a long pause. "Did your dad have any problems in business, maybe an argument with someone at work recently?"

"No. I mean I don't know."

"Matt, you have to think hard," Wojo said.

The young man looked up at Wojo, then turned to Cotter. "Dad got along with everyone. Except the people on the planning commission. He hated them." He looked at Wojo, then back at Cotter. "But he hated them, they didn't hate him. They didn't care enough about him to hate him. I think they resented him but they hardly knew him." He paused, and looked at Wojo again for support. "Dad hated anybody who wasn't born here. He never said it in public. Dad had better manners than that. But he said it enough to me and Mom."

"Are you sure there wasn't someone on the planning commission he had some personal problems with?" Cotter probed. "Someone he may have talked about more than the others?"

"I don't know," the young man said. "Maybe. I haven't been around much this semester. School and all. Maybe Mom can tell you more."

"You hang in there, son," Wojo said. He put his hand on the boy's shoulder. "If there's anything I can do for you, you call me."

Wojo kept his hand on the boy's shoulder and looked at his mother. She was through crying for the time being. Like most native Vermonters, she was more inclined to grieve in private. If there was something she had to do, the crying would wait.

Wojo questioned her gently.

"Mae, is there anyone you can think of who would want to hurt Adrian?"

Mae Bessette looked at Wojo. They had known each other since they were in first grade in the old Eden Falls school house.

"I don't know, Stan," she said. She ignored Detective Cotter. She reached for Wojo's hand. "Who would want to kill Adrian? He never did anything to anybody."

"What about over at the planning hearings, Mae? Did Adrian ever talk about anyone in particular?"

She told Wojo about recent events at the planning commission hearings. She described how local landowner Vesticate Douglas, a friend of her husband, had been trying to get his three hundred-acre farm subdivided, and how some of the planning commissioners had voted Douglas's application down. She explained how Douglas's property would be worth millions if the project was approved because it was so close to the new exit off the interstate. She also described how the new houses would be seen by all the flatlanders who had built expensive homes along Deer Kill Road to take advantage of the view of the valley.

"Adrian said the commissioners didn't want that development because it would spoil their view of the valley," Mae said. "Adrian said that was unfair." She told them how angry her husband had been the last time he came home from a hearing. "He even used a couple of four-letter words. Adrian never swore. Ever! But he did that evening." She paused. "Adrian was mad because he said nobody who was raised in this town should have to get permission from some New Yorker if he wanted to build something." She looked at Cotter, then back at Wojo. "Adrian said there was one person who got into a terrible fight with Vesticate. I don't know his name. Vesticate was pretty mad too."

"You don't remember his name?" Cotter asked.

Mae Bessette looked down. "Adrian was so mad. I never saw him like that." She hung on to Wojo's hand. "Who would do this, Stan? Why would someone want to do this to us?" She stood up and fell into Wojo's huge arms and sobbed.

Cotter looked at Wojo and walked out the front door. He knew he had nothing. It didn't matter that Bessette was fighting mad or that he wanted to shoot someone at a planning commission hearing. Lots of people felt that way when they saw their plans go up in smoke.

A few minutes later Wojo came out of the house. He and Cotter walked silently down the porch steps toward the driveway.

"Hopefully one of the neighbors saw something," Cotter said. "Otherwise it's going to be a long one."

Chapter Ten

Downey's House

On the other side of the woods, Downey kissed his wife and his son and said good-bye as they left for school. Downey watched his son as he walked out the door. He just kissed a murderer, he said to himself. A hot shower and dry clothing made him feel much better. After a cup of coffee he pulled a green parka over his head and went into the garage. He opened the wooden box and removed the gun and his coveralls. He placed the coveralls on the handle of the lawnmower, which groaned under the weight of the heavy, saturated garment before it fell backwards. Downey caught it before it hit the ground.

He looked at the gun. It was one of the few elements of his plan that left him exposed. There was always a chance things would fall apart and the police would somehow connect him to Adrian Bessette's murder.

He reached into the box and pulled out a rag, a bottle of denatured alcohol and a large roll of cellophane wrap. As he opened the bottle of alcohol he thought about a story he had read in the paper a few weeks earlier. The story told of a man who had shot his brother in New Hampshire and had been convicted because the police had found his gun, which happened to be the murder weapon, in his basement. The man had hidden the gun in a concrete block in the crawl space foundation. It was a great hiding place, Downey thought, but the police found the gun anyway.

Downey pulled a pair of disposable rubber gloves from his pocket and put them on. Then he dampened the rag with alcohol and wiped down the gun to remove his fingerprints. Starting at the tip of the barrel and working his way down the stock, he wrapped the gun in tight layers of cellophane, more than a dozen in all before he emptied the roll. Later that day he would drive a few miles up Town Rd 4 to where there was nothing but thick woods for several miles. He would bury the gun in the woods where it would be safe until he could dispose of it permanently. Or, until he needed it again.

An hour later there was a knock on the front door. Downey had settled into his routine with an array of financial reports, sales receipts, inventory figures, purchases, returns, monthly bank statements, upcoming wholesalers' promotions and other items spread out on the kitchen table. He got up from the table to answer the door. Wojo and Cotter were standing on the landing looking in.

"Morning, Mr. Downey," Wojo said. "Do you mind if we ask you a few questions?"

Downey looked confused. "Come in," he finally said. He stepped back into the front hall to allow the two men to enter the house. They were dripping wet. Downey led them into the kitchen so they could see his papers all over the kitchen table.

"This is Detective Cotter, State Police Special Investigations Unit," Wojo said. He looked at Cotter and pointed to Downey. "Mr. Thomas Downey." He shifted his attention back to Downey. "Seen anybody walking around the woods this morning, Mr. Downey?"

Downey tried his best to look surprised at the question. Who would be out in his woods on a morning like this? "No, why?"

"We're looking for someone who may have been hiking through your woods early this morning," Wojo continued. "He may have parked along the road, maybe in front of your house. Have you seen any cars parked out there this morning?"

"I don't think so." Downey shifted his glance from one to the other. "I haven't been out of the house this morning, except to get the paper. Leah left around ten after eight with Tommy." There was a pause. "Who are you looking for?"

"Did you or your wife hear anything unusual this morning, maybe in the woods behind your house?" Wojo asked. Cotter stared at Downey.

"Unusual?" Downey thought for a second. "I don't think so." He looked at Cotter. "Tommy heard some fire trucks, we assumed it was a chimney fire. That must have been around," he paused, "I'd guess around seven or a little after."

Neither cop responded.

"Was it arson?" Downey asked.

"Adrian Bessette was shot this morning," Wojo said. "He's dead. Right in front of his house. We think the killer came through the woods behind these houses here and we think he left the same way."

"Is it possible to speak with your wife, Mr. Downey?" Cotter asked. "If you tell us where she works, we can ask her if she saw anyone in the road when she left for work."

"Adrian Bessette is dead?" Downey asked incredulously.

"Mr. Downey," Cotter said. "Can you tell us where we can reach your wife?"

"She teaches," Downey said. "At the elementary school on Route 14. Why don't you come back this afternoon. She'll be home about three o'clock."

"That'll be fine," Cotter said. He wanted to leave. He saw the picture, another dead end, no leads here. Wojo must have agreed because he didn't say anything else. Cotter handed Downey his card.

"If you think of anything or if your wife saw anything unusual this morning, Mr. Downey, please call me or Sheriff Wojohowski. Anything, even if it seems remote. Please call us."

"I'll ask Leah," Downey said as he took the card from Cotter. "What do you think happened? Is this something we should be concerned about?"

"Times have changed," Wojo said before Cotter could answer. "I'd lock my doors, if that's what you're asking. The days of leaving your keys in your car and going to bed at night without locking your doors are over. You should know that, Mr. Downey."

The two men thanked Downey and left.

Chapter Eleven

Home

Simeon Cotter was, in the eyes of his colleagues, the finest detective in the state. Few, in fact, doubted the SIU would still exist if it weren't for Cotter. He had an outstanding arrest record and he was singled out by his superiors as a prime reason for keeping the SIU every time the Vermont legislature tried to take away its funding.

There was also a sordid side to Cotter's exploits. The unexplained death of a suspect under investigation for robbing and beating an elderly man in Rutland occurred around the same time Cotter had been stationed at the Rutland Barracks. Though Cotter was never implicated in any wrongdoing, his superiors suspected he was in some way involved. Their concerns seemed well-founded. The intrepid Cotter had little regard for procedure and less when he picked up the scent of a perp. He was that way from the day he joined the force fresh from the law enforcement program at Champlain College, to the day he set up Governor Haley's brother in an investment scam sting. He once posed as a DEA agent to shake down a witness in a drug-related homicide in St. Johnsbury. That one landed him in the custody of the FBI and almost cost him his badge. A year later he took off to Albany, New York, and kidnapped a man he believed had raped several coeds at Bennington College. Cotter was out of his jurisdiction and he had no warrant. He brought the man back to Vermont and took him to the local landfill late at night and threatened to bury the man in a landfill with a backhoe, alive, if he didn't confess. That one did cost him his badge, but he was reinstated two weeks later on the condition he change his ways.

His accomplishments were appreciated, nonetheless, especially by the governor who campaigned on a "Keep Vermont Safe!" platform after a series of gang-related homicides in Rutland. But many, from Reggie McHue, his immediate supervisor, to the governor himself, worried about Cotter's methods. Nearly everyone who knew him, or knew of him, expected he would one day self-destruct. The hope was, he wouldn't take the whole department down with him.

By the Wednesday following the murder there was little else for Cotter to do. He had looked for a motive but had come up empty. He had interviewed all of the members of the Eden Falls Planning Commission, with the same results. There were simply no clues.

It was the lack of motive that really bothered Cotter. The usual suspects had all been ruled out - members of the victim's family, business partners, estranged lovers. Cotter was stumped. This was not a random act. There had to be a motive. Until he figured it out, the investigation was going nowhere.

Cotter left Eden Falls Wednesday afternoon to go home to see his wife, Janie, and to ponder his next move. He hadn't seen Janie for over a week, but that wasn't unusual. He was often away from Janie for two or three weeks at a time. As lead detective for the SIU on all homicide cases, his work took him all over the state.

Janie was Janie Dalrymple, a native Vermonter and a graduate of Brattleboro High School, the University of Colorado, and George Washington Law School. She was a beautiful woman, blonde, tall and perfectly proportioned. She was the daughter of George Dalrymple, one of the state's richest and most influential men and six-term lieutenant governor of Vermont. She was raised with much privilege and every advantage a member of her social class can enjoy. She was used to being around important people and she exuded a natural charm, an air of self confidence that, together with her good looks, drew men to her like a magnet.

Despite the benefits of power and wealth, Janie Dalrymple's life had not gone according to plan. At the age of fourteen she was raped by a close business associate of her father. The man was never prosecuted. Two years later, she was nearly killed in a car accident and wears a scar that runs up the inside of her left leg and another just above her left eyebrow as reminders of the terrible event. Her boyfriend wasn't as fortunate. He died in the crash.

Janie met Simeon Cotter in the main lobby of the courthouse in Montpelier while representing a pregnant woman who was suing the state for wrongful termination. Cotter was appearing as a state's witness in the trial of an East Montpelier man who shot his wife of forty-two years because she objected to what he was watching on TV. "I just blew her away 'cause I had enough," the old-timer said in his confession.

Cotter was leaving the courtroom when he saw Janie. He didn't hesitate to approach her. She had seen him the day before and welcomed his introduction. The two decided to have lunch together at a local coffee shop during the noon-hour recess.

There was an immediate electricity and within two weeks they fell madly in love, two adults feeling the puppy love of teenagers, a true love, a physical and emotional passion. They craved each other. Six months after they met they were married.

Cotter thought about Janie as he moved up the ramp onto interstate 89 in Williston late Wednesday afternoon. He knew she'd be out visiting a family in Vernon and wouldn't be home until around nine. It was unfortunate timing but it was something Janie couldn't put off. This would test Cotter's willpower, for he had thought about little else than Janie from the time he left Williston.

Interstate 89 was a clear shot down to White River

Junction with little traffic and wonderful scenery. Cotter put his cruiser into the left lane and took it up to ninety. Another unmarked cruiser with a uniformed trooper came up behind him just south of Royalton but the trooper recognized Cotter's car and backed off. At White River Junction, Cotter picked up Interstate 91 south and was in Brattleboro by six-thirty. In another thirty minutes he was pulling into his own driveway in front of their farmhouse on Route 112.

The Cotters' house straddled the Massachusetts-Vermont line. It was built in 1792. Locals on both sides of the border referred to the house as the state-line homestead. Built by settlers of the Green River Valley, the house had a rich and romantic history. During the Civil War it was used as a way-station of the underground railroad. During prohibition it was rumored that smugglers were provided with lodging and a place to hide if the authorities were hot on their heels. The house reportedly had secret passageways and false walls concealing small chambers where smugglers would lie silently while the feds and local police searched the building.

Cotter looked at his watch. He had time to kill as Janie wouldn't be home for a while. He went inside, had something to eat and took a hot shower. When he got out he wrapped a towel around his waist and scampered up to their bedroom on the second floor. To his surprise, Janie was standing next to the bed. She had nothing on.

Cotter's eyes moved slowly up and down her slender body before settling on her eyes. He knew this tantalized her. "You're home early," he said.

She moved toward him until she could reach the towel. Cotter gently placed the back of his index finger against her chin and ran it slowly down her neck, in between her breasts and down her abdomen to a few inches above her hair.

Janie tilted her head back as he moved his finger down another inch, and stopped. She tilted her head forward and smiled at Cotter. She removed the towel. "I missed you," she said.

Chapter Twelve

The Mud

The week following Adrian Bessette's demise was uneventful for Thomas Downey. He opened the store each morning and went about his routine as if nothing had changed. Leah was unaware of what her husband had done, although she told him he had been unusually moody the past few days, "even for you," she observed. He said he probably had some sort of a bug that didn't manifest in symptoms, but made him feel a bit tired. She accepted this explanation without much protest.

The murder of Adrian Bessette was the lead story in the Burlington Free Press for several days and was the subject of several on-the-scene reports by each of the three local TV channels. But the local media began to lose interest when it became apparent that the state police hadn't a clue about the identity of the killer. The story was soon relegated to old news and dropped out of the local news entirely by the end of the week.

Mud season, however, was always news. Eden Falls had escaped much of the spring thaw without too much damage to its dirt roads. The talk at Toot's General Store was that it was as mild a mud season as locals had experienced in recent memory.

Since the advent of weather forecasting, most Vermonters accepted the fact that there were only three seasons in their state: winter, July and mud season. Most

Vermonters hated the mud. It covered everything from their cars and trucks and animals and children to their kitchen floor. The term *mudroom* was an accurate description for Vermont foyers, as this room was the mud lock for those coming into the house, and those inside who had already taken off their boots and anything else that was covered with the chocolate-brown ooze.

Mud season was a part of Vermont's culture, arriving every spring to signal the end of winter. Mud season also meant brisk sales for Downey's Outfitters. Every April, Downey ran a mud season sale offering hundreds of pairs of boots at discounts up to seventy-five percent off; leather boots with Vibram soles, Sorrell boots with insulated felt booties, work boots, Timberland, Wolverine and Merrell boots, rubber boots for wearing on top of street shoes, hiking shoes, walking shoes and casual footwear. It was Downey's way of paring his unsold winter inventory and making lots of local residents happy, people who would think of Downey's Outfitters when it came time to buy clothing and camping gear at full retail prices.

On Wednesday afternoon, the same day Cotter left for home, Wojo entered Downey's store looking for a deal on a pair of boots. Downey watched him from the storeroom as Burt, the assistant manager, tried to help him. Downey came out of the storeroom to greet the sheriff.

"Is Burt helping you find what you need, Sheriff?" Downey asked.

Wojo looked at Downey and smiled. "Just lookin' for a cheap pair of boots." He picked up a pair of hiking boots with green leather uppers and black soles. It wasn't anything Wojo would ever wear and Downey knew it.

"Ask your wife if she saw anyone in the road that morning?" Wojo asked, looking at Downey.

"As a matter of fact I did, Sheriff." Downey folded a pair of chaps the last customer had tried on. Then he turned to Burt. "Did he buy anything?"

"A pair of chaps," Burt said. "He said if he liked them he'd come back in for another pair. He said he almost tore his thigh up with his chain saw last week. He's never worn chaps but he said he figured his luck's run out."

"Sooner or later everyone's luck runs out," Wojo interjected. He looked at Downey. "So how about it, Mr. Downey, did your wife see anything?"

"No, Sheriff, she didn't. She said it was raining really hard and she was late so she might not have noticed even if there was a car there, but she's pretty sure there wasn't." He looked at Wojo for a second, then busied himself straightening the sweaters that were also on sale and had been rifled through by another customer.

"I'll take these," Wojo said to Burt. "My wife's nephew is here from St. J. Forgot his boots. If these don't fit can I bring 'em back?"

"Of course you can, Sheriff," Burt said. "Just make sure he doesn't wear them outside."

Wojo paid cash for the boots and walked out.

"I don't think I've ever seen him in here before," Burt said. "I wonder what brought him in today?" He looked at Downey and laughed.

Downey didn't respond.

Chapter Thirteen

The Second

Three weeks later Downey made a phone call to a local excavation contractor named Peter Roi. He had known Roi since elementary school, but they weren't friends as children and had nothing to do with each other as adults. Downey tried to remember the last time the two men had spoken, even a few words, but he could only remember a nod or a grunt at the gas pump in front of Toot's General Store. He was sure Roi wouldn't recognize a voice he hadn't heard in more than twenty-five years. He was right.

A man picked up the phone after the second ring.

"Mr. Roi?" Downey asked.

"Yup," the man said.

"My name is Wickham, Nate Wickham. My wife and I just purchased a piece of land off Sage Road, just north of the Eden Falls Fire Department. I'd like to get a price from you for constructing a driveway and digging our cellar hole." Downey paused. "We'll need a septic system and a well, too." He paused again. "Do you do that kind of work?"

"I guess I might," Roi said. He sounded indifferent. No matter how much a Vermonter's family went without, he would never sound anxious for work when asked. It was unbecoming. Besides, Roi hardly needed the work.

"Where about's yer land?" Roi asked. "Lots of ledge up that way."

"You go a mile past the fire station and turn left onto

William Day Hairston Road. There's no sign but..."

"I know where it is," Roi snapped.

Roi's curt interjection broke Downey's concentration. He assumed Roi didn't know who it was but he couldn't be certain. His mind began to run. Did Roi know what he was up to? Obviously not, but Downey still had a sinking feeling he had made a serious blunder. Had he forgotten about a recent encounter with Roi? Could Roi possibly recognize his voice. Not possible, Downey said to himself. Not possible.

"Continue up William Day Hairston Road for several miles to the end," Downey continued. "There's some surveyor's tape on wood stakes that the surveyor put in, on the left..."

"Who did your surveyin?" Roi interrupted.

For the second time in the conversation Roi had caught Downey off guard. That wasn't good. It disturbed Downey. Why would he ask that? Was it a test? That's ridiculous, he said to himself. But Roi knew every surveyor from Manchester to St. Albans. Downey felt like he had lost control of the situation.

"My brother in-law did it. He's from New York." Downey bagan to regain his confidence. "I'd like to meet you there some time this week, preferably in the evening, if that's convenient."

This time the silence was on the other end of the line. "I can do that. Me and Rick can come up most anytime. Evenings are tough though, Rick can't make it..."

"Days are impossible for me," Downey quickly interjected. It was imperative that it happen in the evening for his plan to work. It was also imperative that Roi come alone. "Somebody I spoke with at the post office said you were good, so I'm quite anxious to meet with you up at the site. Money is not an issue. I'd like to get going with the project right away." Downey paused to catch his breath, then went for the setup. "I know you're busy, so we should meet soon. How about tomorrow, early evening, say, about six o'clock?"

"Who said I was good? Lew?"

Downey felt as if he was in control once again. He knew the man couldn't resist a compliment.

"A lady who was getting her mail. She said you did some work for her and she was very satisfied. She told me her name but I don't remember."

This seemed to satisfy Roi's curiosity. The man had worked for nearly everyone in town over the years. Some would say good things about him and others would not, depending mostly on whether or not they were locals.

Peter Roi worked as a logger like his father, but when Eden Falls started to grow, he was smart enough to trade in his log skidder and chain saw for a backhoe and a bulldozer. He saw the hand-writing on the wall, the influx of people with money who wanted large homes far off the main roads, which meant long driveways, long days and lots of profit. Soon he had more work than he could handle, but he never turned down a job, or an opportunity to take someone's money, especially a flatlander.

The voice Roi heard didn't have much of an accent, but it had the unmistakable edge of a man who was not originally from Eden Falls, or Vermont. It was subtle, unlike most of the newcomers, he thought, but it was definitely there, the polish of an IBMer or a lawyer or a man with a college degree, the accent of an educated man, a flatlander with a large checkbook.

"Tomorrow will do," Roi said. "Six o'clock, sharp."

"I'll see you then." Downey hung up.

The next morning Downey told Leah he wanted to go trout fishing after work and asked if she would mind.

"Take Tommy," she said agreeably.

Taking Tommy would be one way of getting Leah's blessing, Downey thought, with obvious complications. He stumbled for something to say and he knew he looked stupid. He was almost amused, until he realized if he didn't come up with something quickly the hole into which he had just dug himself was about to get ten times larger.

"The water's pretty high this spring," he said to Leah.

He wasn't very convincing and he knew it. He didn't have to be. He knew Leah would sense what he really wanted, like she always did.

"Besides, I'll take Tommy plenty of times this year." He came over to her and kissed her on the cheek. "I'd like to go by myself, just this time. You know how I am." He put his hands on her shoulders.

"Unfortunately I do," Leah said. "Go ahead. Have a good time." She looked at him and smiled. "I'll take Tommy out for pizza. He's been begging me all week."

"Thanks," Downey said. He smiled and kissed her again and drew her toward him. He hugged her, and closed his eyes and pictured the woods next to William Day Hairston Road. He didn't want to let go of her.

"Thomas," Leah said gently.

He finally released her but kept his hands on her shoulders.

"Are you all right, Honey?"

He pulled his hands away and backed up. "I'm fine. Really, I'm fine. I have to go. Thanks for tonight." He pulled her to him again and kissed her on the lips. "Bye. I love you. Give Tommy a kiss for me." He picked up his briefcase and left for work.

At four-thirty that afternoon, Downey came home to change and pick up his fishing gear. Leah and Tommy were on their way out for pizza.

"Bye," they said to each other and exchanged kisses.

A few minutes after they were gone, Downey went upstairs and changed into an old pair of blue jeans and a dark green flannel shirt. It won't be cold and rainy this time, he thought. He stopped dressing for a moment and thought about the first one.

This one would be different. It made him nervous. He would be taking more chances. At six p.m. the sun would be over the horizon but it would still be light enough for him to be seen near William Day Hairston Road, possibly by one of

Leah's friends, a parent of one of Tommy's friends or a customer of Downey's Outfitters.

Yes, officer, I saw Thomas Downey driving up William Day Hairston Road about five-thirty last evening, he said to himself.

But that wouldn't happen. Downey knew there were only two houses on William Day Hairston Road and both of them sat way off the road hidden in the woods. Details. One couple had no children and was away for the week visiting grandparents in Newton, Massachusetts. They had been in Downey's store the week before to buy a gift, a UVM sweatshirt, for the wife's nephew. Their travel plans were discussed at the store. More details. That's why Downey planned the event for this week.

Downey would have to take his chances with the second family who, like the other couple, had no children. Downey had called them earlier in the week pretending to be an engineer working for the state. He had told them his crew would be blasting some ledge down the road and wanted to make sure the neighbors knew. He had said his crew would be working late, till about six-thirty, and wanted to know if the people had a problem with that. The man who answered the phone said he and his wife didn't come home from work till seven and wouldn't mind. More details.

Downey finished changing his clothes and looked in the mirror. Everything he wore that night would be discarded, including the shoes. He purposely selected things he never wore anymore so they wouldn't be missed, including an old pair of hiking boots he hadn't worn for several years. Seeing them in the mirror reminded him of earlier days; the blue jeans Leah had bought him, the flannel shirt Tommy had given him for Christmas five years ago. He hated to part with them. But he would. Nostalgia had no place in his life at that moment. He had to become more focused. It was about to happen, again.

With everything else ready to go, Downey went down

the basement steps and headed for the utility room. He reached behind the water heater and grabbed the rifle that he had buried in the woods off Town Rd 4. He went into his shop and removed the cellophane wrapping.

He admired the rifle, the wonderful interplay of precision-machined parts so meticulously assembled and painstakingly finished. Was the man who made this fine piece of machinery any less of a man than one who makes a machine used for another purpose? Downey stared at the gun. Why was it any different than a rock, or a fist? Or an unkind word?

He put the gun in a sports bag with his fishing gear and a small, rolled-up piece of clear four-millimeter polyethylene plastic. He reached into the pocket of his coat which hung on the coat tree in the mudroom and took out a set of car keys. They were from the local Avis dealer. He put the new set of keys in another pocket and walked through the garage, opened the back door of his Land Cruiser and put his gear into the back seat. Then he walked back into the house and picked up the phone. He dialed Peter Roi's number.

"Is Mr. Roi there?" he asked a woman who sounded tired but business-like.

"Nope. He's not back from work yet."

"Do you know where I can reach him, Ma'am?" Downey asked.

"He has an appointment tonight, so you can call back around eight," the woman said.

Having said what she needed to say she started to hang up. Downey marveled at the way Vermonters conserved words. It was as if they cost money, the more words you used, the higher the price. The lady on the phone was no exception.

"I need..." He raised his voice slightly. "I need a load of gravel tonight, Ma'am!" Downey shouted into the phone before she could hang up. She heard him and came back on the line.

"What's that?" she asked.

"I'm just finishing up a small job here and I'd like to

finish tonight. I need a small load of gravel, about five or six yards. Can't Rick bring it up?"

"No, he can't," she said. "He's going to a planning commission meeting tonight. He's trying to get on the commission...Adrian Bessette's seat."

"What about Peter?" Downey asked.

"I already told you, he's gone up to an appointment. He said where but I can't remember. Do you want me to have him call you?"

"No thanks, Ma'am," Downey said. "I'll call him later if I can't find any gravel tonight."

"Suit yourself," she said and hung up.

Downey drove into Eden Falls and parked his Land Cruiser in the parking lot in front of the Grand Union at the opposite end of the complex from Downey's Outfitters. He took his sports bag out of the back seat, walked down a long aisle of cars, turned right and slipped between two mini vans. He crossed two more aisles and stopped in front of a nondescript, gray, American-made late model compact. He took the Avis keys out of his pocket and opened the door. He reached around, unlocked the door to the back seat, opened it and tossed in his sports bag. He closed the back door, got into the car, started it up and drove away.

A mile past the fire station on Stage Road Downey turned left onto William Day Hairston Road. It was five forty-five p.m. Roi wouldn't be there for fifteen minutes. Perfect. Downey drove past the house belonging to the couple visiting grandparents in Newton. The end of the driveway was all that could be seen from the road as it turned dramatically to the left and cut back into the woods. No problem here. Suddenly two deer jumped out in front of the car. Downey swerved to the left and went into the ditch on the opposite side of the road. The deer stood in the middle of the road and stared at him. Downey took a deep breath and looked back.

Despite his predicament he marveled at their beauty, their innocence, just standing there thinking who knows what.

Then, as quickly as they jumped into the road they bounded off into the woods. They were out of sight but they were right there, ten feet into the woods in the shadows of the trees. Downey looked for them. He studied the treeline. He knew they were there just a few feet away, watching him, oblivious to how close they had just come to death.

Downey tried to back the car out of the ditch but it was stuck. This was a most unsettling development. He got out of the car and figured out the right front tire wasn't making contact with the ground. He got back in and turned the wheel sharply to the right. He got out again and pushed the car further into the ditch until all four tires made contact with the ground. It hadn't rained for several days and the ditch was bone dry. Downey put the car in gear and pulled forward, slowly out of the ditch and back up onto the road.

Shaken but not discouraged, Downey continued up William Day Hairston Road, past the second house for another mile and a half until he came upon the surveyor's tape he had tied to a tree near the edge of the road two days before. It was exactly how he had left it. It looked like a surveyor had set benchmarks and property lines for a building site. It was perfect. It would be as Roi would expect it to be. The land owners who lived in New York would never know.

Downey parked the car on the side of the road and got out. He opened the rear door, took the rifle out of the bag and put three cartridges into the magazine. He did a three hundred sixty-degree scan of his surroundings. As expected, the area was deserted.

Just because this isn't the first time doesn't mean I can take things for granted, Downey said to himself. He was amazed how calm he was, perhaps too calm. But that's what he wanted, to be methodical, like a robot, unfeeling, as much for his victim as for himself. It was a state of mind that one had to have to do these things, he believed. It wasn't like the first time. It will be better. "I will be better," he said softly.

And what of remorse? Why didn't he feel any

remorse? He didn't care for this feeling. It was the feeling he had feared the first time. Was he becoming desensitized to the enormity of this act? Or worse, did it give him a certain pleasure? When would he start to feel the reality of what he had already done and what he was about to do again? Would it be when Roi pulled up, or when he had Roi's head lined up in his cross hairs? Would he feel it when he pulled the trigger? Would it come with the second bullet? He hoped it would come soon. His indifference made him more nervous than anything. It told him he was what he didn't want to be, a cold-hearted killer who felt nothing for his victims. This was not Thomas Downey, son of James Downey, husband of Leah Downey, father of little Tommy Downey, a good man.

He shook the distracting thoughts from his head. They were not real, but camouflage was. If Roi spotted him through the trees he would recognize him immediately. It was one thing not being able to recognize Downey's voice on the phone, but there was no chance Roi wouldn't know who he was if he saw him. But if Roi didn't see him there, by the road, waiting for him, would he get out of his pickup? That was a concern. Downey was sure he would. Vermonters are curious by nature, like deer attracted to the sound of the chain saw or the rumbling of a bulldozer on a construction site. Roi would see the car and he'd have to get out of his truck. He'd figure it's a flatlander and a profitable job. "He'll see dollar signs," Downey murmured. Then he'd walk into the woods following the crude path Downey had made, to just the right spot about fifty yards from the road. He'd stop to read the notes on the surveyor's tape which had been tied to a small maple tree. Downey played it out in his mind. "Yes," he said softly. "It will work."

When he finished writing STATION ONE on the tape, Downey carefully stepped over a downed ironwood tree and worked his way through a group of small maples to a clump of white birch so thick it would be impossible to breach with the human eye, especially in the evening light. Downey knew ahead of time this would be his perch. He had been here two days earlier when he had tied the red surveyor's ribbon to the trees on the side of the road. He had carefully selected the tree on which the marker would be attached, and had chosen the ideal spot from which he would fire his rifle. The birch trees were the perfect cover. They were far enough away from the STATION ONE marker that Roi would never know Downey was there, yet they were close enough for Downey to get off a clean shot.

Standing behind the birches, Downey looked at the ground around their base. He would lie on his stomach and fire from a prone position, much like the small, green plastic soldiers he had played with when he was a child.

He unrolled the three-foot by six-foot piece of four-millimeter poly and positioned it on the ground. It would prevent clothing fibers from being left for the Special Investigations Unit. There was also the possibility the FBI might be brought in if SIU thought it was a serial killing. Even though he intended to destroy his clothing after his mission, he decided to be overly cautious. Nothing would be left to chance.

Downey lay down on the poly, placed his left elbow on the ground and his left hand firmly under the barrel of the rifle. He pressed the butt end of the rifle against his right shoulder and peered through the scope. Perfect. He had an unobstructed view of the area by the ribbon at STATION ONE. Now all he had to do was wait.

Before long he heard the sound of a pickup truck coming up William Day Hairston Road. It sounded as if it stopped by Downey's rental car but it was hard to tell exactly. When he heard the door open and slam shut he knew.

Downey could feel his heart beat. What was Roi doing? Suddenly he appeared from the right. He was not following Downey's path. It looked like he was headed straight for Downey. Downey's head was swirling with options. Why wasn't he on the path? Had he spotted Downey behind the birch trees? Downey knew what he had to do. He would have to jump up and shoot Roi before Roi could react. But he only had three shells. What if he missed or the shots weren't killing shots? His heart pounded like a cannon. He gripped the rifle and started sweating and was about to spring to his feet when, as quickly as he appeared, Roi turned to his right. He must have spotted the ribbon because he headed directly for it. Downey's heart continued to pound, heavy and deep. It almost comforted him because he felt it was a normal reaction, something others might feel at a time like this.

Roi made it to the clearing where the STATION ONE ribbon hung. Downey closed his eyes tight, then opened them and looked down the barrel of the rifle at Roi, who had his back to Downey. He was two or three steps from the ribbon.

Downey put his right eye to the scope and found the ribbon in its cross hairs. Within seconds Roi's hand and arm appeared in the scope, then his face. The hairs of the scope crossed at his cheek bone. Roi stood for a moment to look at the red tape, then reached up to grab it. It was securely tied. He began turning the tape in the direction in which he could make out the words. He started to say them to himself, Sta...

The hot lead penetrated his jaw, ricocheted off a vertebra and tore a path out of the back of his neck. It wasn't a killing shot but it crushed the spinal column. Roi stiffened for a split second then collapsed to the ground. The muscles and nerves below his neck were unable to communicate with his brain. His head felt ice cold, like someone was blowing cold air on the back of his neck. He was still conscious.

Downey got up and hurried over to Roi. The shot had silenced the woods. Downey stood above Roi and knew that Roi could see him, and that he recognized him. It didn't matter. Downey stepped back six feet and aimed the gun directly at Roi's head.

Roi couldn't move, but he knew what was coming and his eyes opened wide, as if to plead for a reprieve. It didn't come. The second bullet entered his throat and came out through the bottom of his neck and lodged about six inches into the ground. Blood poured from the wound and the ground became saturated. This was the killing blow.

Downey stood above his victim. A wad of papers stuck out of Roi's shirt pocket. Downey removed them carefully with a stick. The top sheet said *Nate Wickham, six o'clock, W.D.H.Rd., driveway, found-septic.* He put the papers back in Roi's pocket, minus the one with Nate Wickham's name on it.

Downey felt nauseous, not from what he had done but because it had gone so poorly. He was angry that he had almost been compromised, angry that Roi hadn't followed his path. But even though things had almost fallen apart, his plan still worked. Roi was dead.

He picked up the poly and removed the ribbons from the trees. He put everything into his sports bag. Satisfied he had left no incriminating evidence, he got back into the rental car and drove away from the scene. He went over everything, the poly, the surveyor's ribbon, the two shell casings. He couldn't leave any clues. He knew the car tires would leave tracks, but he didn't care since the tires on the rental car were a common make and size. He had checked several dealerships that sold the same model before he rented it.

It was nearly six-thirty. The couple who worked in Burlington were probably on their way home by now, but Downey had more than enough time before they started up William Day Hairston Road. He passed the couple's driveway on the way back, passed the area where the deer had jumped out in front of his car and sent him into the ditch and passed the lower driveway leading to the house belonging to the couple visiting relatives in Massachusetts. Downey looked down the last driveway as he drove by. These must be expensive lots, he thought. His mind wandered. Privacy, great views. And just down the road from Peter Roi's body.

At the bottom of the hill Downey made a right onto Stage Road and another right onto Route 14. He pulled into the parking lot of the Grand Union and parked next to his Land Cruiser. He transferred his gear, locked the Land Cruiser and got back into the rental car. He drove to the airport in South Burlington where the Avis office was located, turned in the car and asked for a ride in the courtesy van back to the Grand Union in Eden Falls.

A young man wearing an Avis jacket directed Downey to the Grand Caravan just outside the door.

"No suitcases, sir?" the young man asked.

"No." Downey said. The last thing he wanted was a thirty-minute ride down Route 14 with a talkative kid wearing an Avis uniform.

"Where to?" the driver asked. "I've been all over the place, today, Shelburne, Waitsfield, Middlebury..."

"Eden Falls," Downey interrupted. "The Grand Union on Route 14."

"I know where that is." The young man seemed excited. "I haven't been out there in a while. We don't get many customers from Eden Falls." He looked in the rear view mirror to see if Downey was listening. He wasn't but the driver kept talking. "I guess they rent from Hertz." He laughed and looked in the mirror. Downey forced a smile. The young man started the van and made a u-turn out of the Avis lot and navigated the van through a maze of ramps and construction to the airport exit.

"Left or right?" the driver asked.

"What?"

"Interstate or Route 14?" the driver asked again. "Route 14 is shorter, but the interstate's faster. No lights." He turned around to look at Downey.

"The interstate," Downey said.

"So what do you do?" the driver asked.

"I'm in the clothing business."

"Did they catch that murderer yet?" The young man looked back at Downey. "I'll bet a million bucks it was a drug hit. You gotta figure, all this stuff coming in and out of Vermont these days. And it's not only the blacks coming up from New York. Course, they bring the hard stuff in, you know, the coke, heroin. I'm not racist or anything, that's just a fact. That's all gang-controlled anyway, you know, that gang down in Rutland, the one they did that big article on in the paper. Anyway, you know how much pot we grow here in Vermont? I'll bet half the farmers out there are growing it. They can make more from a couple of pot plants than they can growing corn or raising cows. Crazy, isn't it? I'll bet the guy was growing it and he stiffed someone. Boom! That's how they take care of that stuff. That's if it's not his wife. Maybe she did it. I saw a program on TV that said if a man gets killed, odds are his wife did it."

Downey stared at the condominiums between the interstate and Route 14. They were pale-colored, wood-framed buildings made to look expensive but built as cheaply as the codes allow. Downey thought of all the people living inside, couples relaxing after dinner or cooling down from an evening jog up and down the condo bike path, children taking baths and getting ready for bed. Downey thought of Leah and Tommy and wondered if they enjoyed their pizza. He was sorry he wasn't with them.

"I've been in Eden Falls a few times," the driver continued. "It's a weird town, kind of." He looked back at Downey to see if he was offended. "I mean, the people, they're not really..." he looked back at Downey again. "Friendly, I guess. One time my friend and I were coming back from St. Johnsbury, late, about nine-thirty, a weekday night, during the summer." He looked into the rear view mirror once again but Downey didn't make eye contact. "We stopped at this garage to put air in one of my tires. I don't remember which one. The guy at the garage was kinda spooky. There were a couple of other guys there that gave us the creeps. So we left. Screw that. We kept going till we got to Williston and we stopped at the convenience store at Taft Corners, you know, the new one?"

Downey nodded and forced a smile.

"My girlfriend works there. Well, she actually works for Dunkin Donuts. They have a concession there, so she sort of works for both. I can get free doughnuts any time I want. They're great." He looked back at Downey who smiled slightly. "We're supposed to go out tonight but I may not get off work in time."

"Oh," Downey said. "I hope I'm not the cause of that."

The driver looked back at Downey and laughed. "No, no, definitely not. I have to close tonight. We don't close till nine but I won't get out till around ten. I have to clean all the cars, you know, empty the ash trays, vacuum, gas 'em up, normal stuff. I'm actually glad you needed a ride because I wanted to get out of there. It gets pretty slow sometimes. Sometimes I just need to get out. Anyway, I like driving the shuttle because you get to meet all kinds of people. I really like that. It makes the job kind of interesting."

The van pulled up in front of the Grand Union.

"This will be fine," Downey said. He reached into his pocket and pulled out a five-dollar bill and gave it to the young man. "I'm sorry you had a bad experience in Eden Falls. Please don't judge everyone in our town by what happened to you that night."

"I won't," the driver said. "Hey, you take care now." He waved to Downey as he pulled away.

Downey walked over to his car and unlocked the door. He knew he had to face Leah and tell her all about his trout fishing. He didn't care. He'd tell her he didn't catch anything but he had a nice time anyway. She'd believe him and not pursue it, not that it mattered. He wanted to see her. He wanted to go home. He got into his car and left.

Chapter Fourteen

A Similar M.O.

Wojo arrived at the scene a few minutes before Cotter. Roi's body was swollen and the smell of decomposition hung in the air. The body had been discovered when Roi's wife finally remembered his meeting was up on William Day Hairston Road. That was three days after she had reported him missing and nearly a week after Roi's demise.

Roi's body was still intact. The heavy scent of after-shave and the smell of human waste that oozed from his body at the time of his death discouraged the local scavengers from making a meal of him. Except for the bloating and black, crusty blood all over his face, Roi's body looked the same as it had when Downey left it.

William Day Hairston Road was lined with police cars, an ambulance and a TV wagon from WCAX-TV news. Two murders in one town in less than a month was big news in the Green Mountain State. Roi's death would make the headlines in the papers the next day. WCAX would air a taped report from the scene on the six-o'clock news.

At least a dozen state troopers and members of the SIU combed the area. Sheriff Wojohowski, State Trooper Barnes, Detective Cotter, Reggie McHue and Deputy Cain stood over the corpse. Cotter had been summoned back to Eden Falls by McHue two days ago when Peter Roi was reported missing, with foul play suspected. McHue thought there might be a connection to the Bessette killing. So did Wojo.

"Similar M.O.," Wojo said. The scene was eerily similar to the morning Adrian Bessette lay in his driveway, except there were more cops and a TV camera hovered over the victim's body. Wojo looked at Cotter.

"I tend to agree with you," Cotter said. "And it's not the work of a copycat killer, either. There's no way he'd know how the Bessette killing went down."

This type of case was Cotter's specialty. He had attended a program for state and local police at the FBI training facility in Quantico, Virginia, last year, courtesy of the SIU and Vermont taxpayers. The program was designed to teach local law enforcement professionals how to use the latest techniques of psychological profiling. The SIU could afford to send only one of its top detectives. Cotter was the obvious choice. He excelled in the classes and especially in the mock investigations, to no one's surprise.

"The M.O. is consistent with a serial killing," Cotter said. "Same caliber bullet, entry and exit wounds in the same part of the body, an operation meticulously planned from beginning to end by someone who could anticipate every turn, who could place himself in the right place at the right time and who could extricate himself from the crime scene without leaving a trace."

But something puzzled Cotter. There was something about this killer that was different. There were no signs of sexual molestation or mutilation of the victim's body before or after death. There was no sign of physical assault, no deliberate clue or signature like most serial killers leave, a cryptic message, a word or shape carved into the victim's flesh.

"It's almost like a hit," Cotter said. "But what's the motive?"

All of the cops, including Cotter, continued to look down at Peter Roi.

"Maybe I'm wrong," Cotter said to McHue who was standing next to Wojo. "Maybe it's not a serial killer. Maybe it's just a regular Joe who thinks he has a pretty damn good reason to knock off these two men." He continued to stare at Roi's body. "I need a motive," he said to no one in particular. He looked up at the others. "Any ideas?"

Nobody said anything.

"Great." Cotter looked at one of the troopers. "Have 'em check the slugs. I think we'll find they're from the same gun that killed Bessette." He turned to McHue to say something but was interrupted by Sheriff Wojohowski.

"You can have your boys look for prints or any other evidence if they like, Detective, but they'll be wasting their time. They won't find anything. This guy's a pro. Smart." He paused and looked directly at Cotter. "We better go talk to Fanny." He turned and headed out of the woods toward the road. Deputy Cain followed.

Cotter stayed back with McHue and the medical examiner. Then he joined Wojo who was waiting for him by his cruiser.

When Cotter reached the road he was approached by the cameraman and a WCAX-TV reporter.

"The sheriff told me you were in charge," the reporter said. "You're Detective Cotter?"

Cotter didn't respond. He felt uncomfortable in front of the camera.

"Can I ask you a few questions?"

Cotter tried to walk past him but the reporter persisted and dragged the cameraman by the arm as he hustled to stay between Cotter and the road.

"Is this the work of a serial killer, detective? When do you think he'll strike again?"

Cotter stopped and faced the reporter. "Serial killers rarely prey on middle-aged men. We'll know more in a few days."

"Are there any suspects?" the reporter asked.

"None at this time." Cotter excused himself.

The reporter seemed somewhat satisfied with the interview. He had enough tape to bring back to the studio. He backed off Cotter and started talking furiously to the cameraman.

Cotter felt like he had said too much and walked over to Wojohowski who was watching the interview while leaning against his police cruiser. He had a smug grin on his face.

"You know something I don't know, Sheriff?" Cotter asked.

"Nope," Wojo replied. His smile slowly disappeared. He stared at Cotter. "Get in your car, Detective, and you can follow me to the Roi place."

Chapter Fifteen

Fanny Roi

They arrived at Roi's house a few minutes after Deputy Cain, who was sitting with Fanny Roi, the victim's widow, on the front porch. Wojo looked at Cotter while they started up the path to the porch.

"Can you imagine that?" Wojo said. "I have to send a fucking mute to be with Fanny at a time like this." He shook his head. "He can't say anything to her." He looked at Deputy Cain sitting on the porch with Fanny Roi as they walked toward the steps. "All he can do is just sit there." He was disgusted. "Maybe it makes 'em feel better, just having a uniform around...makes 'em feel like we have everything under control." He turned to Cotter. "Know what I mean, Detective?"

At the top of the stairs it became apparent that Peter Roi's widow had taken the news of her husband's demise with more stoicism than Mae Bessette. She looked shaken, but composed.

Fanny stood up when she saw Wojo and Cotter walking towards the house. She was dressed in a brightly colored, hand-embroidered wool sweater and polyester knit slacks. She was a natural redhead, but her hair was dyed an unnatural shade of orange to cover up the gray.

As the two cops started up the porch steps, Wojo removed his hat. Cotter tried to look sympathetic. When the two men reached the top step Cotter was struck by Fanny's expression. He thought she looked angry more than sad.

Fanny put her arms around Wojo.

"I knew this was going to happen someday. I knew he'd wind up in the woods somewhere, tied to his bottle. What happened, Stan? Die in a drunken stupor?"

"No, Fanny," he didn't. It wasn't like that." Wojo held Fanny's hands in front of him. "Look, Fanny, Peter was shot, up near the top of William Day Hairston Road. He's been dead since Tuesday evening as far as we can tell."

"Shot?" Fanny asked in amazement. "By who?"

"We don't know, Fanny, but we're working on it." Wojo put his hand on Fanny's shoulder.

Fanny's demeanor changed with the news of the shooting. She told Wojo she thought Peter had been out on a bender with his two sons, for whom she obviously harbored intense dislike.

"When was the last time you saw Peter?" Wojo asked.

"Tuesday morning." Fanny stared straight ahead through the railing at the edge of the porch into the hay field on the other side of the road.

Wojo continued. "When Peter left for work Tuesday did he say anything or do anything unusual? Did he talk about who he was going to meet with Tuesday after work?"

Fanny looked up at Wojo. "He was supposed to meet some man who just bought some land. Up on William Day Hairston Road. I'm not sure where."

"What was his name, Fanny?"

The woman looked baffled. "I'm not sure. I don't think Peter told me his name. All he said was he was angry because the man insisted he meet him right away and made him go out after work and he doesn't like to do that." She looked up at Wojo again hoping that information was important.

Cotter looked at Wojo and suggested the owners of the land where Roi was killed might be able to help. Wojo told Cotter they were an old couple who didn't live in the area and probably knew nothing.

"The killer obviously picked that land because it was secluded," Wojo said. "I don't think there's any connection, Detective, but if you want to waste your time, go ahead."

Cotter didn't say anything. He knew Wojo was right.

"Are you sure you can't remember a name, Fanny? Maybe you could remember what it sounded like. Was it a short name, or a long name? Maybe a local name, Fanny. Did you recognize it as a local name or do you think the man was a flatlander?"

"I don't know." The woman seemed upset about her ignorance and her inability to help.

"Fanny, did anyone call that night looking for Peter?"

Fanny hesitated. "A man called looking for a load of gravel, around suppertime."

"Do you remember *his* name, Fanny?"

Fanny looked quizically at Wojo. "No."

"Are you sure, Fanny. He might have been part of it. Checking to see if Peter was coming." He paused. "A local, Fanny? A flatlander, maybe? It might help us to know."

Fanny's expression became twisted. "Dammit all to hell. I just don't remember."

"Mrs. Roi," Cotter interrupted.

"Fanny, this is Detective Cotter of the state police," Wojo said. Fanny looked at Cotter.

"Mrs. Roi, I have many questions I'd like to ask you and we should really do it now. Time is very important in cases like this. Do you feel up to going inside and spending some time with us? I know this is a difficult time for you, but it would be very helpful. I know you want to help."

Fanny agreed and she, Wojo, Detective Cotter and Deputy Cain went inside the house. Wojo sat down with Fanny at a large table in the kitchen. Cotter and Deputy Cain remained standing.

"Mrs. Roi, where did your husband go to work on Tuesday?"

"Up to the Town Hall," she said. "They're regrading

the parking area and widening the drive around back. Peter had the contract to do that."

"Last planning commission meeting they had cars parked all the way down to the turn on Route 14," Wojo added. "By the church. Had to have Deputy Cain here direct traffic."

Cotter looked directly at the distraught woman. "Mrs. Roi, is there anyone you can think of, personally or through your husband's business, who might want to hurt him, someone he may have had an argument with, a customer, or maybe a supplier or a competitor?"

"I don't think so," she said. "Peter was very busy and things were going well with the business." She paused for a moment. "There was someone who sued him a couple of years ago, but that's been over with for awhile."

"Who was that, Fanny?" Wojo asked.

"Martins, up near the school. They said their driveway didn't have enough gravel on it so they sued us instead of letting us put more gravel down. They never paid Peter, either. Can you imagine that?" She looked up from her lap. "And they sued him." She paused and lowered her head. Then she looked up, at nobody in particular. "Can you imagine that?" She looked directly at Cotter. "That's the kind of people we have here now."

"How was it resolved, Fanny?" Cotter asked.

"Peter offered to put more gravel down but only after they paid him for the work he did up till then. They refused, and they refused to pay him for the gravel he'd already delivered. So the lawyers all agreed Peter could go in and scoop out the gravel he'd already put down. But the Martins knew he'd never do that, so they got the gravel for nothing and Peter never got paid. Damn lawyers ain't worth nothing. I think that's what the Martins wanted from the get go. They just figured they'd sue him so they wouldn't have to pay him, and their lawyer was a damn sight smarter than ours." She paused again. "Reed Torgeson up in St. Albans. I told Peter to get some Jewish lawyer in Burlington, but he insisted on Reed.

The only thing that son-of-a-bitch did was send Peter bills and collect his own money. Never did anything else."

"Mrs. Roi," Cotter interrupted. "Please tell me the names of your husband's employees."

"He only has one, my son Rick."

"Your son?"

"Peter's not his real father. Peter adopted Rick after we were married." She looked at Cotter. "I had Rick before I married Peter." She paused and turned to Wojo. Her voice cracked as she continued. "Peter dropped me when I got pregnant." She looked back at Cotter trying desperately to regain her composure. "But we eventually got back together, after Rick was born." She turned toward Wojo. "Peter and I were married ten years ago."

"Who is Rick's real father?" Cotter asked.

"It doesn't matter," she said.

"It might, Mrs. Roi. You never know when..."

"Trust me, Detective," Wojo interrupted. "Some stones are best left unturned. Rick's father isn't involved in this. Take my word for it."

Cotter looked at Wojo in amazement. "How can you expect me to do that? How do you know he's not involved?"

"He's dead!" Wojo snapped. "Does that explain it, Detective?"

Cotter stared at Wojo. Nobody spoke. Cotter reluctantly turned back to Fanny Roi. "Mrs. Roi, Rick works full time with your husband?"

"Yes. We sub out everything else, no employees except himself and Rick. It's easier that way. Rick helps Peter with everything, especially the business part. He works very hard. Peter was going to give him the business when he retired. Peter loved my son."

"Your husband was going to give your son the entire business?" Cotter asked as he made notes in a pad he had removed from the inside of his jacket pocket. "There's a lot of heavy equipment in a business like your husband's, isn't there?"

"We own everything outright," Fanny said. "It's all ours. Business was good to us in the eighties so we paid everything off. That was Rick's idea. We made double payments during the summer when we were busy and we were able to keep making payments through the winter. Rick is smart when it comes to money. He said we saved thousands in interest and taxes."

"So what happens to the business now that Peter's gone?" Cotter asked.

"Rick gets it."

"Is there a will, Mrs. Roi?" Cotter asked sheepishly. "I know this is very difficult for you, but we need to look at every angle. I hope you understand."

"Rick loved my husband and my husband loved Rick," Fanny snapped. "They worked together to build this business. Peter took Rick under his wing and treated him like his own son."

Wojo reached across the table and covered Fanny's hands. "Listen, Fanny, we're not accusing Rick of anything. We just need to talk to him, see if he knows anyone who would want to hurt Peter."

Fanny started to calm down.

"I know Rick didn't do anything wrong, Fanny," Wojo continued. "So does Detective Cotter." His tenderness brought Fanny around. It was a part of Wojo that the public never saw, but it was there and it worked on Fanny Roi.

"Mrs. Roi, I appreciate what you're going through." Cotter tried to soothe her anger which was obviously directed at him. "If you could provide Sheriff Wojohowski with a copy of your husband's will and insurance documents, it would be very helpful. Can you do that for us?"

"Yes," she said. She looked at Wojo, then back at Cotter. "They're in the drawer in the bedroom. We have nothing to hide, Detective."

Cotter shifted his weight. "I'd like to ask you a few

more questions if you wouldn't mind, Mrs. Roi. Do you and Peter have any other children?"

"Peter has two boys...with the first wife. A couple of wastes."

"I'm sorry? Wastes?"

"They're no good. They drink, do drugs. We keep them on the payroll as subcontractors. They work for my husband and Rick when they're not drinking, or off on a bender with one of their girlfriends. Two peas from the same pod. No good."

"Is there a chance they may know something about what happened to your husband?" Cotter asked. He looked at Wojo. "We'll need to talk with them." He looked back at Fanny. "What are their names?"

Wojo answered for Fanny. "Russell's the older one. He's thirty-one. Ron's the younger one. He's a year younger. I don't think they'll be much help. Doubt very strongly they had anything to do with this," Wojo said. "These boys may be 'wastes' as Fanny here says, but they're not bad boys. They loved their father in spite of everything, I'm sure of that."

"What do you mean, in spite of everything?" Cotter looked at Wojo, then turned to Fanny.

Wojo and Fanny looked at each other. Wojo said nothing, expecting Fanny to answer. It was, after all, a situation of her own making.

"The two boys get nothing. Peter hated the way they didn't take the business seriously. He warned them, a hundred times. He told them if they didn't change their ways he'd give everything to Rick. Rick deserves it. He helped my husband build that business. They didn't. They're leeches. They live off my husband's guilt."

Cotter was amazed. "Your husband didn't plan to give them anything? That must have put a rather nasty wedge between your son and your husband's boys."

"Not really. They don't care. They never had anything to do with Rick anyway. They're a few years younger. Rick went into the Marines right after high school and started working for my husband when he got out. They never had anything to do with him." She paused. "I don't think they resent him. You have to be sober to do that, Detective." Fanny looked at Cotter. "These boys don't qualify."

"You only have to be sober and care for a brief moment, Ma'am," Cotter said. "Sometimes that's just enough time to kill someone."

"Fanny, where was Rick Tuesday evening?" Wojo asked. "Why didn't he go with Peter up to William Day Hairston Road?"

"He had a planning commission meeting," she said.

"Is Rick applying for a subdivision permit somewhere?" Wojo asked.

"No, no. He's trying to get Adrian 's seat on the commission. If Rick doesn't get it, or someone else who's lived here for awhile doesn't get it, then another flatlander's gonna get it and that'll kill this town once and for all. That'll be the end of it for all us landowners. No one will be able to do anything. Rick knew that and he talked with Peter about that Monday night. Peter wanted Rick to go to the meeting instead of with him because he didn't want Rick to miss out on his chance of getting on the commission."

"Who decides if he gets on?" Cotter asked.

"The selectmen," Wojo answered. "Fortunately we still have a majority on the selectboard. Rick should get the appointment."

Cotter looked at his notes and thanked Mrs. Roi for her help. He asked her to call him or Wojo if she thought of anything else that might help. Then he reminded her about the will and life insurance policies and stood up. She got up and went into the bedroom which was down the hall from the kitchen. In a moment she returned.

"Here," she said. "I hope this satisfies your curiosity." Then she turned to Wojo. "Thank you, Stan." She ignored Deputy Cain. The three men walked out of the house and back onto the front porch.

"By the way," Cotter said, as he turned back toward Fanny who was standing in the doorway. "Where is your son now?"

The question took her by surprise. She thought for a moment before answering. "He's at work." she finally said.

"Doesn't he know about Peter yet?" Wojo asked sympathetically.

"I don't know," Fanny said. She looked at Deputy Cain.

"Have you sent anyone to inform Rick yet?" Wojo asked Cain.

Deputy Cain shook his head from side to side.

"Do it!" Wojo snapped. "Then get back here and stay with Fanny until Rick gets home."

Roi's two sons pulled up just as Wojo and Cotter were getting into their cars. Both men drove late-model pickups with *Roi Excavating* painted on the doors in gold lettering with black trim. As the drivers got out of the trucks it was obvious they were brothers. They were both tall and lanky and they both had large heads full of kinky black hair. They looked just like their father, especially the thick black eyebrows and chiseled noses.

Neither man was athletic looking. To the contrary, they looked soft, their bodies neglected, except for the beer they poured freely down their gullets at all times of the day. Both men were in their early thirties but they looked much older. Hard living does that. They moved quickly up the steps toward the porch where their stepmother stood. The older one spoke first.

"What the fuck's going on?" he said to Fanny.

"Russell!" Wojo yelled to the older boy. "Come 'ere!" The older boy didn't move. Wojo got back out of his cruiser and walked deliberately up the steps and stood mere inches from the boy's face. The boy backed away.

"You boys know about your dad, I suppose?" Wojo

asked.

They both nodded.

"Know anything I should know?"

The two brothers looked at each other.

"I don't suppose either of you has been sober enough during the last few days by the looks of you, but you boys know anything at all, like who might've had a reason to shoot your father?"

"Who did it?" the older boy snapped.

"Don't know," Wojo said.

"I'll bet it was Rick," the younger boy said, looking at Fanny. "Find Rick and you got yourself the killer. Son of a bitch. He gets every fuckin' thing Dad owns."

"That's enough!" Fanny yelled. "At least he worked for it, you lazy sonofabitch. Both of you. Look at you, driving those trucks. Neither one of ya could afford a bicycle if your father didn't support you."

"Fanny, that's enough," Wojo said sympathetically.

"Things are gonna change now, for you two," she continued. Better get used to walking cause those trucks belong to Rick now. You want 'em, you're gonna have to work for 'em."

"Fuck you!" Russell said to Fanny.

Wojo hauled off and slapped the young man with the back of his large hand and sent the boy reeling backward against the railing and onto the seat of his pants. Only the railing kept him from tumbling off the porch.

"You ever talk to her like that again and I'll haul your sorry ass into that jail and kick it from one cell to the other." Wojo gritted his teeth as he spoke. He moved forward two steps and stood directly above Russell. "You got that, boy?"

Russell picked himself up and slowly headed back down the stairs and across the yard to his truck. He didn't look back, nor did he look at or say anything to his brother. Ron followed after making a pitiful attempt to say good-bye to Fanny and Wojo. He ignored Deputy Cain and Detective Cotter, who had followed Wojo back up the steps when the boys arrived.

"I'm gonna watch that pair for ya, Fanny," Wojo said. "You don't need that kinda trouble now." He took her hands in his own. "Have Rick come see me when he gets back, Fanny. I'll need to talk to him."

Fanny Roi said she would, and thanked Wojo for his help. Then she started to cry. She drew Wojo toward her and hugged him.

Wojo looked uncomfortable.

Cotter finally said he was sorry about Peter and looked at Fanny. "Mrs. Roi, please call me or Sheriff Wojohowski if you remember the name of the man who asked Peter to meet him Tuesday evening." He paused, then turned to leave. A few moments later Wojo met him where their cruisers were parked.

"A God-damned fucking mute," Wojo said. "Christ!"

"Excuse me?" Cotter said.

Wojo turned to Cotter. "Feel like a home-cooked meal, Detective? Must be tough eating in restaurants every day. Muriel's a real good cook. Best damn Yankee pot roast in Vermont. Come over to my house tonight. Figure about six o'clock." He looked pleased. "Bring an appetite, Detective, or you'll insult the woman."

Chapter Sixteen

A Motive?

If Muriel Wojohowski didn't make the best pot roast in town, it was certainly the best that Cotter had ever eaten. After two platefuls Cotter couldn't fit another bite into his stomach.

"Mrs. Wojohowski, your husband didn't lie," Cotter said. "That was the best pot roast I've ever had."

"Did he put a gun to your head to make you say that, Detective?" She looked at her husband. "He's been known to do that, you know."

Cotter smiled and looked at Wojo. "No, Ma'am, he certainly didn't. That's the best pot roast I've ever had and that's no lie. Honest. Hell, state troopers don't lie."

"Huh!" the hefty woman said as she lifted Cotter's empty plate off the table. "Policemen lie more than anyone. I know. I'm married to one, and he's the biggest liar I've ever known."

Muriel Wojohowski was a hard-core native Vermonter. She married Stan Wojohowski at the age of eighteen. Wojo represented her ticket off the farm. There was little romance in their marriage, and no kids. Like her father's livestock, life to Muriel Wojohowski was birth, struggle with little reward, and death. There seemed little point to it all except to live out the cycle.

Later that evening, Wojo and Cotter retired to Wojo's study, the inner sanctum of police headquarters.

"I'm getting too old for this shit," Wojo admitted. "It

used to be my sheriff's work was fun. There'd be some old-timer beating up his wife, or some poacher jacking deer up behind Grishom's, lost dog, couple a Sunday speeders coming back from the slopes. Now it's a fucking pain in the ass every day. People move in and before you know it you have burglaries, people complaining about everything from noise to dogs running free, taking a shit on someone's lawn. We had a guy call in one Sunday morning, I guess around eleven or so, not too long ago. The son-of-a-bitch complains his neighbor's cutting firewood with a chain saw. Dave Gerrity. 'Been cutting firewood for years. Nobody ever minded before. Now this guy moves into town one day, from some place down in Connecticut, and goes up to the town hall and finds some statute that says you can't cut firewood on your own property, not just Sunday, but anytime, if it's in the town district, except what you burn for yourself. Up to six cord a year I think it says. This guy's got the statute right there when I pull up. Now Gerrity's been cutting firewood for folks as far back as I can remember. Sure he sells it. That's how he lives. He's been retired for years. Now this guy wants me to shut him down. I explain to the guy how Gerrity's been doing this his whole life. Hell, everyone in town who doesn't put up their own wood buys from Dave. Then I tell him how Dave needs the money to live on, but nope, this son-of-a-bitch don't care. Makes me shut the old man down right on the spot. Just like that, and there's nothin' I can do about it. I gotta shut him down, so I do.

"That's the problem in this town these days," Wojo continued. "It used to be a nice place to live. Nice place to raise a family. Not anymore. Another ten years we'll all be gone. Won't find another native Vermonter anywhere in Eden Falls. It's a shame. A God-damned fucking shame. Know what I mean, Detective?"

Cotter shook his head and said he understood.

"Your daddy was a dairy farmer, wasn't he? The Cotter Farm, up to Washingtonville? That was your family?"

"My uncle," Cotter said. "My father worked for the

town."

"I think I knew your uncle. Died recently, didn't he? What's your aunt gonna do with the farm?"

"I don't know, actually. I really don't know." It was obvious Cotter hadn't thought much about it. Now that he did, it seemed to bother him, but not for long. He needed to pick Wojo's brain. His family's problems didn't matter right now. "What about Deputy Cain?"

"I'm not sure I understand your question, Detective."

"What does he do for you?"

"He's a big help. Helps me out a lot. Can't talk though." Wojo looked at Cotter. "So there ain't much he can do that way." He shifted his weight and laughed. "Kinda stupid, too. But he can do some things if ya show him. Follows orders real good, too. So he's real good that way." He paused, then changed the subject to the two murders. "Anything new on the Roi killing, Detective?"

"I think I've made some progress," Cotter said. He leaned forward as he spoke. "I examined Roi's will and life insurance policy. First of all, Fanny was telling the truth about Rick inheriting the whole business, the equipment, the dump truck, everything, including the two pickups Russell and Ron drive." Cotter looked at Wojo and removed his glasses. "I don't want to tell you how to run your town, Sheriff, but I'd watch those two if I were you. I don't think they had anything to do with their father's murder, that was the work of a pro, but they look like trouble."

"They look worse than they are. But you're right. I'm not so sure they're gonna like it when Rick takes their trucks away. I'll watch 'em. Bet on it."

Cotter put his glasses back on. "I also found out Rick gets a million dollars from a life insurance policy he and Peter Roi took out on each other a few months ago, key man insurance it's called. Each named the other as beneficiary if one died. Pretty suspicious in my book, don't you think, Sheriff?"

Wojo didn't react. Cotter found that somewhat odd.

"There's something else," Cotter said after a brief pause. "Rick was late for the planning commission hearing Tuesday night. And, I can't find anyone in town who's seen Rick since the hearing." Cotter paused again and stared at Wojo to emphasize the point. "That sends up a very large and very red flag in my book, Sheriff. How about you?"

Wojo listened to Cotter but didn't say anything..

"I'm real curious about that, Wojo. Aren't you?" Cotter pressed for a response. He was beginning to get annoyed at Wojohowski's indifference to what he considered enlightening information. "His mother said he was at work. That was a lie. That doesn't look very good for either of them. Does it?"

Cotter knew Wojo didn't like where he was going. It was obvious Wojo had feelings for these people.

"I'm not accusing either of them, Sheriff, I'm merely suggesting they may know something that could help the investigation. Considering we have absolutely nothing else to go on right now, I'd say we should look at every possibility."

"That's a hard one for me to swallow," Wojo said. "I can see your point because of the insurance, but what about Bessette. Where's Rick's motive for killing Adrian Bessette?"

"Planning commission? Business deal? Love triangle? Blackmail? I don't know yet," Cotter responded. "You tell me."

"Adrian was fine on the planning commission. Same views as Rick. I don't see a motive there. Anyway, it sounded from what Fanny said that it was Peter's idea to put Rick on the commission more than Rick's idea.

"Look, Wojo," Cotter said. "I don't know that there's a connection between Rick and Adrian Bessette. The problem is, we have two men dead and the only one who has even the remotest possibility of being a suspect has a strong motive to kill one but maybe not the other." He paused. "We need to find a motive for Bessette."

"You can't convince me Rick would kill Peter for the life insurance, Detective," Wojo said. "I've known the boy his whole life and he's not that way."

Cotter was mystified. "A million dollars is a pretty damn good motive in my book. Don't you agree?"

"Normally I'd agree with you, but not now," Wojo argued, trying desperately to remain calm. He stood up. "A million dollars is a lot of money, but Peter was overweight, in terrible shape. He had a bad heart, the son-of-a-bitch was gonna drop dead in a few years anyway. Rick knew that."

"The fact that he hasn't been seen since the night of his stepfather's murder doesn't help." Cotter lowered his voice. "If we could find him and talk to him we'd know for sure. Then we could at least eliminate him as a suspect and move on. As long as he stays away, he's still a suspect."

Cotter stood. Wojohowski moved over to the window and looked out.

"I used to smoke a Cuban cigar after dinner every night. Got 'em from a friend of mine." Wojo looked at Cotter. "Don't know how he got 'em and never asked. Used to relax me, take my mind off things." He looked out the window. "Muriel said they made me stink." He looked at Cotter and laughed. "I started smoking Camels in sixth grade. She made me quit those two years ago, said it would kill me. So what, I said to her. What the fuck do you care? I'm gonna die sooner or later. Might as well make it sooner, that way you'll get everything I own and have enough spunk left in ya to marry another poor slob." He looked over his shoulder directly at Cotter and laughed again. "Then she said no more cigars. Why not, I asked her. Stinks up the house, she says."

Cotter didn't say a word. Wojo kept staring out of the window.

"Sheriff Wojohowski, there's something you can do for me," Cotter finally said. Wojo turned around. "There's something we're missing here. Both men were killed in town. The killer, we assume, is the same man, or woman, for that matter. Whoever the killer is, he knows exactly where his victims will be. He knows their routines, when they're vulnerable, and he knows exactly how to get at them. I think he knows his victims very well. He also knows his way around town, not only the roads but the woods. That suggests he grew up in Eden Falls. That narrows it somewhat. I think it's a foregone conclusion our killer's a local person. And I think he's right under our noses."

Wojo looked at him but said nothing.

"If that's the case," Cotter continued, "we need to find a common thread, something that was common to both Adrian Bessette and Peter Roi. That will help us find a motive. Once we have a motive, we can come up with a psychological profile of the killer. Once you have that, we can look for someone in the community who fits that profile, like someone who has a reason to hate doctors or someone who was just jilted by a blonde lover or whatever. You get what I'm trying to say, don't you?"

Cotter looked at Wojo with great anticipation but Wojo just smiled and shook his head in disbelief.

Cotter wondered if he was wasting his time, but he continued. "We know our killer has the ability to plan and execute covert assassinations, right? So maybe we look for a person with a military background, a Marine, for example, Special Forces, or a Navy SEAL."

Wojo laughed again and looked at Cotter. "No offense, Detective, but the shit they teach you boys in detective school isn't gonna find this killer. This is a small town. Things don't work that way around here. You know that as well as me. People don't talk here. They solve their own problems."

"Not anymore," Cotter insisted. He sat down again.

"Damn, Cotter, are you thick?" Wojo turned away, then spun back at Cotter. "You state boys are out of touch." He leaned forward, put his large hands on the corner of his desk and stared at Cotter. "I'll find out who's doing this but it ain't gonna be your way. You want to help? Fine! I ain't got no jurisdiction anymore so I can't tell you what to do or where to go. But it's my god-damned town and I'll be a horse's ass if I'm gonna let a couple of smart-assed state police detectives run around here upsetting everyone while I sit back and do nothing. We did fine before you guys came along and we'll do fine now."

"Look, Sheriff, we're on the same team, remember?" Cotter shot back. He looked Wojohowski in the eye. "I need your help. You can either give it to me, or I'll bring so many detectives and state troopers into this quiet little town of yours that they'll be reading about it in Los Angeles. I'm trying to run this thing your way, low-keyed, no press. Isn't that what you want?"

Wojohowski straightened up, walked around the corner of the desk and sat down. He looked at his desk and made a funny motion with his mouth. "I wish I had a God-damned cigar," he said. Then he looked up at Cotter. "What do you want to know, Detective?"

Cotter leaned forward in his chair. "I need to know if there's anything about either man that you can think of that can tie the two victims together. Anything at all. From childhood, school, their families, their business dealings, investments, maybe a girlfriend they shared, anything."

Wojo leaned way back in his chair and thought for a moment. "Maybe," he said. He paused again. "Maybe there's some business dealings. I can talk to a few people in town who may know something about that. Shouldn't be too hard. People'll talk to me who won't talk to you, Detective. Know what I mean?"

Cotter accepted the offer and told Wojo it was late and he ought to be leaving. The two men went back into the large kitchen where Muriel was still puttering.

"Thanks for dinner, Mrs. Wojohowski," Cotter said. "It was, and I promise you I'm not lying, the best pot roast I've ever eaten." He turned to leave, stopped and turned back to Mrs. Wojohowski. "By the way, what's your secret ingredient?"

"Truth serum," she replied.

Cotter looked at Wojo. "I'll have to remember that."

Chapter Seventeen

The Red Bird Motel

The Red Bird Motel on Route 14, just outside of Eden Falls, used to be a thriving business, but years of neglect and an influx of new chain motels around the Burlington area like the Holiday Inn, the Sheraton, the Radisson, the Marriot, Motel Six and a handful of others, changed all that. The only people who stayed at the Red Bird were hunters who didn't mind the decaying decor and the overflow of tourists who couldn't find lodging at the better motels or quaint B&B's during foliage season.

The Red Bird Motel was a two hundred fifty foot-long, wood-framed building with clapboard siding. Twenty rooms faced Route 14 with another twenty facing the parking lot in the rear. Each room had a bright red door. The building hadn't been painted in two decades, except the bright red doors.

Cotter walked into his room about nine-thirty. He was logy from the amount of food he had eaten and he was disturbed about the evening's events. There was something about Sheriff Wojohowski that bothered him. It was what his wife had said.

"You policemen lie more than anyone."

Cotter knew it was a deliberately cutting remark from an angry wife.

"I know. I'm married to one and he's the biggest liar I've ever known."

What bothered Cotter the most was he knew it was

probably true.

"You policemen lie more than anyone."

She meant it, too, Cotter said to himself. The words played over and over again in his head.

"I'm married to one and he's the biggest liar I've ever known."

Thinking about Muriel Wojohowski and her wonderful pot roast made Cotter miss Janie more than ever. He sat on the bed, picked up the phone and dialed their number. The phone rang three, four, five times until the answering machine picked up.

"Hi," Janie's voice said. "Sim and I can't come to the phone. Leave a message." A short beep followed.

"Hi, Babe," Cotter said. "I guess you're not there." He paused. "Don't call back, I'm going to sleep. I'll call you tomorrow." He paused again. "I love you, Janie." He held the phone next to his ear. He hoped Janie would somehow rush into their house at the last minute and pick up the receiver. The line remained silent. After a few more seconds he hung up, took off his clothes and got into bed. He picked up the Burlington Free Press and pulled out the crossword puzzle. He tried to concentrate. "A four letter word for sassy." But his thoughts kept returning to Sheriff Wojohowski. "He's the biggest liar I've ever known." Cotter fought back. "Sassy." He closed his eyes and repeated the clue. "A four letter word...for sass..."

Before he could finish the word he was asleep, crossword and pencil on his chest, Stanley T. Wojohowski very much on his mind.

Chapter Eighteen

A Common Thread

Eight hours later Cotter woke up. The crossword and pencil were on the floor next to his bed. The sleep had revived him and the pot roast had run its course. He took a long, hot shower, put on a pair of tan Dockers and a light blue dress shirt and headed for Wojo's office.

Wojo was on the phone when Cotter arrived. He got off when he saw Cotter, stood up and greeted the detective. He hesitated for a moment before dropping back into his seat. "Deputy Cain still hasn't located Rick," he said abruptly.

Cotter plunked himself down in a green vinyl chair opposite Wojo's enormous desk. The seat cushion hissed as Cotter took the weight off his legs.

"I think we're gonna have to move on Rick," Cotter said. "Maybe I ought to alert the dispatcher in Williston to have our boys look for him. Maybe he left the state. I'll have to notify the feds."

"Don't do that," Wojo said. "Not yet." He looked at Cotter and paused. I'm working through some personal contacts to try to track him down. It's gonna take me a little time but I'll find him. You boys have to stay out of it for a few more days." He paused again. "You'll drive him away. Let me find him." He got up and walked over to the gun rack.

"Know much about guns, Detective?"

"Some," Cotter answered.

Wojo pulled a rifle off the rack. "This is the same

model our killer used," Wojo said. "Stop a man cold at a thousand yards." He turned to Cotter. "Ever kill a man, Detective?"

"No," Cotter said. "Have you, Sheriff?"

"Never kiss and tell, and never kill and tell, Detective Cotter." Wojo smiled. His features looked contorted when he smiled, as if the smile was forced onto his face against its will. Then his expression became more serious. "Those are the two things that'll get you into trouble."

Cotter didn't respond.

Wojo put the rifle back in the rack and ambled over to his desk. He became analytical as he walked. "Kiss and tell...that'll run you afoul of your wife. Kill and tell...that'll run you afoul of the law. Personally, I'd rather run afoul of the law. Know what I mean, Detective?" He looked at Cotter and laughed.

"By the way, Detective," Wojo said as he sat down in his chair and shuffled a few papers on his desk. "I found out some things this morning that might interest you." He took a large cigar out of his drawer, removed it from its metal shield and bit off one tip. He tore two matches out of a matchbook and lit both of them with one sweep. He watched the tips of the matches as they ignited. Within seconds, white smoke billowed up from the end of the cigar, thicker and more grand as Wojo sucked on the other end. He looked at Cotter and winked. "She never said nothin' 'bout my office." He sucked on the cigar again, three or four times, his large cheeks imploding with each suckle. The lit end glowed bright orange. His face was barely visible behind the smoke. He finally took the cigar out of his mouth and held it at eye level in front of him. He looked at it lovingly, then turned to Cotter. "It looks like Peter Roi was in line to get a hefty excavation contract when Vesticate Douglas's permit goes through." He paused and watched the smoke trail. "You know Vesticate Douglas, Detective Cotter?"

"I've heard of the Douglas farm in Eden Falls."

"Same one," Wojo said. He studied the cigar which he held about eight inches from his face. "Vesticate's trying to develop his land, build some houses. If he gets his permits, that whole area's gonna be worth a small fortune." He looked at Cotter. "You're talking a couple hundred thousand worth of work for Peter and Rick if they get that contract. Roads, sewer system, what-not. Set Peter for life." He put the cigar back in his mouth and took several puffs.

"You mean Rick, now that Peter's dead," Cotter said.

"No, I don't. Rick's gonna have to sub most of it out now that Peter's gone. Now let me finish." Wojo said. He took the cigar out of his mouth and looked at it for a few seconds, then shifted his eyes to Cotter. "Rick won't make anywhere's near as much on that project as he would if Peter were still alive. But he'll do O.K. just the same." He put the cigar back in his mouth and took another mighty puff. A new cloud of white smoke shot out of his mouth in a stream shaped by his lips which he pursed around his tongue.

He's making love to his fucking cigar, Cotter said to himself.

"Fanny was wrong about something, though," Wojo continued. "The equipment might have been paid for, but not the house. Roi mortgaged the house a while ago to buy a small piece of land next to the Douglas property. Needed the money to buy it. The land'll be worth a half million when it's developed, if planning commission lets him develop it. Worthless if they don't." He put the cigar back in his mouth and sucked on the end which was becoming moist and pliable. He took a few enormous puffs. White smoke gathered around the ceiling fixture above Wojo's desk. He fondled the cigar with his lips rotating it clockwise a half a turn, then counterclockwise and back again.

"It keeps looking worse for Golden Boy, doesn't it, Sheriff?" Cotter could tell Wojo didn't appreciate the remark. "I mean Rick."

Wojo threw it off. "There's more. Apparently Peter Roi

and Adrian Bessette were partners in the land deal."

Cotter perked up. Was this the connection, he wondered?

"Looks like Adrian had to co-sign the loan Roi took out on his house to buy his half of the land. It seems the bank said Peter had plenty of equity but not enough income. Bank said the construction forecast for the area was poor. If the Douglas project fell through, the bank says Peter wouldn't have much work and wouldn't be able to make his payments. So Adrian had to co-sign the note."

"Why didn't he mortgage the equipment?" Cotter asked.

"Don't know," Wojo responded. "Same reason I guess." Wojo reached into his briefcase and pulled out a copy of the deed for the land next to the Douglas Farm purchased by Bessette and Roi and showed it to Cotter. The names of both men appeared on the deed.

"Who inherits Roi's share of the property?" Cotter asked.

"Looks like Rick does," Wojo responded.

"Looks like he also gets Adrian Bessette's share," Cotter said as he perused the deed.

"How so?" Wojo asked, leaning forward in his chair as if he had missed something.

"Seems Roi and Bessette put a clause into their agreement that calls for the surviving partner to inherit the share of the deceased partner should one of the partners die," Cotter said. He continued to look at the deed.

"Hell, Detective. Maybe they didn't want their wives to get it." Wojo roared with laughter.

"So Adrian Bessette dies and Peter Roi gets his half of the land, then Peter Roi dies and Rick Roi winds up with the whole thing." Cotter looked up at Wojo and smiled. "You see what I'm getting at here, Sheriff?" Cotter said. "There's Rick's motive for killing Adrian Bessette. Right here in the deed."

Wojo's face turned red and he leaned forward. "Don't

start that again, Detective. Rick Roi didn't kill anybody! I'd stake my life on that." He raised his voice and he spit as he talked. Then, almost as quickly as he had lost it, he regained his composure. He leaned back in his chair, cleared his voice and spoke in a low tone.

"Don't ask me how I know, Detective, just take my word for it." His shoulders settled back and he became more relaxed. "There has to be another explanation. I'm not exactly sure what it is right now, but you can bet your ass I'm gonna find out."

Tough shit! Cotter said to himself. When Wojo finally calmed down, Cotter continued to read the deed. He looked at the description of the property on the second page. *"...a plot of land located on the southeast side of land owned by the State of Vermont, Department of Transportation as described in the Town of Eden Falls Land Records, Volume VIII, page(s) 244, 245 and 246, and more fully described in Warranty Deed of..."*

When he was finished, Cotter looked up. "The reference to DOT...that's the interstate, isn't it?" He paused. "I'd like to see this property, Sheriff. I'd like to see the Douglas Farm too." He got up to leave. Wojo jumped up to join him and suggested they ride together in Wojo's cruiser to continue their conversation.

The Douglas Farm was located about six miles outside of Eden Falls on Route 14. The soil in that part of the valley was outstanding, a rich loam that had supported generations of Douglases for nearly two centuries.

Next to the Douglas farm was a small piece of land that also abutted the new interstate off-ramp planned for construction in 1998. Both properties were worth little more than their back taxes. With development permits, however, the Douglas Farm would be worth millions and the parcel owned by Adrian Bessette and Peter Roi would be worth nearly five hundred thousand dollars. Bessette and Roi paid thirty thousand for it.

Vesticate Douglas had fought to get permits for the

Douglas Farm Project and had failed for more than six years. The majority of Eden Falls Planning Commissioners opposed the project citing environmental considerations as their reason. To make matters worse, Douglas's project had become the rallying point, the line in the sand, for an anti-development group called Eden Falls Citizens for Responsible Land Management, whose mission was to preserve the town's rural character. The CRLM was able to convince the planning commission that the project violated the town's new development laws and would change the character of Eden Falls from a small rural village to a sprawling suburb of Burlington.

The Douglas Farm ceased operations in 1995, suffering the same fate as so many family-owned dairy farms throughout Vermont and especially in Chittenden County. More than one hundred cows and all of the farm machinery were auctioned off to pare down the property's large delinquent tax bill. With property taxes skyrocketing from the need to provide municipal services to the hundreds of new town residents, local farmers couldn't make ends meet. Higher taxes, rising operating costs, lower milk prices and no younger generation to pick up the slack forced many farmers to give up. The rich family-farm life that was the fabric of Vermont society up until the 1970's had all but faded away.

Fighting the Eden Falls Planning Commission for what he considered his God-given right to do with his land as he desired had driven Vesticate Douglas to the brink of bankruptcy. His patience had worn as thin as his credit line. After a particularly bitter sketch plan hearing at which several commissioners had made glorious speeches about preserving the rural beauty of Eden Falls, Douglas lost it completely.

"You're destroying us," he lectured the commissioners in a stern voice as the meeting was about to adjourn. He was on his feet and fighting mad. "You've driven up the cost of farming to the point where we can't make a living doing that anymore. Then you want to tax us to pay for all your new schools and your paved roads. Then you tell us we can't develop our land 'cause we'll spoil the town. If we can't develop it we can't sell it. What are we supposed to do with it? How are we supposed to live?"

The commissioners were stunned. No one had ever seen such a tantrum at a planning commission hearing before. And Douglas still wasn't through. He started pointing his fingers at Brian Reese, one of the commissioners who had voted against his project. "You've lived in this community for less than two years. My family's lived here and farmed that land for two hundred years. What right do you have to tell me what I can do with my own land? Can you please tell me that?"

Several commissioners, especially Reese, took offense at Douglas's remarks and started shouting back at him. There were threats of lawsuits and countersuits and Douglas had to be restrained by his lawyer and Planning Commission Chairman Nathan Winters.

Still without permits to build, the Douglas property sat untouched. The large, colonial-style farm house in which Vesticate Douglas and his children were born was all boarded up and looked as tired and outdated as the way of life it supported. Douglas and his wife had moved out the year before. The pasture was overgrown with berries and nettles. The outbuildings, including the large barn that had once housed more than one hundred head of cattle, began to show signs of structural failure and it listed slightly to one side. The barn derived its life from the cows and horses that lived within. Once the livestock was taken away, the barn had no reason to live. Within a very short period of time it began a slow decline. Death would occur when a crew came in to salvage the posts and beams and the barn boards for someone's house; a bit of natural nostalgia, a decorator's delight, a piece of Vermont.

Cotter and Wojo pulled onto the shoulder of Route 14 in front of the Douglas farm and got out of Wojo's patrol car. Cotter wasn't sure what he was looking for. It had something to do with seeing if the land Roi and Bessette bought was worth killing for.

"Used to spend a lot of time up here as a kid," Wojo confessed. "Raised plenty of hell with Vesticate. Put up a lot a hay over the years. Couldn't keep up with his older brother, Ray. Little shit could lift more bails of hay and toss 'em right up to the top of that hay wagon, right in place, perfectly stacked right where Ray tossed 'em. Never had to move 'em when Ray tossed 'em. Not me. Hell, my arms would feel like they weighed a ton after a half dozen bales. Lucky I didn't miss the wagon completely. Not Ray. He'd keep on going till there was no more to do. Never seen another man do that."

The two men stood in front of the main house. Numerous wooden surveyor's stakes had been set on the property. Red flags had been affixed to the tops of each stake and surveyor's marks had been written in magic marker indicating where the stakes corresponded to the map. Rows of stakes ran back into the pasture at ninety degrees to Route 14 to indicate the access road, the lot lines and the common area. Douglas had already spent thousands of dollars on surveyors and engineers to help plan his development. So far he hadn't earned a single penny.

Next to the Douglas Farm was a much smaller piece of land that had also been surveyed with an eye toward development. It was the parcel owned by Roi and Bessette. It was perfectly situated to the planned exit ramp off the interstate for a gas station and convenience store, a few apartments or a row of retail condos.

Directly across the road from the Douglas farm was a large pasture that ran a thousand yards back from Route 14 to the tree line. A partially beaten tractor path made its way across the pasture and up into the woods.

"Who owns that land?" Cotter inquired.

"Deputy Cain."

Cotter looked incredulously at Wojo. "What?"

"I know what you're thinking, Detective. Amazing, isn't it? Hardly think it to look at him. Hard to believe he owns a piece of land that valuable."

Cotter thought he detected a bit of envy in Wojo's voice.

"His mother left it to him years ago," Wojo said. He looked at the pasture.

"How many acres does he own?"

Wojo didn't answer at first. "More than Douglas. I think Vesticate said it was something like five hundred, maybe six hundred acres. Was worthless when Cain got it. Old sheep farm. Mostly second-growth now, some money in timber. Vesticate hayed it for years. In fact, I think Vesticate's great-grandfather owned it once. Don't know how it got into Cain's family. Worth a pretty sum if the town lets Vesticate build. Have to assume if Vesticate gets his permits, the town's gotta give permits to everyone up here. Three to four million the way I figure it." He turned to Cotter. "Never know it to look at him. Know what I mean, Detective?"

Chapter Nineteen

A Recollection

On the way back to the sheriff's office, Wojo turned to Cotter and said he wanted to tell him a story.

"Listen, Detective. There was an incident here in Eden Falls, years ago." He paused and looked over at Cotter. "It's a long shot at best, but it might have something to do with these murders."

Cotter turned toward Wojo. He could see the river along Route 14 as he looked past Wojo's face and focused his eyes on the turbid water. It was a picturesque ride through a green countryside bursting with life. Small gentleman farms followed in succession along both sides of the road. Most of them were owned by people who didn't farm. Their fields were leased for pasture land, corn, and hay fields to the few farmers who remained along Route 14. Cotter thought about his uncle and the wonderful times he had enjoyed as a kid on the Cotter farm. In many ways he thought he had been better off than the kids today. Life was simpler then.

"About thirty years ago," Wojo continued, "thirty-two years ago, to be exact, we had a little problem here in Eden Falls. I was just a kid. It seems this group of boys got this idea that if they gave the new boys in town a rough time, you know, a little rough play, maybe the town would get a reputation that flatlanders weren't welcome." Wojo looked at Cotter. "Well this went on for a bit till one day a couple of our older boys took one of the new kids, a boy about ten, maybe twelve years old, into the woods behind the school. The boy's name was Fischer, I think. I think his first name was Brian." Wojo looked at Cotter, then the road, then back at Cotter as he spoke. "They gave him a pretty good going over. Roughed him up pretty good. Then they pretended they were gonna hang him, so they strung him up on the limb of a nearby maple tree. Except the kid died, Fischer, I mean." He turned to Cotter. "Are you listening, Detective?"

"I'm listening," Cotter said after a brief pause.

Wojohowski continued. "There were three local boys involved, besides the Fischer kid, I mean. They were all about sixteen, so, even though the sheriff finds out who did it, he can't arrest 'em because they're all under age. Can't even tell anyone their names."

Wojo turned to look at Cotter. Their eyes met.

"What, are you sick or something?" Wojo asked. "You look like you're about to puke."

Cotter turned away from Wojo. "I'm fine."

Wojo turned back toward the road. "Peter Roi and Adrian Bessette were two of the local boys involved in the hanging. I heard this on pretty good authority from an older kid right after it happened. The kid said he was best friends with Roi and Roi told him him and Bessette were there. I promised never to tell anyone and I haven't till today. Not even Muriel. Hell, if I told her it'd be all over town in a few hours." He laughed and looked back at Cotter. Then he became deadly serious. "If you tell anyone you heard it from me, Detective, about Roi and Bessette, I'll deny it."

Cotter tried to hide his discomfort. The story brought back memories that were terribly painful. He was a young child when word of the hanging spread to neighboring towns. Rumors traveled like a spider's web. His parents tried to shield the sensitive youth from the news, but they couldn't control what other kids said.

The young Cotter was badly shaken by the gruesome stories of the boy who was hanged by local teenagers. His imagination ran wild with images of the hanging, the older boys tormenting their victim as a cat teases its prey before inflicting the fatal wound. He felt the terror the Fischer boy must have felt. He suffered for the boy's physical pain and worse, he thought about what must have gone through his mind at the final moment. It haunted him. He couldn't sleep at night, pleading with his mother not to leave him alone when she tucked him into bed. If he awoke during the night he went immediately to his parents' room and crawled into their bed. For weeks after the incident he had terrible nightmares. He dreamed he was drowning, or in a cave where the walls were closing in on him. In all of his nightmares he came close to experiencing his own death. He often awoke from his nightmares crying like an infant with his mother at his bedside trying to comfort him.

For several days after he had heard of the hanging, the young Cotter was reluctant to go to school and he feigned all kinds of illnesses to stay home. The incident affected his childhood as had no other event or influence. It would be his personal demon, and it would be with him forever.

"I remember when it happened," Cotter finally said.

"Sure ya do. Opens up some pretty good possibilities too, doesn't it?" Wojo suggested.

"What?"

"I said it opens up some pretty good possibilities, doesn't it?" Wojo paused and looked at Cotter. "Are you listening to me, Detective?"

"Like revenge?" Cotter snapped.

"Seems pretty obvious, doesn't it?" Wojo said. "Except *they* didn't do it." Wojo looked at Cotter again. "The boy's family, I mean. The Fischer kid was an only child and his folks left the state after it happened. Moved to Florida I think. So that kinda kills that theory."

"Don't rule it out, Sheriff. Time and distance don't soften the desire for revenge, they just delay it, sometimes intensify it." Cotter looked out of the passenger window at a bank of storm clouds crowding up around the peak of Mount Mansfield. "Maybe they hired someone to come back and do what they believed the courts should have done thirty years ago. It would give them justice, some sort of redemption." Cotter looked at Wojo. "Maybe they're looking for some acceptable justification for their son's death, you know; it happened so they would in turn take the lives of three evil men, a twisted form of divine intervention."

Wojo looked straight ahead and chuckled at the suggestion. "First of all, Detective, I don't know what the fuck you're talking about. Second, I don't think so. Maybe on TV, but not in the real world."

Wojohowski was beginning to irritate Cotter. "Then what's your theory, Sheriff?"

Wojo raised his eyebrows and smiled. "What do I think? I'm not sure." He pulled the cruiser into the town hall, drove around back and parked by the rear entrance. "Could be someone's trying for the ultimate hush up." He shut off the car and looked at Cotter, but neither man made a move to get out. "Maybe one of the three boys has more to lose now than he did thirty-two years ago. Maybe he wants to make sure his two buddies don't blow it for him by talking. Ever! Maybe Adrian Bessette or Peter Roi reaches a point where they want to spill their guts out about the hanging. Take the other boys down with them." He paused. "Maybe it's someone who just came into money and he wants to be able to enjoy it without any hassles."

"Or maybe he was being blackmailed?" Cotter suggested.

"Maybe."

"Who do you have in mind?" Cotter asked.

"Maybe someone like Deputy Cain."

"Cain?"

"Yup, Cain," Wojo said. "Maybe Cain was the third boy. I never found out who it was. Maybe it was Cain and maybe he's our man."

"That's a pretty big stretch, Sheriff, don't you think? Sounds to me like you're going from A to Z and skipping everything in between. It doesn't compute. Weak motive at best."

"I heard Roi and Bessette have been trying to buy Cain's land ever since his mother gave it to him," Wojo continued. "Maybe they weren't satisfied with their small parcel and they wanted what Cain had. An extra couple of million each can't hurt. Maybe they were trying to blackmail him, like you said, you know, sell us your land or we'll tell everyone you were one of the boys involved in the hanging. Newspaper stories, national news, man loses his job. Not a good situation for Cain. Man likes his privacy." Wojo stared at Cotter. "Besides," he added, "there's no statute of limitation on murder, even after thirty-two years. He could go to jail for the rest of his life." He kept both hands on the steering wheel. His eyes remained fixed on Cotter.

"But that would be stupid," Cotter argued. "By exposing Cain, they'd be exposing themselves."

Wojo smiled. "Not necessarily. Here you got two prominent businessmen, well-respected in the community, against the local mute who's also a bit on the, you know, slow side. Maybe Cain doesn't like it, figures he's gonna get burned, so he takes care of things himself. You know, a little P.O.M.I., piece of mind insurance." Wojo laughed.

"He's your fucking deputy!"

"Listen, Detective, he's my fucking deputy because I've known him and his God-damned mother my whole life and I feel sorry for the bastard. That's it. You think I need a deputy? Hell no. Everyone in town knows that. Now the son of a bitch is about to become a millionaire and he's getting a little more conscious of his public image." Wojo looked at Cotter and laughed again.

"I've heard of crazier things in my day, Detective," Wojo continued. "Cain's been my deputy for twenty years. Never said a word in twenty years. Not that he can. Kinda spooky. Know what I mean, Detective?"

Cotter stared at Wojohowski. There was a prolonged silence. Each man tried to read the other.

"Cain. That's intriguing." Cotter finally said. "But the motive is a stretch no matter how you try to make it work. It's based on a premise of blackmail and we have no evidence. Plus, I'm not so sure Deputy Cain cares what people think of his so-called public image. He's a loner, and loners don't spend a lot of time worrying about what others think of them." He paused. "We'd never even get a search warrant." He paused again. "Besides, do you believe Cain has the intelligence to pull off two perfectly executed murders without leaving a clue?"

The two men got out of the car. "I don't know that Deputy Cain has the intelligence to come in from the rain," Wojo said. "Maybe he had a partner. Someone with the brains to help him come up with a plan of attack while Cain did the dirty work."

That was the first thing Wojo had said that made any sense, Cotter thought. He stopped and looked at Wojo. It was possible, he thought, possible indeed.

"That's an interesting thought," Cotter said. "It would have to be someone Cain trusted. It would also have to be someone who wanted something Cain had, something of value that Cain could give him in exchange for his help."

Wojo didn't say anything.

"The only thing of value Cain has is his land," Cotter continued.

The two men stood near the stairs heading down to the rear entrance.

"What about Rick?" Cotter asked. "From what his mother said, he certainly has the brains."

Wojo snickered at the suggestion and started down the steps to the rear entrance to the town hall.

Cotter followed close behind Wojo as the pair entered Wojo's office. When they were through the door Cotter grabbed Wojo's right arm and spun him around. The two men stood face to face. It was a gutsy move.

"I mean it!" Cotter said. "What about Rick?" Wojo stood his ground and looked at Cotter's hand. He didn't throw it off or heave Cotter through the plate glass door that separated Wojo's Office from the public meeting room.

"I know you don't want to hear this," Cotter continued. "I suspect you care a great deal about Fanny Roi. But look at the evidence. It's compelling. Very compelling."

Wojo just stood there and looked at Cotter. Cotter didn't flinch.

"Look at it objectively," Cotter continued. He kept his hand on Wojo's arm. He didn't know how far he could push Wojo. "The guy inherits a million dollars. He's given a company with more than three hundred thousand dollars in assets and no debt. He inherits a piece of prime land owned by Adrian Bessette and Peter Roi. He stands to gain a lucrative contract that will take him into the next decade. Better still, he gets a chunk of Cain's land as payment for coming up with a plan that Cain executes. Roi doesn't even have to get his hands dirty. It's as clear as day. And where is he? Nobody knows." He looked at Wojo for a reaction. "Maybe his mother was in on it too. She stands to gain as much as he does."

"Don't even suggest that, Detective," Wojo snapped. He yanked his arm away from Cotter and headed into the office. He stopped and turned to face Cotter.

"I've known Fanny my whole life. The woman's never had anything worth shit and she doesn't give a pig's ass about money or material things. When she married Peter she had all she ever wanted. She didn't kill him and I don't wanna hear..."

"O.K.," Cotter said. "Well, it's nice to know I have your attention." He paused to let Wojo cool down. "But what about Rick? You didn't come to his defense like you came to his mother's."

"I don't know," Wojo shook his head. "It bothers me, too. You know, that he took off like that. That's wrong. If he had a problem he should have come to see me. I know it makes him look bad. His mother and I were very close when we were younger. He should have come to see me."

Wojo sat down behind his desk. His huge torso barely fit into his leather-covered, cushioned arm chair. "I could help the boy."

Cotter stepped up to the front of the desk, directly opposite Wojo, and leaned over the desk until he was only a foot or so from Wojo. Wojo wasn't pleased. It was the second time Cotter had been in his face in less than five minutes. Wojo was finding it increasingly difficult to restrain himself. He wanted to smash Cotter's head into the desk.

"You know who the third boy was, don't you, Wojo?" Cotter said. He looked Sheriff Wojohowski right in the eye. Wojo didn't blink or turn away. "You sure it was Deputy Cain?"

Wojo looked directly at Cotter. He still didn't blink. There was fire in his eyes. Then, as quickly as it came, it went. "Not sure," Wojo said. He leaned way back in his chair and put his feet up on the desk. He wished he had another cigar. "Just surmising."

Chapter Twenty

A Patch Of Snow

The following day was Thomas Downey's day off. He arose from bed after Leah and Tommy had left. He wished he had gone to work. These were the hardest times, the moments when the realization of what he had become threw him into a state of melancholy. He sat on the edge of his bed with little motivation to move. He knew these moments would come and he knew if he didn't get up and find something to do, anything, as long as it occupied the whole day and exhausted him so he could sleep that night, it would be a very difficult day.

Twenty minutes later Downey was dressed and standing at the top of the driveway holding a mug of hot coffee Leah had left for him. He gazed into the woods behind the house as he took a sip of the coffee. It was his first sip and it tasted delicious. He took another sip. He continued to gaze into the woods. He thought about taking a walk behind the house, past the horse paddock and up toward the stream, like he used to, like he loved to do. But he decided against it. He hadn't been in the woods since he shot Adrian Bessette. "Not today," he mumbled.

His eyes rested on a small patch of snow, no larger than a dinner plate, which clung to life under a tree not far into the woods. It had defied the forces that had caused everything else to melt away, the forces that transform the forest from stark white to various shades of brown and green. The small patch of snow marked the spot in the woods that received the least amount of sunlight. The proof was in its solitary existence.

A red squirrel sat on the patch of snow. He was old and his fur was ragged and thin. Downey watched the squirrel but it didn't move. He wondered about the squirrel's demise. Would it be from natural causes, or would he fall prey to a hungry fox? He wondered if the squirrel understood death. Did he know that, like the patch of snow on which he sat, his time was limited?

Downey turned quickly away from the squirrel. To his surprise Wojo was walking up the driveway. He had parked his cruiser down in the road. Wojo seemed remarkably fit for a man his size, making it up to the top of the driveway in less than a minute. When he reached Downey he smiled, took a deep breath and let it out. He appeared unfazed by the incline.

"Morning, Mr Downey. Coffee break?"

"Good morning, Sheriff," Downey replied. He looked down at his mug. "No, actually, I slept late." He looked up. "Today is my day off." He thought Wojo was staring at him but he wasn't certain if it was Wojo or his own paranoia. "Are you here to talk to Leah?"

Wojo didn't respond at first. "Nope," he finally said. "I've been thinking. I've been wondering where the man who shot Adrian came out of the woods, and I figure it had to be somewhere around here." He looked at the woods behind Downey's house.

Downey turned and looked into the woods.

"I was thinking I might take a walk in the woods behind your house." Wojo paused and turned toward Downey. "And your neighbors' houses. If that's all right with you." He paused again and turned back toward the woods. "Maybe I can find something. You never know." He looked at Downey. "Know what I mean, Mr. Downey?" He smiled at Downey. "What do you think?"

Downey had difficulty forcing a smile. He worried that even if he smiled it would look contrived. He looked away from Wojo and in the direction of the horse paddock. "If it were me," he began. "I don't know." He looked at Wojo. "I don't know what I would do. Why would he necessarily come this way?"

"Which way would you go, Mr. Downey?"

Downey didn't answer at first. "I have no idea, Sheriff." He waited for a response but Wojo didn't speak. It's Wojo, Downey said to himself. It's definitely not me. He cleared his throat which felt sore. "Well," he said, breaking the interminable silence. "Ordinarily I would consider going with you but I have a very busy day ahead of me." He excused himself and went back into the house.

Wojo stood at the top of the driveway. He surveyed the house, the front and side yards, the horse paddock and the woods. Then he started walking toward the woods behind the horse paddock following the path Downey had taken weeks before.

Downey watched Wojo through the kitchen window. Wojo stopped at the tree line at the far end of the horse paddock. He looked into the woods where the path continued up toward the stream and Adrian Bessette's house. After a few minutes, he turned around and headed back across the paddock toward the driveway. Downey lost sight of him and went into the den. Within a short period of time he saw Wojo walking down the driveway. When Wojo reached the road he got into his cruiser and drove off.

"What about the neighbors?" Downey said.

Chapter Twenty-One

Enlisting Help

That afternoon Cotter drove to the State Police barracks in Williston. Williston was about forty-five miles down Route 14 from Eden Falls, but it was a pleasant drive with only two traffic lights along the way and one of them was a yellow blinker.

The Williston Barracks was the state police headquarters for all of Chittenden County. It was also the headquarters of the Special Investigations Unit. Cotter walked in the front entrance and waved to Evalyn Massey, a large, uniformed woman who monitored the main lobby from behind a glass-enclosed reception booth. Everyone who sought access to the rest of the building, including the cops, had to go through a security area in the lobby. It was the only way into the building except through a rear door that could only be opened with an I.D. card issued to troopers stationed in Williston.

Cotter was greeted on the other side of the metal detector by Dave Nichols. The detector went off when it picked up Cotter's gun, but nobody said a word. Nichols was the SIU's inside man, a computer whiz and first-class forensic technician. Nichols and Cotter went upstairs to an interview room on the second floor to meet with Barracks Captain Walter Freeman, Lieutenant Fred Graham of the SIU, Detective Reggie McHue and several state troopers who were helping out on the Roi-Bessette murder investigations. The meeting was called by Cotter.

The interview room was undecorated and it smelled like an antiseptic cleaning liquid. Its cinder-block walls were covered with a high-gloss canary yellow paint and the floor was wall-to-wall linoleum. Light came from a row of windows that ran all along the outside wall and from five rows of fluorescent fixtures that made the room vibrate. It was called the interview room but it wasn't used for interrogations. Those were conducted on the first floor near the holding cells in ten-by-ten cubicles with no windows. The interview room was used for press conferences, conferences with victims' families, and office meetings.

"Let's skip the bullshit and get right down to business, if you don't mind." Cotter looked around the room. Nobody said a word. "Good," he continued. "Here's what we have so far." He summarized the events surrounding the two murders, the similarity in M.O., the interviews with Fanny Roi and Mae Bessette, and the unusual lack of evidence at the crime scenes. He talked at length about the business relationships between the victims and Rick Roi and he alluded to Sheriff Wojohowski's suspicion of Deputy Cain, although he didn't elaborate on the reasons for that suspicion. It took Cotter about a half an hour to bring everyone up to speed.

"I'd like to focus on Rick Roi," Cotter said. "To a lesser extent, I'd like to look at Deputy Cain as well. Reg, I'd like to put as many people as we can spare on finding Rick Roi. We may want to contact the feds because chances are real good he's no longer in Vermont. We also need to put a tail on Deputy Cain, find out what he does and where he goes when he's not with Wojohowski. Fred, can you get a warrant to look at Cain's financial records? Go to the town clerk and look at his deed to the land on Route 14. See if he has any mortgages or liens."

"I'm gonna need help, Sim," Lieutenant Graham said.

"Walter will assign someone to work with you," Cotter responded. He looked at Captain Freeman, who nodded in approval. Cotter continued.

"Call a local real estate broker and find out what the Douglas Farm is worth right now and what it will be worth once it's developed. Do the same for the land owned by Roi and Bessette, and Deputy Cain's land too. Check all the financial records for Mrs. Roi and her son Rick. Dave will help you." Cotter looked at Dave Nichols, then back at Fred Graham. "Maybe she inherited some money she didn't tell us about. Look at the financial records for Peter Roi's excavating business. Let's see who has the best motive individually, or in partnership with someone else." Cotter paused. "Who knows, maybe all three of them conspired to kill Peter Roi and Adrian Bessette." He paused again and waited for someone to say something. No one spoke. "That would make it easy."

Everyone mumbled something in agreement.

Cotter looked around the room, then directly at Captain Freeman who had his hand up to get Cotter's attention.

"What about Bessette's wife and kid?" Freeman asked.

"You're right, Walt," Cotter answered. "Except I honestly believe the answers to our questions lie with the Roi family, possibly in conjunction with Deputy Cain. If we strike out there, we can always look at Mae Bessette and her son."

Cotter looked around the room. No one else raised a hand.

"One more thing," he said. "So far, the press has kept its nose out of this. I'm not sure why, but I'd say we've been very lucky. Gentlemen, I want to keep it that way. The only person outside this room who knows what you know is Sheriff Wojohowski, and he's not telling anyone. If there's a leak from this room," he looked at Walt Freeman, "heads are going to roll."

Freeman nodded again in agreement.

"I mean it, guys. Keep your fucking mouths shut." He made eye contact with everyone present, then he turned to Captain Freeman.

"Walt, it's imperative we put as many people on this as

possible without raising eyebrows. Time is our enemy. I believe we're dealing with a conspiracy that involves more than one individual, and I think it's going on right under our noses. Worse, I don't think it's over yet. We need to push hard on this, gentlemen. We need to find Rick Roi."

Chapter Twenty-Two

The Second Interview

After the meeting at the Williston Barracks, Cotter drove back to Eden Falls and headed straight for Wojo's office. Wojo and Deputy Cain were sitting at their desks. Neither man looked busy when Cotter walked in. Wojo greeted Cotter, then looked at Deputy Cain. Cain got up, put on his Deputy Sheriff's hat, and walked out.

Cotter sat down and told Wojo about his meeting at the Williston Barracks. He left out most of the details.

"We're looking at Rick Roi and we're looking at Deputy Cain," Cotter said. "Every resource we have will go into finding Roi. There's no arrest warrant, we just want to talk to him."

"I appreciate your holding back on the arrest warrant, Detective. I don't know why he ran. Maybe he was confused, young as he is." Wojo sat for a minute, his huge hands folded behind his equally large head. "Do me a favor, Detective, call me when you find Rick."

"You have my word, Sheriff." Cotter paused. "I'd like to ask you for a favor in return."

"Shoot," Wojo said.

"I'd like to take you up on your offer to look at the high school yearbooks from the years Bessette and Roi were in school."

Wojo sat back in his chair, his hands still clasped behind his head. He was smiling.

Cotter continued. "If our killer is someone local, someone who was somehow connected to Bessette and Roi, maybe we can pick up a lead. The yearbooks are a good start, anyway. Maybe we can put a few things together and figure out who the third boy was." He paused. "I'm still not convinced it was Deputy Cain."

Wojo didn't say a word.

"If we can determine who the third boy was," Cotter reasoned, "we may have our killer." He paused again. "Or our next victim."

"Not a bad idea, Detective." Wojo pulled his legs off his desk and got out of his chair. He put on his hat and told Cotter the new high school library would be the best place to find all the yearbooks from that period.

On the way over to the school, Wojo was unusually effusive. "You know, back then we all went to one school, from first grade right through graduation. That's if you graduated. Years ago most of the kids looked forward to taking over the family farms, so there was no reason to stay in school past ninth or tenth grade. Most people wanted their kids to learn to read and write. Once they could do that, they had as much education as their parents, sometimes more." He pulled into the school parking lot. "Some of the smart kids wanted to be doctors and lawyers. That was fine. We can always use another doctor." He paused and chuckled. "Can't say that about lawyers." He parked the cruiser by the main entrance to the school, shut off the engine and looked at Cotter. "You must've graduated high school to become a detective," Wojo said.

"I did."

"Bet you went to college, too."

"Champlain College. Four years in law enforcement."

"God-damn, I'm sitting here with a college professor."

"Hardly," Cotter said. "By the way, did the older kids mix with the younger kids, you know, use the same classrooms, lunchroom, in the hall..."

"Everyone knew everyone else," Wojo said. "Every damned person in that school knew everyone else's business.

If you were sticking it to some girl, everybody knew about it. Except the girl's father, of course." Wojo laughed. "There was this teacher, Mrs. Shuman, I think her name was. She was new and she was pretty young for a teacher. She was getting it pretty regularly from this senior because her husband traveled most of the time. She didn't think anybody knew about it. But we did. Hell, the whole town knew. Used to make heavy breathing noises in the back of the classroom when she spoke. Laughed our heads off. She only lasted one year before she got fired." Wojo finally opened the car door to get out.

"Must've been rough for the younger kids," Cotter suggested.

"Sometimes the older kids gave you a rough time. But you also got to hang around with them, so that was O.K. That's how you learned about sex. But you could get your ass kicked if you weren't careful."

"Especially if you were a flatlander?"

Wojo looked defensive for a second, then he chuckled. "Flatlanders took it pretty hard at first. Like Washingtonville." He looked at Cotter. "Isn't that where you went to school?"

"Yeah, but it wasn't that way when I was there," Cotter said. "Not that I can remember much. We didn't mind the new kids, flatlanders or not. There were so few of us in town we welcomed everybody."

Both men were out of the car and on their way across the parking lot to the front door. "That's because you weren't as close to IBM when it opened," Wojo said. "You didn't get the ones we got here. They were different. They didn't belong here and they still don't." He looked away from Cotter, then turned back to face him. "I was always kinda big for my age so I didn't have it too rough. Older kids didn't mess with me." He looked Cotter in the eye. "In fact, Detective, I kicked some major flatlander ass myself, you know."

"I'll bet you did," Cotter said.

The new Eden Falls Regional High School replaced the old wood-frame, three-story, white clapboard schoolhouse that had five classrooms, each one heated by a pot-bellied stove. The old schoolhouse had character. The new building looked like a thousand other high schools in America. Its architectural style was nondescript, a single-story U-shaped building made out of brick, stamped metal building panels and glass with a flat roof that was designed to take the heavy snow loads that accumulated during the winter. Inside there was a half-mile of brightly lit corridors lined on both sides with rows of lockers painted a hideous pea green and interrupted every forty feet by a door to a classroom. A very large three-story, windowless brick cube was stuck on one end. That was the gymnasium. Another brick cube of equal size was stuck on the other end. That was the auditorium.

The new high school was completed by the start of the school year, September 1980. Since then there have been three additions. Eden Falls's first graduating class, the class of 1981, had twenty-nine students, four of whom went on to four-year colleges. The graduating class of 1996 numbered three hundred thirty-one students. Two hundred forty-eight moved on to four-year colleges, and sixty-seven enrolled at two-year schools.

The difference in the number and type of students at the new Eden Falls Regional High School from 1980 to 1996 reflected the changes in the social makeup of the town itself. The new high school building also reflected those changes. It was cold and impersonal. Instead of interacting with everyone, students tended to stick to their own clique. There were jocks, preppies, hippies, crunchies, techies, suckups, losers and the local kids, referred to by the others as rednecks. The rednecks were at the bottom of the social ladder.

As Cotter and Wojo entered the building, Cotter wondered what it must be like to go to a school like this. The main lobby was enormous and filled with activity. On the far side of the lobby were the administrative offices, the principal's and vice principal's offices, the attendance office, the guidance office and the new security office, all separated from the throngs of students in the lobby by floor-to-ceiling glass panels.

The library was next to the security office. It was the only room in the entire building, other than the principal's office, that was carpeted. The two men found Mrs. Weiner, the school librarian, at the reference desk.

Mrs. Weiner took the two men to the shelf containing the school yearbooks, which went back to 1921. Adrian Bessette and Peter Roi were in the graduating class of 1967. Cotter wanted to look at the yearbooks from the ten-year period between 1959 and 1969, since it was possible some of the kids from that period still lived in town and might be able to provide answers to Cotter's questions.

Wojohowski was also in school during that time, as was Fanny Roi, Mae Bessette, Vesticate Douglas, Deputy Cain and two dozen other people who graduated in the sixties and still lived in town. Thomas Downey was among another group the two men identified as having been in the school in a younger grade during the same period. Of the twenty-eight former students still living in Eden Falls who were in school at the same time as Bessette and Roi, Cotter and Wojo selected a dozen who might have some knowledge of who the third boy might be. Thomas Downey was on the list because he was the same age as Brian Fischer.

Cotter knew the interviews might be a waste of time. After all, it was a strange community that pretended something as awful as what happened here thirty two years ago didn't happen. Cotter always wondered about that. It was something he could never come to grips with as a child. Why weren't the kids involved in the hanging punished? Isn't that the way it's supposed to be? He suspected those who remained in town wouldn't be forthcoming, especially if they were closely associated with those involved, and the chances of that were pretty good. Shame, fear, and total denial would prove difficult adversaries in extracting information from those selected for interviews. But Cotter wanted to proceed nonetheless.

Wojo and Cotter decided to interview Downey first because his store was right across the street from the school. They left Wojo's cruiser in the school parking lot and walked across Route 14.

The two men walked into Downey's Outfitters about three-thirty. Downey was behind the counter. The store was fairly large, about sixty feet wide by a hundred feet long. It featured everything from name-brand casual outerwear and footwear to outdoor wear for tradespeople, to canoes, snowshoes, climbing gear, backpacking and camping gear, camping supplies, thermal blankets, tents, tarps and an assortment of Swiss army knives and other cutlery, fishing rods, reels, hooks, lures and everything else the serious angler would want or need, except live bait. Downey's Outfitters did not carry firearms. It was all high-quality merchandise and very expensive. Downey's Outfitters guaranteed everything and people came to appreciate Thomas Downey's sincerity and genuine interest in taking care of his customers.

As the two men approached the counter, Downey excused himself from Jamie LeTourneau, a twenty-one-year-old sales clerk who had worked for the Downey's since she was in ninth grade.

"Afternoon, Mr. Downey," Wojo said. "You remember Detective Cotter?"

Cotter looked at Downey and put his hand out. Downey shook it and made eye contact with the detective.

"Yes, Detective. Good afternoon."

"The Detective would like to ask you a few questions, Mr. Downey, if that's all right," Wojo said.

"Of course," Downey replied.

"Mr. Downey, how well did you know Adrian Bessette and Peter Roi?" Cotter asked.

"Hardly at all."

"They didn't shop here?"

"Actually, neither one did. I don't remember either one

ever coming in here. I knew them both, but I never had anything to do with them. I don't believe I've ever had a conversation with Peter Roi. I knew who he was, but that's about it."

"How about Adrian Bessette?" Cotter asked.

"Same thing. I knew Adrian because he was a neighbor, but I never had anything to do with him in school, either. He picked me up once, about five or six years ago on Route 14, when my car went off the road. He drove me home. We didn't say much except that we didn't care for mud season. That was probably the first and last time we ever spoke."

"They were a few years ahead of you in school, weren't they?" Wojo asked.

Cotter looked at Wojo. Wojo knew the answer to that.

"Four or five years ahead of me," Downey said. Then he thought for a moment. "Four."

"Do you remember an incident when you were in school where a boy was accidentally hanged?" Cotter blurted out unexpectedly.

Downey didn't answer for a second. He was surprised by the question. "Of course I do, Detective. How could any of us forget that?"

"Do you have any idea who the three boys were, the ones involved in the hanging?"

Downey looked at Wojo, then back at Cotter. "They never told us. As far as I know, nobody knew but the police, and the boys' parents."

"It's important, Mr. Downey," Cotter said. "Very important. Maybe you can remember who the local bullies were, not necessarily the ones involved in the hanging, but just, you know, the ones who were just plain mean. Maybe they seemed to pick on the newer kids more than the others." He looked hopefully at Downey. "Maybe there was a group of older boys *you* were afraid of."

Downey didn't respond at first. "All of the older boys were frightening, Detective. I guess that's the way it is when you have elementary school kids in the same schoolhouse as high school kids."

"Certainly some of the older kids must have frightened you more than others."

"Perhaps," Downey agreed. "But that was a long time ago, more than thirty years ago. You're asking a lot, Detective." He looked at Wojo again.

Cotter was frustrated. He'd hoped for more than Downey was able, or willing, to provide. "Maybe I am, Mr. Downey," he said. But if you think of anything that might help, as obscure as you might think it is, please call me." He reached into his pocket for a card and handed it to Downey.

"I will," Downey said. "If I remember something, I'll call you."

"Thanks," Cotter said. The two men turned to walk out.

"By the way, Mr. Downey," Cotter stopped and turned back toward Downey. "Did you go to school at the same time as Deputy Cain?"

Downey thought for a moment before answering. "I did, but he's a few years older than me, too. I think he was in the same grade as Adrian Bessette and Peter Roi, maybe even a year ahead of them." He looked at Wojo. "I think Sheriff Wojohowski would know. Sheriff Wojohowski was in the same class."

"Was Cain friendly with Bessette and Roi in high school?"

"I'm sorry, Detective?" Downey said. He had made eye contact with Wojo and didn't hear Cotter's question. He looked away from Wojo and turned back to Cotter. "You're asking me if Deputy Cain was friendly with Adrian Bessette and Peter Roi?"

Cotter nodded.

"I don't know. I don't think so. But I think Cain's brother was. He was older though, maybe a year or two. I guess he was left back." Downey looked at Wojo again. "He and Sheriff Wojohowski were pretty good friends, as I remember."

Cotter finally turned to Wojo.

"We *were* good friends," Wojo said. He looked very uncomfortable, as if his enormous body prevented him from slipping into the woodwork.

"Where is he now?" Cotter asked Wojo.

It was obvious Wojo didn't like being questioned by Cotter, especially in front of Downey. He turned sharply to Cotter. There eyes met. Neither man blinked.

"Dead," he said. "Died in Vietnam." That seemed to satisfy Cotter, who turned back toward Downey.

The three men stood motionless. Cotter finally broke the silence. "Thank you, Mr. Downey. Once again, it's very important that you contact me if you think of something that might help. If you know something, anything, that you've kept inside for all these years, and you want to ease your conscience, this is your chance."

Downey looked at Cotter. "That sounds very inviting, Detective, but I'm afraid the things I'd like to get off my chest might even bore the daylights out of a psychiatrist. They'd surely be of no interest to you gentlemen."

Cotter and Wojo left the store. Cotter would use that same line with everyone interviewed that day. *If you want to ease your conscience about something you've been holding in all these years, now's your chance.* He was sure someone would take him up on the offer.

He was wrong. The rest of the interviewees turned out to be as forgetful as Thomas Downey. Nobody remembered anything about the hanging, except that nobody ever talked about it. To Cotter's chagrin, nobody could come up with the names of the three boys.

Chapter Twenty-Three

A Search for the Truth

The interviews lasted the better part of Thursday and all day Friday. Instead of going home Friday evening, Cotter called his wife and told her he'd be home late Saturday afternoon. There were a few things he wanted to do in Burlington before bagging it for the weekend, or what would be left of it by the time he got home.

Cotter was away from home about fifty percent of the time. When he was called into an investigation, he would be gone anywhere from a couple of days to several weeks. It was nearly five weeks since Adrian Bessette's murder. Cotter had spent most of that time in Eden Falls, running back and forth to Brattleboro on weekends. He hadn't been home in over a week and he was tired of the Red Bird Motel.

He left his room early Saturday morning and made the one-hour trip into Burlington along Route 14. The interstate would have cut nearly half an hour off that time, but it was early and Cotter wanted some time to think. He parked a few blocks from the Fletcher Free Library and walked the rest of the way at a rapid pace. The crisp air coming off Lake Champlain gave him a chill. It also invigorated him, as did the prospects of what he might find within.

The Fletcher Free Library was built during the Great Depression. It was a wonderfully old, field stone structure with enough European influence to look important, if not grand. When it was built, engineers designed a state-of-the-art steam-heating system that was to defy Vermont winters. Defy them it did, as well as the staff and the patrons. The library was a sweat bath most of the year. It was either that or freeze. The custodial staff, unable to contain the amount of steam that rose up through the cast-iron radiators when the boiler was lit, couldn't do anything about the library temperatures that hovered somewhere around ninety degrees during all but the summer months. It wasn't uncommon for all the windows to be open in the middle of January. In October and April, when morning temperatures started off in the low forties, librarians and patrons froze because the cold was preferable to turning on the heat. Even with the windows wide open, the tepid outside air during the spring and fall months wasn't frigid enough to moderate the equatorial temperature inside, steam hissing away, doing its job, keeping Vermonters warm.

Faced with the enormous research task in front of him, Cotter wished he had paid better attention to his teacher and less attention to Sally Hunter the last time he was at the library. He was lost. The center lobby was as active as a bee hive, with librarians working the counter, answering questions and stamping the due dates on patrons' books. Two large rooms full of book shelves and reading tables, one to the left of the main lobby and one to the right, loomed in front of Cotter. He had no idea how to proceed. A retired volunteer with white hair saw Cotter's bewildered look and asked if he could help.

"I'm looking for copies of the Burlington Free Press from 1965," Cotter said.

"In the reference section to your left," the man responded, pointing the way.

Cotter thanked him and went into the reference room. A small work area with a sign that said: *reference librarian*, greeted those who needed help. A stout woman who wore a pair of thick glasses that made her look like an owl was directing a young lady to the stacks of over-sized books. After waiting his turn, Cotter asked the woman for back issues of the Burlington Free Press, specifically, those from September and

October, 1965.

The lady told Cotter the copies he needed were on microfilm. "Unfortunately there's no index from that period," she said.

Cotter spent more than an hour fumbling through many reels of microfilm on a machine that was hardly cooperative before finding an article about a hanging behind the Eden Falls Center School. The headline read:

Eleven Year-Old Boy Dies In Eden Falls Accident.

The article told of the death of Brian Lewis Fischer, eleven, son of David and Janice Fischer, formerly of Bayside, New York, who had moved to Eden Falls the year before. It attributed the death to asphyxiation. There was no mention of foul play. The article said several local youths were with Fischer at the time of the accident but it didn't say if or how they were involved. Cotter wrote down the name of the medical examiner, Dr. Jessup, who had determined the cause of the boy's death.

By noon Cotter had gone through eight reels of microfilm. After he put them away he went back to the lobby and asked the librarian if there was a pay phone he could use. The librarian directed him upstairs to a hallway next to the public restrooms. There was one phone and several teenagers gathered around it while another talked into the receiver. Cotter didn't want to cramp their style so he waited around the corner. After a few minutes the teen who was on the phone hung up. He and his cohorts bolted down the stairs until they got to the bottom step, which was in full view of the librarian's counter.

Cotter put a dime into the pay phone and asked the operator for the number of Dr. Jessup. Dr. Jessup's phone rang several times before a young lady answered and said the good doctor and his wife would be back around supper time. Cotter asked if he could come over that evening, but the lady said evening would not be a good time for an interview since the doctor would be quite tired and not in a talkative mood.

Cotter agreed to come by Sunday morning after the family returned from church.

Cotter called his wife next to explain why he wouldn't be home Saturday night. Janie said she expected as much and had made plans with her sister earlier in the day to visit their mother that evening in Brattleboro.

"Are you sure it's O.K.?" he asked.

"Sim, Honey, you can have a free conscience. I don't mind, really I don't. Marie's coming for dinner after we visit Mom. I'm making everything I can't make anymore since I married you, all the things you refuse to eat."

"What, no meat?" Cotter joked.

"No meat, just healthy, delicious vegetables and tofu. We don't all have your pedestrian palate, you know."

"Janie, I love you. I'd even eat tofu to be with you tonight." He paused. "I'm onto something pretty crucial here and I don't want to walk away from it, even for a day. Besides, even if I was there you'd only have my body, my mind would be here, on the case."

"That's all I want, Detective, just your body. That's why I married you. Didn't you know that?"

Cotter laughed. He longed for Janie's touch. "You can have my body tomorrow night. My mind, too." He paused. "I love you, Janie." He paused again. "Say hello to your sister and mother for me."

"I'll save some leftovers for you," Janie said. "Je t'aime."

As many times as he called Janie at the last minute to say he was hot on the trail of some criminal and would be late coming home, or not coming at all, Cotter still felt guilty. This time was no different. But he had to see Dr. Jessup in the morning.

Investigations were like fires, he thought. The fuel is there from the beginning, like the truth, but it's useless by itself. It searches for a spark, something to get it going, a way out. When the right spark is applied, ignition occurs, like a breakthrough. When an investigation gets hot, it acts the same way. The perps become desperate. The closer the cops get, the more desperate the perps become, until they do something stupid that blows the whole investigation wide open and leads to their arrest. At least that's the way Cotter saw it.

As Cotter got deeper into the investigation, he found the information beginning to feed him. Rick Roi and his mother, Deputy Cain, Dr. Jessup. It was as if the fire was beginning to burn and beckoned him to feed it. But he knew there was still something missing, an element to this thing that defied the obvious, and it made him more determined. It also scared him, for it was forcing him to come to grips with something he had repressed for most of his life.

Cotter hung up the phone. He thought about the day he had found out about Brian Fischer. He remembered the bus ride home from school that day, the descriptions of Brian Fischer's face as he dangled at the end of the rope. The older kids had joked about how he probably crapped his pants when he died. Cotter hated them for it.

He walked slowly down the stairs to the main lobby and through the library door into the overcast day. He looked up Main Street toward the University of Vermont campus, then down toward the lake. He couldn't decide which way to go. So he sat on a concrete retaining wall. He didn't really feel like going anywhere. Even this, he said to himself, is better than the Red Bird.

Chapter Twenty-Four

A Visit to the Doctor

Sunday morning brought glorious sunshine and balmy weather to Eden Falls. Days like that were rare in Vermont and when they occurred, especially on Sunday, the citizenry, human and otherwise, came out to celebrate.

The sudden change in the weather was a favorable omen. The warm weather and cloudless sky improved Dr. Jessup's mood and he was remarkably receptive to visiting with Cotter after church. He was a cynical old man with an assortment of aches and pains. He felt everyone in town should know about them and he never missed an opportunity to remind them. The way he figured, he had listened to everyone else's ailments for fifty years before retiring, so it was time someone listened to him.

Cotter entered the doctor's house through the front door. The lady who welcomed him introduced herself as Mrs. Jessup, the doctor's wife. She was short, round and plainly attired in a mid-calf-length light blue dress with a flowery print. It was the kind of dress that was never in style, and would never be out of style.

Mrs. Jessup was quite pleasant and, like everyone else in Eden Falls, couldn't say enough about the weather. For as long as the warm spell lasted, the weather would be the topic of conversation in Eden Falls, even more than the murders of Adrian Bessette and Peter Roi. At least in public.

"Mr. Cotter," the doctor's wife said as she led the detective into the study in the rear of the house. The house was an old Victorian structure with ornate woodwork. The study was lined with shelves filled mostly with medical books and memorabilia from years of tending to the town's ill and infirm. There were mementos from trips the Jessups had taken all over the world and several scrapbooks full of articles written about their excursions in the old Eden Falls Town Crier.

The shelves were also filled with gifts from families of patients who couldn't afford to pay for medical care when times were bad. The walls were covered with deer racks, eight-pointers and nine-pointers and even a ten-pointer from Tracy McGovern for delivering his son, Tracy Junior, in 1967. McGovern was out of work at the time and didn't have any medical insurance. The rack from the two hundred forty-pound buck was the largest rack ever taken in Eden Falls. Jessup wasn't a hunter, but he accepted it graciously as payment-in-full.

Another family, for whom Dr. Jessup extended free medical care, used to pay him with a steady supply of fresh eggs. Another provided hay for Mrs. Jessup's two ponies. Others gave freely of what they produced: firewood, garden vegetables, maple syrup, a fine piece of furniture, free labor, carpentry, snow plowing, rototilling, a new roof, a new set of brakes or even an apple pie.

"It's a pleasure to meet you, Dr. Jessup," Cotter said as he put out his hand.

Dr. Jessup shook Cotter's hand and looked up and down the taller, much younger man, but didn't say a word. Cotter felt like the doctor was studying his physical features for some clue to his character. Dr. Jessup held onto Cotter's hand for what seemed an interminable amount of time. Finally the doctor spoke.

"Good morning, Detective. Cotter?" He paused. "Your father was Simeon Cotter?"

"Yes, sir, he was. I'm named after my father."

"Simeon Cotter was a friend of mine," the doctor said.

"We served during the war together. I knew a lot of boys from Washingtonville. Do you still live there, Detective?"

"No I don't. My wife and I live in southern Vermont, a little town called Halifax. You probably never heard of it."

"Yes I have." Dr. Jessup peered into Cotter's eyes.

If it's true the eyes are the window to the soul, Cotter thought, then Dr. Jessup was doing his best to look deep into his soul.

"It's a little town just south of Jacksonville," Dr. Jessup said. "Just a few miles down the road from Wilmington. My uncle lived in Jacksonville. He owned a sawmill in Halifax right on Route 112, just up from the Emery farm."

Cotter was impressed by the doctor's memory. It was a good omen. He hoped it would carry over to the forthcoming interview.

"What can I do for you, young man?" the doctor asked.

Cotter decided to get right to the point. "Dr. Jessup, do you remember an incident that happened about thirty-two years ago here in Eden Falls in which an eleven-year-old boy was accidentally hanged?"

The question hung in the air like a bomb. Dr. Jessup was caught off guard. His smile became hollow. He turned away from Cotter and walked behind a broad, black cherry desk and slowly lowered himself into his chair. He seemed to age right before Cotter's eyes. After a few moments he looked up at Cotter and spoke. "Why, after all these years, are the Vermont State Police suddenly asking questions about the hanging?" He looked at Cotter from behind the desk. "Don't you think you boys are a little late?" His entire demeanor had changed. He seemed angry with Cotter.

"What do you mean?" Cotter asked defensively.

"Just what I said," Jessup barked. "Why are the state police asking questions about a crime that took place more than three decades ago? Can you answer that question for me please?"

Cotter was speechless.

"I thought so." Jessup got up from his chair and looked at Cotter. "Surely you're not reopening the investigation, because there never was an investigation."

Cotter looked bewildered. "I'm sorry, Doctor." Cotter said sheepishly. "You have me at a disadvantage. I was seven years old when that happened. I can't answer for the actions of the Vermont State Police in 1965."

Dr. Jessup didn't say anything. He sat down again behind his desk. "What is it you'd like to know, Detective? Not that I'm going to have any answers for you, but go ahead. Ask what you need to ask."

Cotter was relieved but he was more than curious about Dr. Jessup's behavior. He was also curious about what the doctor said. Why, indeed, had the Vermont State Police failed to conduct an investigation into the hanging years ago?

"Can you tell me anything about the incident?" Cotter asked. "You were the M.E. at the time so I'm assuming you were at the scene and examined the Fischer boy."

"Yes I did," the doctor said. "I was at the scene and yes, I did examine the Fischer boy. It was one of the worst days of my life. I've seen more suffering in the war than a man should see in a dozen lifetimes, Detective, but the expression on that boy's face..." The doctor looked up at Cotter. "Four to one." The doctor said. "Some odds." He shook his head. "That boy never had a chance."

"What?" Cotter asked.

Dr. Jessup looked up from his desk.

"You just said four to one, Dr. Jessup. What did you mean by that?"

"Four to one," the doctor said. "Pretty weighty odds, wouldn't you say? Especially since they were so much older. They were men, for Christ's sake, and that boy was just a child."

"There," Cotter said. "You said it again."

Jessup looked at Cotter. "What did I say again, Detective?"

"You said four to one. There were four older boys?"

Dr. Jessup looked confused. "That's right. Of course," He paused. "The Free Press said there were only three. That was part of the cover-up. One of the boys was the son of a local town bigwig so it was decided there, right at the scene, that the official word would be three boys instead of four. Just in case the whole thing got out."

"That's unbelievable," Cotter said. "How many people knew there were four?"

"Back then or who are alive today?"

"Both," Cotter demanded.

"Well, let's see," Jessup said sinking back into his chair. "There were the four boys, me, the parents of the boys," he looked up at Cotter to clarify what he had just said. "Not the parents of the Fischer boy, the others I mean, two of the selectmen, both of whom are dead, and Sheriff Wojohowski."

"Wojo?"

"No, no," the old doctor replied, jerking forward in his chair. "Not Wojo. His father."

"Sheriff Wojohowski's father was the town sheriff?"

"You didn't know that?" Jessup seemed surprised by Cotter's ignorance. "There was a great deal of secrecy surrounding the whole matter. I didn't condone it then." He put his head down. "I've always believed that someday the people of Eden Falls would have to pay for their silence, myself included. I wonder if your visit is the first step in bringing the truth to light." He looked up. "Or is it a sign of trouble?"

A million thoughts rushed through Cotter's head. "Let me ask you something, Dr. Jessup. Did Wojo know there were four local boys involved?"

"Stan?" Jessup asked

"Yes, sir. Do you think Stan knew there were four?"

Dr. Jessup thought for a minute. "I suppose he did. After a while everyone in town figured it out, but only those of us who were there knew their identities."

Jessup got up from his chair and faced the book shelves

behind his desk. His back was turned to Cotter. "There's something else the paper didn't say." He turned around and walked over to the couch on which Cotter sat. He lowered his voice, not that anyone besides Cotter was going to hear him. It seemed natural. Whenever the subject of the hanging was brought up, the people of Eden Falls lowered their voices.

"It was also part of the cover-up," Jessup said.

"What was?"

Jessup paused. "There was another young boy who was beaten and hanged that day."

"I thought only one boy died," Cotter said.

"The second boy survived. He was in the same grade as the Fischer boy, maybe a year younger, I'm not sure. I believe, like the Fischer boy, the other boy's family had just moved to Vermont. I'm afraid I can't tell you much about him, not even his name. He was taken away from the scene before I arrived and I never learned who he was." He looked away. "I suppose I didn't want to know. More secrets to keep. I don't like keeping secrets, Detective, even though I've kept this one for thirty-two years."

Dr. Jessup looked tired.

Cotter watched him sink into his chair. He knew Jessup was retreating. He knew his visit had caused the Doctor to relive something that had tormented the man for many years. Cotter wouldn't have been surprised if Jessup excused himself without further conversation. But the old man continued.

"He was treated by Doc Hughes up in Johnson." Jessup turned toward Cotter. "Doc Hughes is dead, been dead for twenty years. I doubt his records still exist. You're talking thirty-two years."

"No idea who it was?" Cotter asked hopefully. "Surely there must have been some rumors."

"None that I ever heard, Detective. I can tell you the boy was pretty badly hurt but he survived, physically, that is. I imagine he must be carrying around some heavy baggage up here though." He tapped his head with his index finger.

"Is Dr. Hughes's wife still alive?" Cotter asked.

Dr. Jessup stood next to his desk. He steadied himself with his hand. He opened a small leather address book and copied a phone number from the book onto a piece of note paper. He handed the note paper to Cotter. "Mrs. Hughes lives in a nursing home in Manchester, New Hampshire. This is the name of the home."

Cotter looked at the note paper. "How about the names of the four boys?"

"You want me to break my Hippocratic oath, Detective? You know better than that."

"How does that apply, Doctor? How does that apply in this case? I don't see that that applies here," Cotter desperately wanted the names of the boys but he knew if he pushed too hard Dr. Jessup would simply dig in, or ask Cotter to leave. But he had to push. It was the only way. He was too close. "You were called to the scene as a medical examiner. I'm asking you in that capacity for the names of the boys who were involved."

Dr. Jessup sat back down in his chair. He appeared to have aged right before Cotter's eyes. "You didn't treat those boys, Detective. I did," he snapped. He took several breaths before continuing. "You forget that these boys and their families were my patients. I brought all four of them into the world and I treated their mumps and measles and dog bites and I set their broken bones..."

"I know but..."

"Then don't ask me to tell you their names, Detective, because I won't. You boys had your chance thirty-two years ago and you did nothing. Now you come around here expecting everyone to jump through hoops to help you." Jessup had become agitated. "You want to know who they are, Detective Cotter, you're gonna have to find out from someone else. That's final."

Dr. Jessup stood up abruptly and led Cotter to the

study door. Cotter knew he had blown it. He was frustrated but at the same time he was energized by what he had learned. Except now there were three names he needed, not just one, and the number of unanswered questions just jumped through the roof.

"If there are no further questions, Detective, then please excuse me so I may join my wife and daughter in the garden. You can never tell when we're going to have another day like this. I'd hate to waste it. I'm sure you understand."

"Indeed I do, Doctor." Cotter shook the doctor's hand and left.

Chapter Twenty-Five

The Ferry to New York

The more he thought about his meeting with Dr. Jessup, the more confounded Cotter became. Instead of answering his questions, Jessup had confused him. Worse, the meeting had elicited memories from his subconscious that threatened to overwhelm the issue at hand, the deaths of Bessette and Roi. After all, he reminded himself, that's what this whole thing is about.

He wasn't sure if there was a connection between what had happened thirty-two years ago behind the old school house and the recent murders of Adrian Bessette and Peter Roi, but there was enough evidence to suggest there might be. Still, he could easily become sucked into a wild-goose chase to satisfy some powerful inner need to come to grips with his own demons, so he had to keep his priorities in line. As badly as he wanted to focus on the hanging at the expense of everything else, he knew he couldn't, unless further evidence presented itself which drove him in that direction.

It was nearly two in the afternoon when he left Dr. Jessup's house. He wanted to see Janie, but he wasn't up for the long drive down to Halifax, especially since he'd have to leave before daybreak Monday morning to be back in Eden Falls by seven. That was the time he and Reggie McHue had agreed to meet to look at what the other detectives had come up with on Rick Roi and Deputy Cain.

Cotter felt bad he wouldn't see Janie. But he also needed some space, some time alone to ponder the events of the past few days. He was getting nowhere in his murder investigation and now, suddenly, there was a possible connection between the murders and the most disturbing memory of his childhood.

So it was with some, but not total, regret that he called Janie and told her he wouldn't be home for a few more days. Then he drove back into Burlington to spend what was left of the beautiful spring day on the upper deck of the ferry to New York State.

It took about forty-five minutes each way to make the Lake Champlain crossing. Despite the sunshine, it was cold out on the broad lake. The wind blew uninterrupted through Cotter's hair. It reminded him of his childhood and the annual trip his family took each summer to take the very same ferry ride across to NY state, of the hot chocolate his mother used to buy young Simeon and his little brother on the return trip back to Burlington. Simeon and his brother would huddle together on the upper deck with their cocoa, shivering, but refusing their parents' pleas to come inside the cabin. Now, three decades later, sitting on the upper deck of the ferry to Port Kent and chilled by the wind, Cotter took a sip from his hot chocolate, and cried.

Chapter Twenty-Six

Reggie McHue

Back at the Red Bird

Monday morning Cotter was awakened by a call from Reggie McHue.

"Did I wake you, Detective?" McHue teased.

"What time is it?"

"Five-thirty, on a beautiful Monday morning, Detective."

Cotter was annoyed at McHue's bright attitude at such an ungodly hour. No one has a right to feel that good at five-thirty in the morning, Cotter said to himself.

"I called to make sure you're coming to Williston this morning, Sim. Or did you forget?"

Cotter felt like telling McHue to go fuck himself.

"I have some information that might help your investigation," McHue continued.

"You found Rick Roi?" Cotter sat up and spun his legs over the side of the bed.

"Not that good, but we got some stuff that makes him look more and more like your man."

"I'll be right over." Cotter jumped out of bed and into the shower. In twenty minutes he was dressed and on his way. He pulled into the parking lot of the Williston Barracks a little after six-thirty. He went directly to Reggie McHue's office on the second floor.

"Coffee, Detective?" McHue asked.

"Absolutely." Cotter looked at the formica counter and the coffee urn, a half-dozen stained mugs, a jar of store-brand non-dairy creamer and a paper cup filled with plastic stirrers. "Which mug do I use?"

"Take any one you want. When you're ready I'll tell you what we found."

"I'm ready," Cotter said. He poured the dark black coffee into a pale yellow mug with several chips in the rim. It was the best one he could find.

"Still no trace of Roi," McHue started, "but we have some background info that sets him up as a pretty strong suspect, at least based on the M.O.'s." McHue dropped a folder onto the counter next to the coffee mugs.

Cotter picked it up and took out a typed report titled *Military Background.*

McHue continued. "Roi was a Marine. Special Forces." He looked up at Cotter whose head was buried in the report. "Perfect training for someone who wanted to pull off a couple of hits with our killer's M.O., wouldn't you say, Sim?"

"Great. Now the Marines are training killers and sending them into society to practice their skills on members of the public. A great country we live in." He shook his head and looked at McHue who was looking back at him with a wry smile on his face.

"Who pissed you off this morning?"

Cotter realized how he had sounded. "Sorry, Reg. Too many days without seeing Janie."

"I thought you saw her this weekend."

Cotter hadn't told McHue about the hanging or its possible tie-in to the murders. So instead of telling him about his meeting with Dr. Jessup, Cotter told him he spent the weekend going back to the murder scenes to look for some evidence they might have missed before. Then he put the report back in the folder and handed it back to McHue.

"This is real good work, Reg," Cotter said. "But it doesn't say whether or not he had the training to plan the murders."

McHue looked confused.

"Did he?" Cotter asked.

"I don't know, Sim. It wasn't in his record, except that he was Special Forces. No intelligence training or anything like that though."

"I think that's a key element, Reg."

"I know members of the Special Forces are capable of pulling off covert missions but they're training is in combat, not strategy."

"I still don't follow," McHue said.

"Look, Reg, whoever planned these murders knew more than what they teach in the Marines, even Special Forces. Those guys learn how to insert themselves into hot areas and extricate themselves when necessary, but to my knowledge, planning strategy is different, different schools, different skills, more along the lines of espionage than running around like Rambo. Whoever planned these murders was more than a Special Forces op."

"Maybe he was working with someone else."

"Bingo," Cotter blurted out. "Someone with the training to plan the murders. Then Roi carries them out. A partnership, a symbiosis."

McHue thought about that for a moment. "There's one other little thing you have to figure out, Sim. Did Roi hire someone to plan his incursions or did the person who's the brains behind the murders hire Roi to carry them out? There's a major difference there, pal."

Cotter agreed.

"Unfortunately, without Roi, it's gonna be tough going," McHue added.

"Maybe not," Cotter looked at McHue. "Sheriff Wojohowski and I identified a dozen or so people out of the old yearbooks from Eden Falls High School who lived here as kids and are still living in town. It's likely our mystery person is among those on the list. We've interviewed all of them, but no leads." He took a list of names from the yearbook out of his breast pocket and handed it to McHue. "Here's the list. Check 'em out, everything you can find, criminal records, military service, whether or not one of them is in serious debt, anything at all, including something that could be used to blackmail them. It's possible our man is at the mercy of Roi and was forced to do something out of fear. Look for any connections any of these men may have or once had to Roi, especially financial connections."

"What about our Deputy Cain?" McHue asked.

"I'll look into him myself. I'm working on another angle to this thing that's a long shot, but it's just something I need to do by myself, if only to prove to myself I'm wrong."

"Anything we can help you with, Sim? We're here to help, you know."

"Nope. Not yet," Cotter said. "By the way, if you need me I'll be in my car. I have to go to New Hampshire today to visit an old lady."

"A relative, Sim?"

"Nope, someone who may hold the key to all of this, if I'm lucky. Otherwise, just another dead end."

Chapter Twenty-Seven

The Doctor's Wife

The drive to Manchester, New Hampshire was uneventful and gave Cotter time to think. He valued the drives through the Vermont countryside. There were few distractions, few cars, great distances between exits and beautiful scenery.

What bothered him more than anything was the absence of Rick Roi. It just didn't make sense, from any perspective. Why would he run? Cotter kept asking himself. Suddenly he came upon the Manchester exit off Interstate 93. He was in the extreme left lane doing well over seventy. He had to activate the red flasher on the dash of his unmarked cruiser to cut across three lanes of traffic to make the exit. Fortunately there was little traffic. He took the directions to the nursing home out of a clip attached to the visor. It was only a couple of miles off the interstate in an industrial park near the airport. What an awful place to spend your remaining years, Cotter thought, especially for a woman who was born and raised in the most beautiful countryside in the northeast.

Willomena Hughes had lived in the nursing home for less than a year. Her children had offered to take care of her, but her two sons lived in Arizona and there was no way she was going to live in the heat of the southwest. Her daughter couldn't take her because she was single and shared an apartment in New York with two other women.

The nursing home looked nice enough, Cotter thought.

It was clean and most of the residents were outdoors in the lovely gardens that surrounded the main dormitory. An attendant told Cotter Mrs. Hughes had gone out on a day trip with several other residents to attend a movie in town, something residents who were physically able were encouraged to do.

"I'm sorry," the attendant said. "Mrs. Hughes won't be back until four p.m. Are you family?"

"No," Cotter replied.

The attendant became snippy. "Then I'm afraid you can't see her tonight. You'll have to come back tomorrow during regular visiting hours, nine-thirty a.m., till..."

Cotter took his I.D. out of his pocket and held it in front of the attendant. "Detective Simeon Cotter, Vermont State Police, Special Investigations Unit. I'd like to interview Mrs. Hughes about a matter that I'm sure a local judge would find of sufficient consequence to issue a warrant, if that's what it's going to take."

The attendant hesitated. "Dinner is served at five, so you'd best come back around six, or six-thirty. Mandatory bed by eight, so don't be any later than that."

Cotter looked at his watch. It was eleven minutes past two. He decided a movie and a bite to eat wasn't a bad way to kill an afternoon. He'd be through in time to get back to the nursing home by six.

The movie proved better therapy than he thought, though Cotter couldn't figure out how the cop in the film could elude so many bullets from so many automatic weapons without getting hit. Could they all be such bad shots, he wondered? After a sandwich at DeLorio's Pizza next to the Fourplex theater, Cotter returned to the nursing home. It was five minutes to six on an unusually warm spring evening and Mrs. Hughes was sitting on the porch with several other ladies, deeply engrossed in a conversation about today's Hollywood offerings compared to the classics of an earlier era.

"Mrs. Hughes," the attendant said, as he and Detective Cotter approached the group of women. "This is Mr. Cotter.

He'd like to talk with you for a moment, if you're up to it." The ladies all looked up at Cotter. A few giggled out loud and rolled their eyes at Mrs. Hughes. It was to be expected. Most young men who visited were sons or sons-in-law and the reason for their visits was, more often than not, obligation or pure guilt. It wasn't often a handsome young man came to see one of them just to talk.

"About what?" Mrs. Hughes asked suspiciously.

"Oh, Willy," one lady said. "Don't be so rough on him." The lady looked at Cotter and winked. "If you want to talk to me, young man, just sit yourself down right here." She patted the empty seat next to her.

Cotter was a little embarrassed. The attention from all the ladies made him blush. "Mrs. Hughes, I'm Detective Simeon Cotter from the Vermont State Police. I want to talk to you about a patient of your late husband." He looked at the other women. "In private, Ma'am, if I could. I'd greatly appreciate a moment of your time." He put his hand out to help Mrs. Hughes get up from her chair. She accepted his hand and slowly lifted herself up.

Willomena Hughes was a spunky old lady with white hair and remarkably smooth skin. It was obvious from her complexion that she had avoided the sun as a child. Except for her hair and poor posture she could have passed for a woman twenty years younger.

Cotter sensed correctly that Willomena Hughes was a refined, well-kept elderly lady. She was a doctor's wife, the antithesis of Mae Bessette and Fanny Roi, who, despite being thirty years younger, wore the skin of hard living.

"A patient of my husband?" Mrs. Hughes asked as she got up from her chair.

Cotter led her to an empty cluster of chairs and suggested that she sit down.

"Mrs. Hughes, I'm investigating a crime that may have its roots back in Eden Falls around 1965."

"You mean the Bessette murder?"

"You know about that?"

"Do you think we're dead here, Detective? I do read the papers, you know."

"Yes, Ma'am, I'm sorry, I didn't mean..."

"Go on, Detective."

"Do you remember an incident that occurred in 1965 involving an eleven-year-old boy named Fischer? He was hanged by a couple of local youths."

"I haven't lost my memory yet either, Detective." she snapped. "Of course I remember it. It was the most horrible thing."

"Mrs. Hughes, we have reason to believe the murders of Adrian Bessette and Peter Roi..."

"Peter Roi?" she interrupted.

"Yes, Ma'am, Peter Roi." Cotter realized she didn't know about Roi. "I'm sorry, Mrs. Hughes. Peter Roi was killed several weeks ago. Also murdered." He paused. "We've been told that both Peter Roi and Adrian Bessette were involved in the hanging of Brian Fischer behind the old school house in 1965."

"Oh my," Mrs. Hughes said. She seemed to lose time for a moment. "My husband said this would never die. He said someday this thing would come back to haunt this town." She looked up at Cotter. "Eden Falls, he meant."

"You mean because of the cover-up?"

She didn't respond.

"Mrs. Hughes, did your husband treat another boy who was involved in that incident?"

She didn't answer.

"Mrs. Hughes, please. I was told by Dr. Jessup that there was another boy who was hanged. Dr. Jessup said he survived and was taken to your husband for treatment. Ma'am, it's very important. Do you know the name of the boy who your husband treated that day?" He waited but she didn't answer him. "Do you know his name, Mrs. Hughes?"

She looked up at Cotter. She had tears in her eyes.

"He was such a sweet boy. How could anyone do that to such a young boy?"

"His name, Mrs. Hughes. Do you remember his name?"

She stared straight ahead. Cotter held his breath, for he knew the next few seconds might determine the fate of his investigation.

She looked back at him and focused her soft blue eyes on his. She was an extraordinarily beautiful woman, Cotter thought. Her eyes were bright and alert and filled with compassion, and tears.

"They didn't want anyone to know what had happened. That's why they brought that young man to my husband. They didn't want anyone in Eden Falls to know."

"Who, Mrs. Hughes? Who did they bring to your husband that day?"

She didn't say anything at first. Her gaze wandered off as if she had been transported back in time to the afternoon they brought the young man to her home. "He was barely conscious. He had a severe rope burn around his neck. I remember him well. His hair was matted and caked with mud. His arms and hands were cut up and bleeding. He didn't make a sound when they brought him in. He was in shock, I guess. I remember how his mother held him. "

"Mrs. Hughes," Cotter said softly, not wanting to bring her back to his reality too fast. "Mrs. Hughes, do you know the name of the boy who was treated by your husband that day?"

She obviously wasn't listening to him. She seemed to have drifted off into another dimension. She looked up at Cotter and their eyes met again. "Such a sweet boy." She smiled when she pictured him, but her smile disappeared when she remembered why he had come into their lives. Then, when Cotter thought she was too far gone to continue the interview, she looked straight into his eyes and seemed intensely lucid. "His name was Thomas Downey."

Cotter was thinking about his next move when she

spoke. For a second the name didn't register. He wasn't ready for it, not the name of the boy, and especially not Thomas Downey. When the words finally reached his brain he was stunned. Downey! He never would have guessed it on his own.

Mrs. Hughes didn't say anything else. The interview had obviously shaken her. Cotter knew she never expected to confront something as upsetting as the memories of that awful event on this beautiful spring evening.

Cotter thanked her. He knew he was the cause of her anguish and he felt bad. He asked if he could show her back to her room, or get her a glass of water, but she refused.

"Please just let me sit here for a moment, Detective." she said. "I need to rest for a minute. I've had a long day."

Cotter still wanted to know the names of the boys involved in the hanging and the town officials involved in the cover-up, but he knew he'd have to find them out on his own. He thanked Mrs. Hughes a second time, gave her his card and told her she was a big help to the Vermont State Police. She accepted his gratitude and asked again that he leave her alone. Cotter said good-bye and headed back to the visitors' parking lot.

It was getting dark when Cotter pulled onto Interstate 93 on his way back to Vermont. When he reached White River Junction he thought about heading south on 91 and spending the night at home with Janie. He figured he could be home in two hours, have dinner and a passionate evening with her, leave early and be back in Eden Falls by eight, earlier if he had to. But something kept gnawing at him, something that kept interrupting every sweet, sensual image of his wife.

Thomas Downey, he thought. He kept repeating his name. "How does Thomas Downey fit into all of this?" he muttered.

"Shit!" he yelled as he slammed the steering wheel with the heel of his right hand. He put his cruiser into the far left lane and gunned its powerful engine. Within seconds the speedometer read ninety-five and was still rising. Cotter couldn't wait to get back to the Red Bird.

Chapter Twenty-Eight

A Treacherous Road

Shortly before eleven Cotter pulled off Interstate 89 at the Moretown exit and headed up Route 14 toward Eden Falls. It was an extremely dark evening. Thick, black, low-slung clouds had moved into the region a few hours earlier.

Route 14 was a typical Vermont secondary road with numerous bends, steep inclines and blind curves. Many drivers had lost control of their vehicles driving too fast around a tricky bend or trying to pass when they shouldn't, their front tires catching the shoulder, sucking them down an embankment like a whirlpool, or worse, ending up like an accordion pressed against the unforgiving ledge on the side of the road.

A few miles from the Red Bird Cotter noticed a set of head lamps in the rearview mirror. They approached Cotter's cruiser at an unusually high rate of speed. Suddenly the head lamps veered out into the oncoming lane as if the driver intended to pass.

"Asshole." Cotter couldn't believe anyone would be stupid enough to pass on a turn, especially at night. But, to his amazement, a full-size late-model pickup was now abreast of his unmarked cruiser.

"This guy's doing sixty or more," Cotter said to himself. He thought about what he would to say to the driver after he pulled him over. He tried to get a look at his face but he couldn't see him. Suddenly the pickup swerved to the right and careened off the left front fender of Cotter's cruiser. Cotter tried to cut the wheel but his right front tire caught the shoulder and pulled the car off the road. A sixty-foot ledge loomed in front of the car. Cotter cut the wheel again to bring the car back onto the pavement. The ledge grew larger by the second. The cruiser finally responded and jumped back onto the pavement where it was hit, once again, by the pickup.

Whoever was driving the pick-up knew exactly what he was doing. After the second collision the truck sped up and drove off. The second collision drove Cotter's sedan completely off the road. It began to spin sideways as it skidded along the gravel shoulder in the direction of the ledge. Only an old, rusted guard rail kept Cotter's car from hitting the ledge. The car ricocheted off the guard rail and spun around, finally coming to rest facing in the opposite direction in the drainage ditch on the side of the road. The cruiser was still upright. The headlights were still shining but the engine coughed a few times and died.

Cotter sat in the cruiser for a moment, badly shaken, his heart beating rapidly. He did a mental check of his anatomy and decided he wasn't hurt. He knew if it had happened a few hundred feet up the road where there was no guard rail Detective Simeon Cotter would be part of the ledge.

His cell-phone still worked so Cotter called Reggie McHue at home to ask him to come pick him up and drive him to the Red Bird. He didn't talk about his interview with Mrs. Hughes. McHue didn't press it.

"Better send a wrecker, too," Cotter said. "I think this thing's gonna need some body work."

McHue arrived in his wife's Explorer a half hour later.

"Who did it, Sim?" McHue asked.

"If I had to guess I'd say I didn't have a clue. The only one who knew I was going to Manchester was a Dr. Jessup I interviewed yesterday. But he didn't know when I was going."

"Was someone tailing you?"

"That's a possibility. There were no cars behind me, though, for at least the last half-hour." He paused. "Like everything else in this case, it just doesn't make sense." He was tired. Dark rings encircled his eyes. He looked at McHue. "I'm gonna need help, Reg."

Chapter Twenty-Nine

ROTC

When they were a mile from the Red Bird, McHue turned to Cotter and told him the boys at the SIU had run computer checks on the people from the yearbooks.

Cotter perked up.

"Computers, Sim," McHue said. "You ought to spend more time in the office. You might learn something."

"Not now, Reg," Cotter snapped. "Tell me what you have." He was recharged, as if the accident had never happened.

"Pretty boring group of people, actually," said McHue. "Nothing much of interest on any of them, a few DUI's, one bankruptcy. Nothing much to go on, except one."

"Downey?" Cotter asked.

"How'd you know?"

"What do you have on him?" Cotter asked impatiently.

"Well, he's about as average an American as you can get. Good family man, successful business, excellent credit and on and on. But his military record raised a few eyebrows." McHue looked at Cotter then back at the road. "You asked for military records." He looked at Cotter again. "This guy's was outstanding. In fact, he fits your profile to a tee."

Cotter was staring at him intently.

McHue continued. "Downey enrolled in Army ROTC at Princeton, Sim, straight-A student. After graduation he was assigned to a classified counter-intelligence program somewhere out in Arizona. Real hush-hush. I guess they were gonna train him to be a spy." McHue looked at the road and laughed.

The Red Bird came into view a hundred yards up on the right and McHue put on his directional signal. He looked at Cotter who was still staring at him. McHue sensed his friend's frustration and it made him uncomfortable. "Sim, that's all there was."

"What do you mean that's all there was?"

"That's it. The last entry in his military file is his acceptance to spy school."

"That figures," Cotter seemed to slump back wearily into his seat. He looked at McHue. "What about his discharge? Anything on that? Date? Rank? Anything?"

They pulled into the parking lot and parked in front of Cotter's room. As tired as he was Cotter wasn't anxious to go inside. The room depressed him.

McHue turned off the engine. "Nothing, Sim. Strange isn't it? Usually we have pretty good access to military records. If we can't get what we want, then the FBI boys down in Washington get what we need. They probably have so much shit on people down there they can get whatever they want." He paused. "But not this time. Zip! We struck out. Everyone we talked to down there was anxious to help at first. Then they became amazingly tight-lipped when we called 'em back."

The two men sat in the Explorer. There wasn't a sound to be heard inside or outside the vehicle until McHue finally broke the silence.

"How does Downey fit into this whole thing anyway, Sim?"

"I can't say just yet. I'm not even sure he does. It's just a hunch."

"Tell me about it, Sim. I can't help you if you keep me at arm's length. I know you're onto something."

Cotter didn't answer.

"O.K.," McHue continued. "You asked me for help. I didn't offer. You let me know if there's anything I can do. O.K.?" He looked at Cotter who had tilted his head back against the seat and closed his eyes.

"I don't like to see you working this one alone," McHue said. "It's doing something to you, like you're personally involved or something."

Cotter still didn't say anything.

"It's not really kosher either, Sim. If the boys in Montpelier find out you're up to your old tricks, you're gonna be in deep shit. It could cost you your job." McHue looked away. "Besides, you need help."

"I have help," Cotter said. "Wojo."

McHue looked back at Cotter but didn't react.

Cotter got out of the Explorer and thanked his buddy for the ride. He unlocked the door to his room and turned on the light. He went right to the phone on the night stand and placed a call to Bret Stevens, an FBI agent whom Cotter had befriended at the serial killer profiling course he had taken recently at the FBI training complex in Quantico, Virginia.

"Stevens here!" a man said with a thick midwestern accent.

"Bret, Sim Cotter, Vermont State Police, Special Investigations Unit. How are ya, buddy?"

"Sim? Hey, how the hell are ya. Catch that guy yet who's been popping your citizens off up there in the north country?"

"How'd you know about that?"

"Come on, buddy. Don't you think we care about you guys out in the trenches? I make it my business to know what's going on out there, especially when one of my protégés is working the case. Got a tough one, Sim?"

"I don't know yet, Bret. The guy's smart and he appears to be perfectly sane. He's not your everyday serial killer. He may be doing it for what he considers a legitimate reason. His targets aren't random."

"They all believe that, Sim. You know better than that."

"No, no. This one's different, Bret," Cotter insisted.

"Have you constructed a profile of the killer yet?"

"Can't," Cotter said. "There's not enough to go on, except one thing. I'm pretty sure our killer was in the military and he might have had some training as a special forces op, possibly in counter-intelligence."

"Why do you think that?"

"He's good, Bret. Very good. He gets in and he gets out and he doesn't leave a trace of any kind. He's smart enough to predict and control his victims' actions, where they'll be at precise times. And he's there waiting for them. The last victim appears to have been set up. Pretty clever."

"Can't you check the military data base? There can't be too many possibilities up there in Vermont. Christ, how many people up there do you have with that kind of background?"

"Well, I thought I might have a match on a local businessman, but when we pulled up his military record it was blank from the time he graduated from Princeton. He was ROTC and went to some Army intelligence school in Arizona. I don't even know the name of the school."

"That's typical," Stevens said. "Those guys are pretty damn paranoid. Want me to open some doors for you, Sim?"

"Can you?"

"Let me give it a shot," Stevens said. "Get yourself on the next puddle jumper out of Burlington and meet me here first thing tomorrow. You do have airplanes up there, don't you?"

"Yes we do, and fuck you too, asshole."

Be in my office tomorrow, as early as you can, and I'll take you to see a friend of mine who owes me big time. We'll see what we can find out. At the very least, it will be great to see you, Sim."

Cotter thanked his friend and told him to keep the coffee warm. Then he called the dispatcher in Williston and told him he'd need a car and driver first thing in the morning.

Chapter Thirty
Downey's File

Cotter arrived at Dulles International Airport around nine-thirty the following morning on the first U.S. Air flight out of Burlington. He grabbed a taxi and arrived at the FBI training facility in Quantico just after eleven.

"Sim, great to see you."

"Likewise, Bret." The two men shook hands. "So, how's the coffee this morning?" Cotter asked.

"Fully aged and remarkably robust, Sim. Just like my women." The two men laughed. "Help yourself," Stevens said, "to the coffee, that is." He pointed to a pot of java and a stack of foam cups on a desk just outside his office.

Bret Stevens looked like the prototypical FBI field agent. He was dressed in a conservative light gray suit, had short-cropped hair just long enough to part and was clean-shaven except for a large handlebar mustache that hid his upper lip. Just enough wax was applied to the very ends to keep them pointed upwards.

Stevens was an expert at serial-killer profiling. He was in charge of the Bureau's training program for state and municipal police officers. He liked Simeon Cotter. He admired Cotter's unencumbered sense of logic and his willingness to embrace the new profiling techniques. Cotter had performed exceptionally well in the three-week course and the two men had become good friends.

"We don't have much time," Stevens said as he poured

himself a cup of coffee. "A friend of mine's waiting for us downtown at the Pentagon. I'm calling in a favor." He looked at Cotter. "You owe me one yourself now, Cotter. This guy's a colonel and they keep score. Now I owe him and you owe me. That's the way it works here, pal." He got up and put on his jacket. "You'll have to finish your coffee in the car, Sim. We need to go right now or we'll miss him."

The drive from Quantico into Washington allowed Cotter time to brief Stevens on the details of the two crimes. As with Reggie McHue the night before, Cotter left out the part about the hanging. After listening to Cotter's account of the killer's M.O. Stevens said he agreed with Cotter's conclusion that the killer must have had some sort of military training in the planning of covert operations. He also suggested they might find some personal problems in the man's file, a bump or a glitch in his record, even a dishonorable discharge, as most serial killers found military life with its focus on authority difficult to hack.

Cotter still wasn't convinced Downey would fit the profile of the typical serial killer, but he believed his military records would be revealing nonetheless. He was more interested in whether or not Downey had the training to mastermind the murders of Bessette and Roi than in his ability to cope with authority. But he still listened to everything Stevens said with great interest.

The ride went quickly and the two men arrived at the Pentagon around one-thirty. They were given directions to Colonel Malcolm Davis's office and found it rather easily, considering the size and complexity of the building.

"Bret, how you doing?" Davis asked as the two men walked into the Colonel's office.

"Fine, Malcolm." They shook heartily. "This is Detective Simeon Cotter, Vermont State Police, Special Investigations Unit." Stevens said. Cotter and Davis shook hands.

"What can I do for you, Detective Cotter?" Colonel

Davis asked.

Cotter got right to the point. "I'm trying to find the complete military service records of a man we think may have been involved in a couple of murders up our way. Our boys checked out his military file by computer but the file was incomplete. The guy went to some sort of counter-intelligence school after graduating from college. He was ROTC. There are no entries in his file after he was transferred."

"Army, I assume?" Davis said.

"Army."

"Then you're in luck, Detective." Davis pressed the button on his intercom and asked Lieutenant Price to come into his office.

The lieutenant was short and wiry thin and entered the colonel's office with a spiral notebook and a pen. "Yes, sir?"

Davis turned to Cotter. "What's the name of your suspect, Detective?"

"Downey. Thomas Downey."

"Do you have any idea when he was discharged?" Davis asked.

"Just a guess, probably mid-seventies. I'm sorry I can't be more specific."

"Only a problem if we come up with multiple hits," Davis said. "A Vermonter?"

Cotter wasn't sure how to answer that. "No, to Vermonters he's not a Vermonter, but to an outsider..." Cotter hesitated. "The answer would be yes."

"Was he a Vermont resident when he entered ROTC?" Davis asked, somewhat confused by Cotter's answer.

"Yes," Cotter said.

Davis looked at the lieutenant who said he'd get right on it and walked out the door.

"Go get yourselves some lunch, boys," Davis suggested. "Sorry I can't join you. Take as much time as you can because this might take a little digging. These intelligence boys are real protective of their own. They don't like people asking questions. Secrecy is what they do, you know." He looked at Stevens, then turned back to Cotter. "Personally I think they're a bunch of paranoid assholes."

Cotter and Stevens took Colonel Davis's advice and went to get some food and catch up on old times. Stevens asked Cotter if he was interested in joining the Bureau and Cotter declined. It was a conversation they had every time they spoke. They returned to Davis's office around three-thirty.

"Gentlemen," Davis said as they walked in, "Sit down. I have what you're looking for." He looked at Cotter. "Quite an interesting individual, this suspect of yours."

"How so, Colonel?" Cotter asked. He looked at Stevens who winked.

"Thomas Downey was a hot recruit. Several agencies, including the CIA and Defense, had their eye on him when he was at Princeton. But the Army kept him and sent him to intelligence school after he graduated. Some strong recommendations from the folks at Princeton. Four-point-zero average." He looked at Cotter. "He was sent to what was then a top-secret training facility about a hundred miles west of Phoenix. He did very well at first, especially on the academic stuff. Apparently he has the equivalent of a photographic memory." Davis talked as he scanned the contents of the folder. "They were quite high on him till he took a battery of psychological tests." Davis looked up at Cotter. "Then all shit broke loose."

Davis held up a piece of paper on which was stamped, CONFIDENTIAL. "This report was written by a psychiatrist who did a mental evaluation of your suspect. It concludes your guy was unfit for duty. Deep-seated emotional trauma...blah, blah, blah...an inability to manage stress." Davis looked up. "Not exactly what they're looking for over there, Detective." He looked at Stevens, then back at Cotter. "Too bad." He put down the first piece of paper and began to read another. "This progress evaluation says he has a one-sixty I.Q. In fact, according to this, they tried to keep him in spite of the fact he was a wacko. Sort of an in-house agent who wouldn't be exposed to too much stress. They gave him a job writing simulated operations against terrorist installations in the Mid-East. Two-, three-man stuff. Navy SEALS probably. In and out, a couple of Arabs get their throats cut. That sort of stuff. That assignment lasted one year. He was discharged in 1982." He looked up at Cotter again. "Sounds like your man, Detective."

"Maybe," Cotter responded. "What were the conditions of his discharge?"

"Honorable, I assume," Davis said. He looked down at the report. "Exactly two years to the day after he entered the program. The balance of his active duty was waived for psychological reasons."

"I doubt he planned it that way," Cotter said.

Davis got up and said he had another meeting. He looked at Stevens, then back at Cotter. "I hope I've been able to help you guys. Let me know if he's your man, will you?"

"Will do, Malcolm," Stevens said.

The two men exchanged handshakes with the Colonel and left. Stevens asked Cotter if he wanted to stay over and have dinner together that evening. Cotter thanked him but declined. He had too much to do back in Vermont. For the first time since he had become involved in this case he had a lead. He was excited, and desperate to get back to Eden Falls. Even the prospect of spending another night at the Red Bird Motel didn't bother him.

Chapter Thirty-One

Shopping at Downey's

The big box stores like Wal-Mart and Home Depot, which had opened in Williston during the past few years, had wrecked havoc with many of the family-owned businesses in northwestern Vermont. But some, like Downey's Outfitters, survived. Downey lost a few customers at first, but they eventually came back.

Downey opened the store every morning at seven to accommodate early risers, especially his construction clientele who often stopped in for a pair of gloves or other necessities on their way to work. Wednesday morning he pulled into the store's parking lot, an extension of the Grand Union parking lot off Route 14, fifteen minutes before seven.

Downey got out of his Land Cruiser and walked toward the front door. To his surprise, Cotter was standing by the door waiting for him, looking no worse for the all-nighter he had just pulled trying to get back from Washington before daybreak.

"I heard you opened at seven," Cotter said with a smile. "My wife's birthday is this Saturday and I wanted to get her something nice. I looked around the other day when the Sheriff and I were here and I saw some things that she'd love, so...I hope you don't mind..."

"Not at all, Detective," Downey said. "I'm a morning person myself, and so are many of my customers. Please come in."

Downey excused himself to turn on the lights and go through his morning routine. He invited Cotter to look around and to call him if he needed any help. Cotter thanked him and went to the women's outerwear section.

Downey came back out front ten minutes later and Cotter told him he'd found a sweater that his wife would love. But he didn't see it in her size, which was medium.

"Most of these take a while to get, Detective," Downey said as he took the sweater from Cotter and looked at the label. "This one, unfortunately will take about four to five weeks, that's if we can get it at all. These are hand-made. I compliment your taste, Detective."

"That's a shame," Cotter said. "My wife would love it."

"Well, why don't you give her this one," Downey suggested. He held up a similar sweater in a larger size. "I know it's a large, but they run small and it may fit her, who knows. If not, she can exchange it, or she may be willing to wait for a medium, if we can get it. At least you would have made the effort and she'll appreciate that."

Given what Colonel Davis had said about Downey, Cotter wasn't surprised how quickly he had turned Cotter's problem around. It was a cute turn of events, he thought, and so natural. Give Janie the sweater and let her decide. Closure! Best of all, Downey came out looking like he had solved Cotter's problem, and he made a one hundred, fifty-dollar sale to boot.

"That's an excellent idea," Cotter said. "By the way, Mr. Downey, is that your Land Cruiser out there?"

Downey looked out the front window at his vehicle sitting in the parking lot. "Yes. Why?" he asked, turning back to Cotter.

"How about your wife, does she drive a pickup by any chance? You know, a full-size pickup?"

"No, Detective, she drives an Accord. Why do you want to know?"

"I thought I saw you Monday night, a little after eleven, on Route 14 coming from the interstate. I thought I recognized you." Cotter was groping. He didn't have a clue who ran him off the road.

"It wasn't me," Downey said. He put the sweater in a box and took Cotter's charge card from the counter. He slipped it through the tiny slot in the register looking for authorization from the credit card company. He put it through several times but it wouldn't activate the computer. He looked up at the clock on the shelf behind the counter.

"They don't open till seven-thirty. Sometimes not until a few minutes after." It was barely seven-thirty. He tried the credit card again. It still wouldn't activate the computer. "Well, I think we can assume it's good, Detective. I think I can assume a member of the Vermont State Police is trustworthy."

Downey smiled as he filled out the credit card form and handed it to Cotter for his signature. Cotter signed it and pushed it back across the counter to Downey.

"It wasn't me." Downey said, as he tore the perforation from the credit card receipt and handed the pink copy to Cotter. He put the sweater box in a bag and gave it to Cotter. "I was fast asleep by nine-thirty Monday night." He chuckled. "I tried to watch the first quarter of the Bulls-Celtics game, but even Michael Jordan couldn't keep me awake."

"Look, Mr. Downey," Cotter said. "I really did come in here this morning to buy my wife a gift, but since I'm here, I have to be frank. I'm really stumped about the Bessette and Roi murders. Do you mind if we talk about them for a few minutes?"

Downey tried his best not to react. He looked at Cotter. "I suppose not, Detective. I'm not sure how I can help you, though. I really didn't know either man very well. But go ahead."

"You lived here when the Fischer boy was hanged. Isn't it possible the murders have something to do with that?"

"I don't know. I was pretty young when that happened."

"But they were both involved, weren't they?"

"Who?" Downey asked.

"Bessette and Roi."

"Involved in the hanging?"

"Yes, at least that's what I've heard."

"I don't know who told you that, Detective. Nobody was supposed to know who did it. I don't know, I don't think too many people know, except those involved, probably their parents, but most of them are dead. It was very hush-hush. That's what I remember most about it. Everyone in town kept saying you weren't supposed to talk about it, the teachers, pretty much everybody."

"So you don't remember anything about it?"

"I remember when it happened. It was quite a thing. It made quite an impression on me. I was only ten, like I said, but I'll never forget it. Today they'd bring a crisis management team into the school to talk with the kids; psychologists, social workers. But we didn't have anything like that then. We just had to deal with it." He paused. "How about you, Detective. You're from this area, aren't you?"

"Washingtonville," Cotter replied. "I remember hearing about it, but I was younger than you. It had quite an impact on me, too, though." He looked into Downey's eyes and for a moment he thought he saw something. Was it a plea for help, a plea for understanding and compassion? Suddenly it wasn't there. As quickly as it had appeared it was gone. Cotter continued to stare at Downey. Downey remained indifferent. Cotter finally broke off eye contact, thanked Downey for his help, and left with his package.

Chapter Thirty-Two

The Douglas Hearing

The Eden Falls Town Hall was a three-story Georgian Colonial built in 1792 by one of Eden Falls's founding fathers, Jedediah Keane. The clerk's office was on the first floor. Town meetings were held in a conference room located in what used to be the basement, but was now called the lower level. Sharing the lower level with the conference room was the sheriff's office. The two areas were separated by a glassed-in foyer. The entrance to the lower level was in the rear of the building down a flight of concrete steps.

The conference room was about forty feet wide by forty feet long and could accommodate no more than fifty people. More than twice that many were expected for the Douglas Hearing.

Planning Commission Chairman Nathan Winters expected the room to be jammed with partisans of both sides of the dispute. This was the meeting everyone in town had been waiting for. It would decide, once and for all, whether or not the Douglas Farm project would be approved. There was always the possibility of appeal, but that wasn't on anybody's mind. For now, as they had for two hundred years, the people of Eden Falls, through their elected officials, would decide their own destiny.

The Douglas subdivision sparked so much interest in the community that the atmosphere in the conference room was more befitting a championship prize fight than a public zoning hearing. The only thing missing was a cloud of smoke hanging over the noisy crowd, the smell of beer and a microphone suspended by a long cable in the middle of the conference table, Michael Buffer on the end of the mike announcing the combatants: *...in the blue corner, the challenger, wearing Levi jeans, work boots and a flannel shirt, Vesticate Douglas; and in the red corner, wearing Dockers slacks, Air Jordans and a Nike polo shirt, the champion, the Eden Falls Planning Commission.*

What had been a community of five hundred people in 1970 had become a community of three thousand in 1990. At one time cows in Eden Falls outnumbered people five to one. Now, it was said, there were more lawyers in town than cows. The change was too sudden.

What was at stake at the hearing was more than the Douglas Farm project. It was a battle for a way of life that was slipping away from Douglas and the rest of the local people whose ancestors had settled in town many generations before. They had accepted most of the changes to their town, but they could not accept being told by flatlanders what they could and couldn't do with their land. That, they believed, just wasn't right, and they rallied behind Vesticate Douglas to make one final stand.

The most vocal flatlander on the planning commission was Brian Reese. Reese and his family had moved into Eden Falls in 1995, and Reese had a seat on the Eden Falls Planning Commission before he paid his first property tax bill. It didn't take long for his city affectations and hostile attitude toward locals to surface.

As seven o'clock neared, members of the community began shuffling in, anxious to get a seat. Some people wanted to know on which side of the room the Douglas group would sit and on which side of the room supporters of Citizens for Responsible Land Management would sit. As people walked in they looked for their fellows and segregated themselves accordingly. By seven-fifteen the room was full, except for the conference table.

At twenty after seven, members of the planning commission began filtering into the conference room. By seven twenty-eight, everyone was seated, except the Douglas group. At seven-thirty, Vesticate Douglas walked in.

Douglas was a large man with an enormous double chin that shook as he spoke. His waist and hips were larger and fuller than most men, and his posture made him look like he was always searching for a place to sit down.

Vesticate Douglas was an anachronism. He was a man you would trust but not with your most precious belongings. He had influence in the community but it only went so far. People liked Vesticate, but they didn't adore him. They respected him, but they didn't admire him. You wouldn't mind a man like Vesticate Douglas going steady with your daughter, but you wouldn't want your daughter to marry him. He was lukewarm water and a gradual incline. Nothing about him was compelling or definitive. He was just an average man, and that was fine with him.

Douglas was followed by his lawyer, Wilson Turner, of Turner & Boxleitner, a third-generation Burlington law firm that had represented Vermont's lumber barons since before World War Two. Turner wore a wrinkled white shirt, unbuttoned at the collar, with a tie that had been loosened slightly to allow him to breathe. He carried a large portfolio of legal papers under his arm, a hardbound copy of the Vermont Rules of Civil Procedure and Annotated Statutes and copies of the town's zoning and subdivision regulations. As Douglas and Turner sat down at the far end of the table, a man got up from a chair directly behind Douglas and sat in the last empty seat at the table, next to Douglas. His name was Farley Sweet.

Sweet was a tall, rail-thin, rustic old gentleman who dressed in corduroy slacks and a wool plaid shirt. He smoked a cheap pipe from which he had removed the filter because he claimed it intercepted too much of the tobacco flavor. He was slightly hard of hearing. Farley Sweet's even temperament and soft demeanor were a testimony to how few of life's problems bothered him. In many ways, he was the quintessential Vermonter.

By seven thirty-eight everyone was seated and looking at Nathan Winters.

Chapter Thirty-Three

The Third

He was dressed in black jeans and a black, hooded sweatshirt. He carried a small leather pouch out to his vehicle and threw it on the passenger seat as he got in. He pulled out of the side road, made a left at the T intersection and a right, three miles later, onto Route 14. He headed west toward Eden Falls Center. A mile before town he turned right onto Bridge Street and drove over the single-lane steel bridge that looked like a giant erector set. On the north side of the river he made a left onto Green River Road and followed it along the river toward Eden Falls Center.

The Green River was small, no more than forty feet across at its widest point and as little as a dozen feet at its narrowest. It was rarely more than two or three feet deep most of the year. In March, however, it became a raging torrent, a fact to which a number of people who lived along its banks could attest. By late spring it usually relaxed to its normal pace, and by mid-summer it could fizzle to a trickle. Its water was clear and cold. Its gravel banks were lined with small boulders and littered with other natural debris like tree limbs and root balls that were captured and dragged downstream by the river's powerful spring current.

Houses lined Green River Road opposite the river for a mile past the steel bridge. Most of the houses had large, wraparound porches and people were inclined to be outside and about in the early evening. Sounds of children playing and lawnmowers buzzing filled the air.

He knew people would begin to retreat indoors as the sun set and the mosquitoes and deer flies pressed their attack. Some people would remain on their porches with citronella candles burning and zappers zapping, but even those folks would retire soon enough.

He drove past the houses. It was nearly dark. A mile and a half past the last house he came to another steel bridge on the left that crossed the river back to Route 14. On the right there was an old service station that no longer sold gas but still did auto repairs. The gas pumps were still there, but they were 1950s vintage and hadn't worked for ten years.

He pulled into the service station. It had closed hours earlier and there was no one around. He pulled up between two cars parked against the left side of the building and turned off the engine. He got out, grabbed the leather pouch, closed the door quietly and began walking across the road toward the second steel bridge.

Suddenly the steel bridge looked like it was moving. He froze. It was the strangest sensation, as if the steel superstructure was shimmering. Without thinking, he dove into the bushes on the side of the road just before the bridge. The bridge stopped moving but came distinctly into view. Every steel beam, plate and rivet were caught in the high beams of a Dodge mini-van as it approached the bridge from the south side of the river, and headed directly for the man in the hooded sweatshirt on the north side. The van rumbled across the broken pavement. It slowed to twenty miles per hour to avoid breaking an axle or shock. Its head lamps lit up the bushes into which the man had just leaped, but he was well-hidden and his dark clothing absorbed the penetrating light. Neither the driver nor his passengers saw him.

I needed that, he said to himself. He was serious. He had already become complacent, taking too much for granted. It made him sloppy and it angered him.

He waited for the taillights to disappear before venturing back out onto the road to cross the bridge. The bridge was dark once again. He wondered if he should hike down the embankment and traverse the river rather than risk getting caught mid-span in someone's headlights.

He stood at the entrance to the bridge on the north side of the river and listened for the sounds of another vehicle. He heard nothing. He decided to take his chances. He lowered his head and sprinted quietly across the bridge. His sneakers didn't make a sound. He was certain nobody had seen him. On the other side of the bridge he crouched down near the side of the road. He looked back over the bridge, to the corner at Route 14 and at each of the houses within eyeshot. He listened for children stealing their last bit of play, or a couple out for a romantic walk. Nothing.

Satisfied he was alone, he ducked around the metal guard rail on the right side of the road and slid down the embankment toward the gravel river bank. He was now on the same side of the river as the Eden Falls Town Hall, about three hundred and fifty yards downstream.

He followed the gravel bank on the south side of the river around a bend that was imitated thirty feet up the embankment by a curve in Route 14. Around the bend the river straightened out and he followed it for another one hundred yards and stopped. He knew he was behind the town hall, but his landmarks were unclear, and he wasn't certain where along the rear parking lot he would come out when he climbed the embankment.

He worked his way up between the rocks and small vegetation, the former providing an excellent foothold and the latter providing the perfect hand grips as well as cover. He wore leather gloves to protect his hands.

As he got near the crest of the embankment he was careful to avoid detection. He eased his head above the edge of the bank just beyond the parking lot, to find he was nearly one hundred feet to the left of where he wanted to be. Nevertheless, he dragged himself over the crest of the bank and lay prone behind a ten-inch by ten-inch creosoted timber, one of many that had been placed lengthwise along the edges of the parking lot of the Eden Falls Town Hall.

He hoped the pickup he was looking for wasn't too many rows away from the edge of the bank where he lay. The more rows he had to traverse, the greater his chances of being seen by someone leaving the hearing early or arriving late. There were more than seventy-five cars and pickups in the parking lot.

He was looking for a specific truck, but he didn't see it at first. It has to be here, he said to himself. "Unless he came with someone else," he mumbled. It was a disturbing thought and he knew it was a possibility. Then he saw it. He was instantly relieved. It was only three rows away from the bank and it was shadowed from the large spotlight on the pole out by Route 14 by several large oak trees that were full of new leaves.

It was a brand new 1997 Dodge Ram three-quarter ton, four-wheel-drive pickup. It was deep red with chrome trim. It had all of the options one could ask for, including a black leather toneau cover over the custom-fit, hard-plastic bed liner. There was no doubt this was the right truck.

He focused all of his senses on the parking lot. He listened intently for the sound of leather against gravel, a footstep, the scrape of cowhide or Vibram soles against a concrete step, the sound of a car door, a human voice, anything that would alert him to the presence of another person. As hard as they tried his ears couldn't discern any threat. Only then did he slowly raise his shoulders, followed by his hips, until he was on all fours. Still satisfied he was indeed alone, he shifted into a squat position and carefully moved toward the truck. When he reached it, he slid himself, feet-first, under the passenger side of the vehicle just behind the right front tire.

Chapter Thirty-Four

The Hearing Goes Two

"The business at hand, folks, is the Douglas Farm project," Nathan Winters said. He looked at Vesticate Douglas. "Vesticate?"

All side conversations ceased with the announcement of this much-anticipated event. Vesticate Douglas pulled his chair closer to the table and straightened his posture. The commissioners fiddled with their papers and readied their copies of the town's planning and zoning regulations. Farley Sweet opened his briefcase and removed a large stack of folders. All eyes shifted to Vesticate Douglas. Douglas was ready. "Thank you, Nathan," he said.

"Are you going to give us the same story about your land isn't a wetland?" Reese asked, before Douglas could start.

Douglas shot a penetrating look at Reese. "*You* may have determined it's a wetland, but unfortunately for you, sir, the US Geological..." He looked down at his files. "...survey, the State of Vermont Wetlands Division, the Army Corps of Engineers and all your scientific experts don't agree with you. That land's been in my family for..."

"I know that land," Reese interrupted. "I walk my dog on that land every day. I see what's there. There's no way you're going to convince me that land isn't a wetland."

"That's for sure," Douglas said. He turned to Wilson Turner. His voice was still elevated. "If I pissed in the Sahara Desert, this son-of-a-bitch would call it a wetland."

Winters jumped in, raising his voice above the laughter from the Douglas partisans. "Gentlemen!" He stood up. "Gentlemen!" The combatants disengaged in deference to the chairman. "Let's move on."

"Thank you, Nathan. Douglas looked at Reese. "Thank you." He turned to his left and introduced Farley Sweet.

Sweet cleared his throat. He took his thick, black-rimmed glasses out of a leather case in the breast pocket of his shirt and slowly put them on. If Winters had a knack for knowing how to manipulate a crowd, Farley Sweet was a master. The most remarkable thing was that he didn't even know he was doing it. It was his natural tempo, slow, hypnotic. It forced people to listen because they were so anxious to hear what he was about to say.

"You know," Sweet said. He looked down at some notes and shifted his buttocks in his chair. His white hair glistened under the fluorescent lights. A small amount of air came up his esophagus and he burped, but he kept his mouth shut. Then he cleared his throat and everyone knew he was going to speak. "I think." He stopped to shift his weight again, and cleared his throat a second time. "If we put a few hay bales in the right places it'll solve any problems with runoff."

The commissioners looked at Sweet.

"Though I don't think there'll be any," he added.

Those who'd never met Farley Sweet expected more. But that was all they were going to get.

"Everybody should have a copy of Farley's wetlands control plan," Douglas said. "It was approved by the state last week."

Chapter Thirty-Five

The Third (continued)

He took an adjustable wrench out of the leather pouch. He put the wrench on the bolt that attached the cable from the battery to the starter, and turned it counterclockwise. After a few revolutions, the bolt became loose and came off the rest of the way by hand. It was a new truck. In a few years, eaten by the rust from the salt spread on Vermont's roads during the winter, the bolt wouldn't be as forgiving. He pulled the cable away from the starter and let it hang so it would be in plain view to someone looking under the hood.

He was about to slide himself out from under the chassis when he heard the rear door to the town hall open. He listened intently to the sound of human voices. He heard heavy feet walking up concrete steps. "Why don't they pick up their feet," he said softly to himself. He could hear their voices getting closer. The people were coming his way, but he was relaxed. He breathed calmly, slowly, and let his arms and legs relax too. He shifted his weight between his left and right buttocks, undulating his body like a snail to move himself directly under the center of the truck.

It bothered him that he didn't know if the meeting had ended and this was the first wave of people coming out, or just some people who were bored or had other obligations. It seemed too early for the meeting to be over. It was too important to end so quickly.

Still, there was a chance something had happened, the

planning commission relented and approved the plan without a fight, or Douglas said: "To hell with this shit!" and threw in the towel. He thought about that for a moment and realized that wouldn't happen.

Even if it did, no one would spot him. Let them come, all of them, he thought. He was safe in his cocoon under the truck. He looked up at the frame and all the cross members and nuts and bolts and all the parts, the starter, the fuel tank, the transmission, the springs and shocks and brakes and grease fittings and drive shaft and ball joints and manifold pipe and muffler and emergency brake cable. He looked at the tires. He thought about how the whole truck was held up by air. A bullet in each tire would take care of that. Bam! A clean shot right through the belly of the side wall.

He was totally relaxed. He waited for the voices and sloth-like footsteps to go away, but they didn't. Instead they got closer. He could hear the people speaking, laughing at something that had happened inside, no doubt. He wondered if they were laughing at Douglas's futility. Or were they laughing at Farley Sweet's occasional muffled belch? They sounded like school children, he thought, giggling, louder and louder. Finally they stopped. They were about three cars away from the pickup. He could see their feet. One lady wore soft leather boots that extended far enough up her leg that he couldn't see their top. He assumed she worked in Burlington, at a bank or a law office perhaps, and hadn't been home to change. The second set of feet belonged to a man. They were attired in heavy hiking boots, the kind with thick Vibram soles stiffened with steel inserts for rock climbing. He was the heavy-footed one. A third set of feet was clad in white sneakers. This was a woman, the man guessed, by the size of the sneakers and the short strides she took.

After what seemed an interminably long and frivolous conversation about some mundane topic, the woman with the black leather boots got into her small, metallic Japanese sedan. The man and the other woman walked away, down another row of vehicles, and got into a Saab. Both vehicles drove out of the parking lot, turned right onto Route 14 and headed away from the town hall.

That wasn't even close, the man thought. He listened once again for footsteps or voices and heard none. He surveyed the parking lot three hundred and sixty degrees from his vantage point under the truck and saw nothing. He slid his body out from under the truck and stayed as low as he could as he moved back toward the edge of the parking area, over the creosoted logs and over the crest of the embankment. He breathed easily. This was a piece of cake.

Now all he had to do was wait.

Chapter Thirty-Six

The Hearing (Round Three)

"Why don't you send the little shit back to New York," someone yelled from the gallery, referring to Brian Reese. Everyone turned and looked in the direction of the voice and a number of people laughed.

Winters stood up. The hearing had gotten out of control.

"If this doesn't stop I'm going to end this hearing and recommend to the selectmen that they supersede this commission and grant Mr. Douglas his permits."

"You can't do that," Reese said.

"God-dammit, Reese!" Winters shot back. "I'll do whatever the hell I want and you can't do a damn thing about it." It was the first time most of the people present had ever heard Nathan Winters raise his voice. It was also the first time in memory a chairman of the planning commission had disciplined another member in front of an applicant.

A heated debate over a number of issues followed Farley Sweet's testimony. Finally Nathan Winters called for a vote. To no one's surprise, a majority of the commissioners voted against the Douglas Farm project. Nathan Winters was the only vote in favor. There would be no permit.

Douglas's expression concealed his rage. The result of the hearing was what he had expected. He had known his rejection was pre-ordained, given the composition of the planning commission. Still, he was seething inside. He wanted to leap across the table and strangle the diminutive Reese, who sat smugly with his arms folded, staring at Douglas.

All eyes in the room fell on Douglas. He stood up and said he would like to speak. He started off calmly. "We're going to appeal and we're going to have the Superior Court throw this thing right back in your faces," he said. He began to grit his teeth. "What you've done here tonight is not only illegal, as your attorney will tell you, but you've stuck a knife in the back of every one of us who was born in this town. May you people go straight to Hell!"

Turner pulled at Douglas but Douglas pushed his hand away.

"I wish I was on the planning commission when people like you started coming into this town twenty years ago," Douglas continued. "I would've done the same thing to you and none of you would be here now. That's the trouble with this town. You people move in here and think you can just take over. Take away all our rights. Who the hell gave you the right to do that?"

Turner begged him to stop.

"This is my land!" Douglas said as he grabbed a copy of the survey and crumpled it up in his hand. He held it above his head as his voice rose. "My great-great-grandparents fought and died for this land while you people were speaking some gibberish somewhere off in Europe." He looked at Reese. "You little piece of shit, you haven't lived here for two years. Who the hell do you think you are coming in here telling me what I can do with my farm?"

Turner jumped up and grabbed Douglas by the elbow. Reese no longer smiled. Nathan Winters jumped up to prevent his long-time friend from causing more problems for himself.

Douglas turned to Turner. "I know what I'm saying," he said. "I'll see this guy in court because I'm going to sue his ass off."

"Vesticate, please," Turner said. He tried to move Douglas away from the table.

"You're not God," Douglas yelled at Reese. "I'm gonna be back here after my appeal and I'm going to shove my permit down your throat, you little bastard." The veins were bulging from Douglas's forehead. "I'll tell you something else, Reese. I don't want you walking your God-damned dog on my property again. You hear me, Reese? Who gave you permission to come on my land? If I catch your dog on my land again I'm gonna blow his head off and have you arrested."

"Vesticate!" Turner yelled. He grabbed Douglas and spun him around. Two decades of resentment poured from Douglas's mouth as if he were speaking for all native Vermonters.

Reese gathered up his papers quickly and started for the door. Turner took Douglas over to the corner of the room opposite the door and tried to console him. The meeting was over. There was nothing else he could do. For now, the Douglas Farm project was dead.

Chapter Thirty-Seven

The Third (continued)

The doors to the town hall opened and people began pouring out. There was an explosion of energy into the parking lot. Some people talked about what had just happened inside. Others moved quickly to their vehicles so they could get home at a reasonable hour. Pro-Douglas forces avoided the anti-growth forces. Members of each group looked suspiciously at members of the other group as they lingered to dissect what had happened at the hearing. After twenty minutes, however, everyone had gone home and there were only two vehicles left in the parking lot.

The man kept his body hidden as he peered over the crest of the embankment and watched the procession of cars leaving the town hall. He was surprised the owner of the pickup, one of the two remaining vehicles, hadn't come out yet. Suddenly he heard the rear door to the town hall open and close, followed by the sound of a man's voice.

Two men paused outside the door as it latched. One man turned to lock the door behind them. The two men conversed as they walked up the concrete steps. They walked a short distance and stopped. One of the men put his right hand out and his left hand on the other man's shoulder. The two shook hands and parted. One man headed for a Volvo parked just outside the door. The other headed for the pickup.

The owner of the pickup hesitated as he stood by the driver's door, fumbling for his keys. He found them in his coat pocket. He opened the door, tossed a briefcase into the passenger seat, stepped inside, buckled himself in and tried to start the engine. Nothing happened. He looked confused. He was very tired and he thought about leaving the truck and going home with the other man, who, having sensed something was wrong, had driven over to where the dead pickup was parked.

"What's wrong?" the man in the Volvo asked.

"I don't know," the man in the pickup answered. He got out and opened up the hood. The light from the Volvo's head lamps was barely sufficient to get a good look inside, shadowed as it was by the pickup's grill and the man's body.

"Hard to see," the owner of the pickup said, peering into the engine compartment. "Could be the starter's not getting any juice." He moved to the passenger side of the compartment and looked down at the starter. "That's it," he said. "The wire to the starter fell off." He shook his head in disgust. "They can't even check to see if things are tight anymore, damn car makers. Just crank 'em out as fast as they can."

"You gonna be OK?" the man in the Volvo asked. "Do you want me to bring you home?"

"Nope," the other man answered. He looked up. "Thanks anyway. I'll get this thing going in a few minutes. I'd rather not leave it here all night. But thanks, Nathan.

Winters drove off after saying goodnight.

The other man stood at the front of his truck looking into the engine compartment.

The man in the dark, hooded sweatshirt moved quickly into position, eyes wide open, alert, head up, body low, his senses focused on everything around him. He slid quietly over the top of the bank, moving like a cat in a large loop, eyes trained on the man at the truck. He was about thirty feet away.

The owner of the truck was still looking into the engine compartment trying to figure out how a starter cable could come loose on its own. Before he knew it, the other man was only ten feet behind him and had taken a twenty-two caliber pistol out of his leather pouch. Suddenly the owner of the pickup spun around. The two men stood face to face.

For a moment neither man made a sound.

"I thought you might be coming for me," the owner of the pickup said.

The hooded man pulled the trigger and a flash of light followed by a sharp bang filled the air. A small bullet hit the other man in the chest. It lodged in his right lung. He slumped against the grill of his pickup and tried not to fall to the ground. The hooded man walked several paces closer, aimed the gun at the other man's head, and fired a second shot. The bullet hit the other man in the center of his forehead. He let go of the grill and crumpled to the ground. After discharging a third and a fourth bullet into the man's head, the hooded man hurried off to the edge of the parking area and slipped down the embankment to the river below to make his escape.

He followed the river around the bend toward the second bridge. Instead of risking being seen on the Route 14 side of the river, he waded across the swift moving but shallow current and hiked along the north side of the stream until he came to the first bridge. He listened for sounds that would indicate whether or not someone had heard the shots and had called the Sheriff. He heard nothing. He climbed the bank below the bridge and came up by the guard rail near the entrance to the auto repair shop. He moved quickly across the dark parking lot to his own vehicle, unlocked the door and jumped in. He started the engine and pulled out of the lot and headed down Green River Road. He blasted the heater to dry his feet. He was as relaxed as if he were coming home from a movie. He felt invigorated, alive.

As he drove along the river he thought he heard sirens. Was it a chimney fire, or an accident? Or had someone found the body?

Chapter Thirty-Eight

The Investigation

"I don't know why this has to happen at two in the morning," Wojo said as he raised himself out of bed. "Don't know why it can't wait till morning."

Wojo lumbered across his bedroom to the bathroom where he relieved himself. He walked over to his closet and dressed in yesterday's uniform, minus the tie, then went into the kitchen to boil water for a cup of instant coffee to take with him in the cruiser on the way to the scene. "The God-damned body can wait," he said as he waited for the water to boil. He picked up the phone and dialed Deputy Cain's number.

"Vesticate Douglas is dead," Wojo said. "Go get the M.E. and get over to the town hall as soon as you can. Have the M.E. call Detective Cotter and get him over there too. I don't know where the hell Cotter is but find him. Maybe he's still at the Red Bird. Have the M.E. call him at his home in Brattleboro if you have to. Wherever the hell you find him make sure he knows we have another one."

Wojo arrived at the town hall nearly half an hour after state trooper Ben Oaks. Oaks had pointed his cruiser toward the front of the pickup and the high beams threw a terrific glare off the bumper and grill. Vesticate Douglas lay slumped to the ground in front of the truck. His hair was a bloody sponge. Dried blood was caked around three holes in his face, one above his left ear, the other two in his forehead. A patch of blood on his shirt gave away a fourth hole in his chest, just to the right of his sternum.

Oaks was kneeling down over the body when Wojo walked into the light of the high beams and threw an enormous shadow. Oaks was young and educated. He had graduated from Champlain College with a degree in law enforcement before applying for a job with the state police.

"Better not touch anything till your boss gets here," Wojo said to Oaks.

"By the book, Sheriff," Oaks replied. "Did you call him?" he asked Wojo, who was still looking at the body.

"Deputy Cain's gone after him," Wojo said. "And the M.E." Wojo knelt over the body next to Oaks. "That's Vesticate all right. Damn! Any idea who did it?"

"Nope," Oaks said. "A lady heard the shots around ten o'clock last night. She said she heard the cars leaving the parking lot about a half-hour before the shots."

"Why in God's name did she wait till two in the morning to call it in?" Wojo asked.

"She said she didn't think much of it until she let her dog out about one a.m.," Oaks said. "She thought she saw the pickup here and she noticed the driver's door was open and the dome light was on. She said she had a cup of tea and looked back out at the parking area, about a half-hour later, and noticed the pickup was still there and the door was still open and the dome light was still on. So she called 911."

"Who are you talking about, Oaks?"

Oaks looked at Wojo.

"The lady!" Wojo said. "What was her name?"

"Evalyn Gardner. She lives right over there."

"I know where she lives," Wojo snapped. "Who questioned her?"

"Trooper Stanley. He took her home. She was standing out here when we arrived. Right over there." Oaks pointed to a spot under the pole light.

Just then Deputy Cain and Detective Cotter pulled up, followed closely by the M.E., Dr. Donald Smith. Smith was younger than Oaks. He had worked for the county for less than three months when the first killing happened. There had been two homicides in the whole county last year and two the year before. With three homicides under his belt in his first three months on the job, Dr. Smith had become a very busy man.

Cotter hustled over to the front of the pickup. "Anybody touch anything?"

"And good morning to you too, Detective Cotter," Wojo said.

"Good morning, Sheriff. I understand a woman called it in about an hour ago." Cotter finally looked at Wojo. He turned to Dr. Smith before Wojo could respond. "We need to know when he died, Doc. I guess we can assume death was instantaneous, judging from his wounds." Cotter put his hand under the dead man's chin and turned the face slightly towards him. "Vesticate Douglas," he said, mostly to himself. He stood up and looked at Wojo. "Any ideas?"

"Got me, Detective. Could be one of the assholes on the planning commission. I heard Vesticate gave them a pretty good tongue-lashing last night." Wojo paused. "Trooper Stanley here interviewed the lady who called it in. Said she heard shots around ten, just after the meeting let out. Said she didn't think much of it until later when she noticed the truck sitting here with the door open. 'Bout one a.m. That's when she called 911."

"That about cover it, Oaks?" Detective Cotter asked the younger man.

"Yes, sir," Oaks replied.

"Gonna search for clues?" Wojo asked.

"I'd be very surprised if we found anything, Sheriff," Cotter said. "I think we can assume that our killer has struck again, whoever he may be." Cotter looked at Dr. Smith. "See if you can get at least one good slug. Let's try to get a make on the gun, maybe the guy made a mistake and we'll get lucky. Otherwise you can clean up this mess whenever you're ready,

Sheriff. I've seen enough." He started to walk back to his cruiser. "Not even gonna dust the truck, Detective?"

"You can, Sheriff," Cotter yelled back as he walked toward his cruiser.

"Think he's a little weird this morning, eh Oaks?" Wojo said. Then he turned to Deputy Cain. "Clean up this mess after the Doc's through. Then have Earl come up and bring Vesticate's truck back to his home. I have to go tell Grace Vesticate's dead. I don't want people seeing this mess here in the morning. Know what I mean?"

Chapter Thirty-Nine

Roi Found

Cotter's second trip to Manchester didn't bring him back to the Red Bird much before midnight. Wired from the coffee he had consumed to stay awake on the drive home, he lay in bed, in total darkness, thinking about Vesticate Douglas and how he had to be the third boy involved in the hanging. It all made sense, finally. He dozed off and came back into consciousness. He thought about Thomas Downey, the boy who had escaped the same fate as Brian Fischer. He thought about what Mrs. Hughes had told him earlier that day, much earlier, a lifetime ago.

He began to dream about being on a ferry boat with his parents and his younger brother. Then, suddenly, the ferry was on dry land and couldn't move. Then he was separated from his parents who were suddenly home, in his room, and he was still on the ferry which was now a small rowboat. He had arranged his clothing from his closet on the rowboat, but the rowboat became smaller and smaller until it was the size of a toy boat and he tried to contract his legs so they wouldn't hang over the side. And then there was no rowboat at all. Suddenly he was on a bus, a school bus, and he could see his parents but he couldn't touch them. There was a window but it wouldn't open. Then he saw Janie and he wanted to touch her too, but she couldn't see him and then he saw Wojo. He screamed.

He jumped up. The phone was ringing. It liberated him from his nightmare.

"Cotter?" Wojo's voice growled at the other end of the line. "Cotter? You up?"

Wojo was the last person Cotter expected to hear from at four in the morning. Cotter was disoriented. He looked toward the window. No light came through. As he began to gain his wits he realized he was covered with sweat. The dream, he said to himself. It was over, but the terror remained. He switched the receiver to his right hand and put it up against his right ear. "I'm up now, Sheriff. What's up, another killing?" Cotter could barely keep his eyes open. They stung as he rubbed them. His head swirled.

"They found him, Detective."

"Found who?" Cotter squinted his eyes.

"Rick Roi."

Suddenly Cotter sat up straight and his eyes opened wide. "Who got him?"

"Over in New York. Tripp's Corners. Sheriff got him last night. Caught him just outside of town."

"When can we get him?"

"Soon as you get me a warrant, Detective."

"I'll call Judge Twomey first thing in the morning. But right now I'm going to get a few hours of sleep, if that's all right with you, Sheriff."

"Sweet dreams, Detective."

Chapter Forty

The Game Begins

There's a certain magic that fills the Vermont air in the springtime. It's almost as if Mother Nature puts something in the spring air that awakens her creatures, bestows on them a sense of optimism, a fresh start, a feeling of industry mixed with a bit of frivolity that brightens their spirit. On warm, sunny spring days, the feeling is magnified a thousand times.

Cotter arose after sleeping for only an hour. He showered and left the Red Bird about six a.m. He wanted to be in Burlington to meet Judge Twomey at eight, sharp. Twomey always arrived early and, if you caught him at the dot of eight, you could get your warrant and be out of there in ten minutes. If you got there at eight-thirty, you could be there until midmorning.

Cotter made it into Burlington by ten to eight. He parked his cruiser several blocks away from the courthouse on Main Street and walked the rest of the way at a brisk pace to stretch his legs and enjoy the weather. A block from the courthouse he watched a group of girls run across Main Street towards the Main Street Elementary School. A crossing guard held impatient commuters at bay by holding up her left hand, palm out, facing the idling automobiles. She was the quintessential symbol of authority, Cotter thought. She wore a black uniform with polished black leather shoes, white leather gloves, a starched white cap and a white, three-inch wide, heavy cotton strap that ran around her waist, up and over one shoulder and down her back where it was reunited with the waistband. She looked like ten thousand other crossing guards all over the country, doing the same job, and getting the same results. People would steal, murder, even start wars, but they'd never disobey a sixty-year-old, short, plump, uniformed, white-haired, unarmed but stern-looking crossing guard and a group of giggling ten-year-old girls scampering across a busy intersection.

The girls ran across the street unaware of the power that faced them from both directions on either side of their crosswalk. Cotter noticed one little girl, a straggler, for whom the crossing guard held everyone in place by holding her outstretched hand just a little bit straighter and higher. The girl was half-way across Main Street when she broke into a skip on her way to the other sidewalk where a few of her classmates waited. The girl had that look in her eyes, Cotter thought, that spring look, that gaiety, that little stutter step in her stride. Cotter felt it too. Was it the weather, he wondered, or was it his belief that the investigation was about to turn in his favor?

The Chittenden County Courthouse faced Courthouse Park, Burlington's town green. The courthouse was an enormous granite building with nine marble columns that held up a marble facade into which was carved: *With Justice For All.*

Burlington was Vermont's largest city but it was, in reality, just an overgrown town with paved roads, a few more buildings and a few more people. Burlington's population was only thirty-five thousand, not including the college students who swelled the downtown area between September and May. It was an intimate city. All the local merchants and businesspeople knew each other. That was especially true of people involved in law enforcement and the courts.

Cotter entered the courthouse lobby through two very tall, solid oak doors. He avoided the main staircase and headed directly for the door marked *Court Personnel Only.* He zoomed up the staircase to the administrative offices, which contained the judges' chambers on the second floor. His long legs propelled him two steps at a time. He could have taken three, maybe four at a time. He was pumped. He was Rafer Johnson, John Carlos and Jim Thorpe all rolled into one very determined man.

Judge Twomey was standing by the coffee tray next to the water fountain in an alcove off the main corridor when Cotter burst through the stairwell door, about ten feet from where Judge Twomey was standing. Twomey turned around as the door swung open. Cotter had never testified in Judge Twomey's courtroom but Twomey knew of Cotter and recognized him immediately, all six-feet four of him, and breathing heavy.

Cotter stopped in his tracks when he saw Twomey. The door had swung open so violently it had crashed against the wall and swung back at Cotter who stopped it with his left hand. The two men stood face to face, momentarily speechless.

"Why bother opening it at all, Detective?" Judge Twomey finally said. He looked down and poured coffee from the carafe into his mug. "Just knock it down next time." He filled the cup. When he finished, he looked up. "It's just a door, after all."

Cotter stood there, feeling somewhat embarrassed.

"So, where's the fire, Detective...Cotter, isn't it?" Twomey asked as he put the carafe back in the coffee-maker.

Judge Rocheford Twomey was a small man, about five feet eight inches tall and one hundred forty-five pounds. His staff and most of the lawyers around town referred to him as *Judge Roquefort*, or *the Big Cheese*. He wore a small goatee which came to a point about an inch below his chin. He was a sharp dresser who looked more like a movie producer than a judge.

Judge Twomey was a volatile man whom many considered emotionally unstable. Neither was he blessed with a great legal mind. He was a one-way judge. Despite a long list of successful appeals by criminals convicted in his courtroom, he continued to be as hard on the accused as he had been when he was a prosecutor. There was nothing subtle about his pro-cop attitude.

With that in mind Cotter asked the Judge if he could have a few minutes of his time before the judge settled in for the day's work.

"Come on back, Detective, but go easy on the furniture," Twomey said, as he led Cotter toward his chambers. He led Cotter through the main work area, past the clerk's office, the bailiff's office, the juror's room, the hallway to the rest rooms and the door to the courtroom. They finally entered Twomey's office. Twomey walked around his desk and sat down. "Now what can I do for you, Detective Cotter?"

"You've read about the killings in Eden Falls?" Cotter started. He didn't wait for a response. "We've located the man we think may be involved in at least one of the killings. He's over in New York State. Tripp's Corners."

"Where the hell's that?"

"Up near the Canadian border, near Messina. Anyway, Judge, I don't know if he's involved or not but we need to interrogate him to find out. There's a strong chance he may be associated with another man and they're in it together. I need to get him and bring him back to Williston. I need an arrest warrant to do that."

"Of course you do, Detective. Christine will be here at nine. If you'd like, you can go ahead and drive to...what's the name of the place again?"

"Tripp's Corners, Judge."

"Tripp's Corners. As soon as Christine comes in I'll have her prepare the warrant and fax it up to the sheriff up there. Call over here when you arrive and give Christine all the information, his name, the fax number. You know the ropes I'm sure, Detective."

"Thanks, Judge."

"Don't mention it, Detective." Twomey paused. "What's the man's name, anyway?"

"Rick Roi, Judge."

Twomey wrote it down on a pad on his desk.

Cotter waited for Twomey to finish writing. "His father was one of the three victims."

Twomey looked up. "And you think he's involved?"

"Stepfather, Judge, I'm sorry. And there is a chance he's involved. The problem is, we don't have a lot to go on and we hope to shake things up by questioning Rick Roi, and possibly arresting him. It's about the only thing we have."

Ordinarily Cotter would never tell a judge he wanted a warrant just to shake things up. But Cotter knew Twomey was a cop's judge and would do whatever he could do to help him. Twomey was only too happy to oblige.

"You know," said Twomey. "You and I are a lot alike. I've watched your career develop, particularly in the SIU. I like your style, Cotter. You don't put up with any of the bullshit most of your colleagues get hung up on. The Miranda bullshit, I mean. I'm glad to see you don't let it get in your way, off the record of course, Detective."

"Of course, Your Honor." Cotter felt very uncomfortable. A sentiment of that sort from Judge Twomey carried two edges. It was like having Ivan the Terrible pat you on the shoulder and say, *Son, I like your attitude.*

Cotter chuckled to himself as he left Judge Twomey's chambers.

Chapter Forty-One

The Game Continues

The blood of a cop without caffeine is like a V-8 engine running on crude. It has no pop, but that's nothing twelve cups of java a day can't help. Cotter hadn't had a sip of coffee when he pulled into the Eden Falls Town Hall parking area a few minutes after nine. He had, indeed, been in and out of Twomey's chambers in less than ten minutes. He jumped out of his car and headed for Wojo's office. He didn't hesitate as he walked in the door. He knew what he had to do was going to be difficult and he wanted to get it over quickly. Wojo stood up from his desk when Cotter walked in. He was smiling. The smell of Old Spice was fresh on his clean-shaven face.

"Morning, Detective," Wojo said. "Got the warrant for me?"

"I have it but it isn't for you, Sheriff. I came all the way back here from Burlington just to give you the courtesy of hearing it from me...in person."

"What the fuck you talking about?" Wojo's smile was gone.

"I'm going to get Rick Roi in Tripp's Corners, Sheriff. Myself!"

"Hell you are! I found him. I'm bringing him back."

"It's not gonna happen that way, Sheriff Wojohowski. It's my decision and it's not up for debate. It's the SIU's case now, not yours. Plain and simple."

Wojo stared at Cotter. His face was bright red. Neither

man flinched.

"What's the name of the sheriff up in Tripp's Corners?" Cotter asked.

Wojo sat down without taking his eyes off Cotter. Then he broke off eye contact and reached into the front drawer of his desk. He removed a large cigar. He stood up and moved toward Cotter. "I found Rick because I wanted to protect him from you and your little shit-eating over-funded pals at SIU. I hope you're not assuming you're gonna bring him back here and charge him with anything...like murder, for example. Because you'd be making a big mistake." He walked out in front of his desk holding the unlit cigar. He stared at Cotter who was within arm's length. He pointed the cigar at Cotter. "I won't let you make that mistake, Detective. I promise you that." He put the unlit cigar in his mouth.

Cotter didn't react. He knew Wojo had threatened him but he didn't care. It didn't matter. He knew what his course was and Wojo's threats would have no effect on what he had to do.

Cotter turned to leave, stopped, and turned back toward Wojo. "Let me ask you something, Sheriff Wojohowski, if you don't mind. How is it that you were able to find Rick Roi without leaving Eden Falls, when the combined efforts of the FBI, the Vermont and New York State Police couldn't find him?"

Wojo lit his cigar and took several enormous puffs until the tip of the cigar was bright red and smoke began to billow around his head. He walked back to his chair and sat down. The chair hissed. He took several more titanic puffs and the tip of the cigar glowed red once again and the smoke began to collect near the ceiling. He leaned back in his chair and looked at the cigar. The end that went into his mouth was beginning to develop that moist, masticated look.

"I used my personal contacts, son." Wojo took a deep breath and sighed. He clenched the cigar between his teeth, rolling his jaw from side to side to spin the cigar. "Something they don't teach you college boys in your little police school."

"Well, then," Cotter said. "I guess I learned a pretty good lesson today, Sheriff. Didn't I? A lesson in the power of personal contacts."

Wojo took another puff and smiled. He took the cigar out of his mouth and admired it. He didn't look at Cotter or acknowledge his departure.

Cotter walked out of the sheriff's office, went up the steps to the parking lot, got into his car and drove back into Burlington. There he picked up Route 2 and headed north towards the Champlain Islands. At Grand Isle, he took the ferry across Lake Champlain to Plattsburgh, New York. From Plattsburgh he took Route 27 north towards the Canadian border and Tripp's Corners. He was there by noon.

Tripp's Corners was a small town, not unlike Eden Falls. There were more businesses along its main street than along Route 14 in Eden Falls, but none of them looked like they were thriving and some were boarded up. The area hadn't seen much prosperity since the Plattsburgh Air Force Base was shut down a few years earlier.

The sheriff's office was on Cobb Hill Road, about a block off Main Street. It was located in a two-story red brick building that it shared with Franco's Pizza and Dillon's Barber Shop. Cotter parked in front. When he entered the sheriff's office he noticed a foul odor. He must have made a face because a man's deep voice greeted him with an apology,

"Sorry about the smell. Sheriff's dog just took a shit right where you're standing." The man pointed to a spot about a foot from Cotter. Cotter looked at the dark stain and took several steps to the side. Then he turned to the black man standing in the doorway to the hall behind the sheriff's desk and introduced himself.

"Simeon Cotter, Detective, Vermont State Police. I'm here to pick up Rick Roi."

"Paul Reynolds, attorney at law." Reynolds stepped toward Cotter and put out his hand. The men shook heartily.

"Unfortunately, you're going to have to wait for Sheriff Lanphere," Reynolds said. "If that's who you're here to see."

Cotter noticed that his features were true African with little, if any, white blood mixed in. He wore a beige suit and the contrast between his ebony skin and his light beige suit was striking. His proud, yet gentle demeanor relaxed Cotter.

"By the way, Detective, do you have a warrant?"

"It's on its way, as soon as I can get to a phone."

Reynolds directed Cotter to the phone on Sheriff Lanphere's desk. "Just dial nine to get out," he said.

A copy of the warrant arrived a few minutes later on Sheriff Lanphere's fax machine. Lanphere came in as the cutter snipped the fax paper and a copy of the warrant slipped into a bin in front of the machine.

Sheriff Auggie Lanphere was a medium-sized man, five-ten and a trim one hundred sixty pounds. He was in his early-fifties. His graying, short-cropped hair was neatly groomed. He looked like a drill sergeant. His uniform was heavily starched and formed into pleats where it was tucked into his belt. His stomach was flat as a board and he held himself proudly.

Sheriff Lanphere looked at Cotter as he walked in. Cotter was still at Lanphere's desk.

"Sheriff," Cotter said. "I apologize for taking over your office." He walked toward Lanphere and put out his hand. "Detective Simeon Cotter, Vermont State Police, Special Investigations Unit."

The two men shook hands. Lanphere didn't say anything.

"I've taken the liberty of having Judge Twomey fax you a copy of the warrant for Rick Roi," Cotter said. He handed Lanphere the copy of the warrant. He sensed Lanphere had an attitude. Was he expecting Wojo? Was that a problem, he wondered? Either way Lanphere was out of line and Cotter decided he'd had enough.

"If that's in order, Sheriff, I'd like to get back over to

our side of the lake." He glared at Lanphere and lowered his voice. "And let's cut out the bullshit."

Lanphere looked at Cotter, then he turned to Paul Reynolds. "Paul, would you mind?"

"Not at all," Reynolds said. He looked at Cotter as he turned to walk back into the holding room. Lanphere walked behind his desk and sat down.

"How are things on the Vermont side, Detective?"

Cotter didn't answer at first. He knew Lanphere was patronizing him. "How about if I ask you a question, Sheriff?" Cotter put his hands on the edge of Lanphere's desk and leaned forward until his face was no more than a foot from Lanphere's nose. "Why don't you tell me why you notified Sheriff Stanley Wojohowski about Rick Roi when you knew both the Vermont State Police and the New York State Police were looking for him?" Lanphere didn't move, nor answer the question. Paul Reynolds and Rick Roi suddenly appeared from the hallway. They stared at Cotter and Lanphere. Lanphere got up and walked away from his desk.

"Thanks, Paul," Lanphere said. He turned to Cotter. "Bring your own cuffs, Detective? Budget's tight, can't let you have any of ours." He took a set of keys from his pocket and unlocked Roi's hands. Roi didn't look bad for a man on the run. He didn't look worried or upset either, as one would expect.

Cotter looked at Roi. "I don't expect any problems, Sheriff. I think Mr. Roi would like to get back and clear things up as much as we'd like him to do that. Besides, if he goes on the run again, he'll have a much rougher time of it when we catch him, which we will. I don't imagine he wants that, especially if he didn't do anything wrong." He looked at Rick. "Do you, Rick?"

"No, sir," the young man replied. "I won't be a problem, I promise."

"If that's all, Sheriff, we'll be on our way," Cotter didn't wait for a response. He grabbed Roi by the elbow and led him toward the door. He caught Paul Reynold's glance as he walked out. It was a strange look, Cotter thought, but he didn't have enough time to try to figure it out. Getting out of Tripp's Corners was all he cared about for now.

On the ferry from Plattsburgh back to Grand Isle, Cotter turned to Roi and told him that they needed to talk. "Off the record," Cotter insisted. The sun poured through the rear window and both men were sweating. The sound of the ferry's two enormous diesel engines and the steady vibration of the two props seemed to relax both men.

"How old are you, Rick?"

"Twenty-six," Roi said.

"Do you believe me when I say I don't think you killed your stepfather, or the others?" Cotter asked.

Roi didn't answer.

"I mean I believe that personally. I'm not speaking as a cop."

"I guess so," Roi said. He looked terribly uncomfortable. "I wasn't involved, Detective Cotter. I swear, I had nothing to do with it."

"I know that." Cotter paused. "Listen to me, Rick. I believe I know who the killer is and I intend to catch him, but I need you to disappear for a few days to do that."

Roi looked confused.

"If I bring you back to Williston you'll be the bait at a press-feeding frenzy. You'll be tried and convicted in the paper. My colleagues will be rough on you, too. Worse, with everybody focusing on you, it's going to be harder for me to catch the man who killed your stepfather." He searched Roi's face for a signal, anything that would let him know he understood. "Do you follow me, Rick?"

"I guess so," Roi replied.

"I can't bring you back to Williston today, Rick. Unfortunately, that's not going to look very good for you, especially when I tell my superiors you escaped."

Roi sat up in the passenger seat and looked surprised.

He was about to say something, but Cotter held up his hand.

"I know this sounds pretty fucked up, Rick, but it has to be this way. Neither one of us has a choice. I need you out of the way to catch the real bad guy, and you need to disappear to avoid the lynch mob. When it's all over, in a few days, I'll come get you and straighten everything out. I promise, you won't get hurt." He stared at Roi who seemed like he finally grasped what Cotter was trying to say. "Are you with me, Rick?"

"I don't think I have a choice," Roi said sheepishly.

"That's good," Cotter replied. "I'm glad to hear that. Your best shot here is to cooperate with me. Again, I promise you, you won't regret it."

"I believe you, Detective."

The two men sat in the front seat looking at each other.

"Do you want me to take off again?" Roi asked.

"No, no. You need to be somewhere where I can reach you and no one else can find you. You need to stay in one place. Don't forget, when I tell them you escaped, you're going to become one hot commodity. Your face and vitals will be all over the place. Your best bet is to stay low."

"I understand," he said. "But what I don't understand is why you're doing this for me."

"I'm not doing it for you," Cotter snapped. "I'm doing it so an innocent man doesn't get caught up in the system. That could be anyone. It just happens to be you. I'm also doing it because with you in custody, more than likely with three murder charges hanging over your head, my job is going to be a lot more difficult, maybe even impossible."

"Where do you intend to stash me away?" Roi asked, with a hint of sarcasm.

"I'm taking you to my house. Nobody will look for you at my house. You'll be safe there and you'll be comfortable. That's the best place." Cotter stared at Roi until the younger man looked away. "Look at me, boy," Cotter snapped. Roi looked back. "I'm putting a whole lot of faith in you, boy. If you're not up to it, tell me now. Don't let me find out you fucked up and took off, because if I do, I'll have every state, federal and local cop in the northeast on your ass until I see it in a fucking jail cell. And I won't care whether you did it or not. You take off on me, boy, and I'll fuck you over like you wouldn't believe. I'll fix things so you serve life times three!" Cotter looked directly into Roi's eyes. "I promise you that." He paused again. "Do you understand me?"

Roi's eyes bugged out of his head. He believed Cotter because he saw something in his eyes, something frightening. Cotter wasn't joking. The younger man didn't speak at first. Then he said in a calm voice, "I understand."

The two men pulled into Cotter's driveway in Halifax, Vermont, about five p.m.. Janie's car was in the barn. Neither man had said a word during the three-hour ride. Cotter turned off the engine and looked at Roi.

"Are you sure you're prepared to go through with this?" Cotter asked.

Roi shook his head affirmatively.

"Then I want you to get out of the car and go sit on the stoop in front of the side door. Don't move from there." Cotter dialed Reg McHue on his cell phone.

"Reg, this is Cotter."

"Where the hell are you?" McHue demanded.

"I'm sitting in my driveway. Listen, Reg, I need your help."

"You're in your driveway? Where's Roi?"

"He's gone." McHue started to babble but Cotter cut him off. "Reg, shut the fuck up!"

"What do you mean he's gone? Gone where? What's going..."

"Reg, I mean it. Shut...the fuck...up! O.K.?" McHue didn't respond. "Listen to me, Reg. I lost him on the ferry. I don't know how, but he slipped me. I let him out to piss and he never came out of the head. When I tried to go in, the door was locked. He could have slipped out through a mechanical chase. Assuming the guy could swim he could have easily made it to shore. It happened just after we left Plattsburgh."

"Christ."

"Look, Reg. I don't want anyone to know yet. I think I know where he is. I just need twenty-four hours head start. I'm afraid if word gets out, they'll chase him underground, then I'll never get him."

Cotter knew McHue suspected something was up. This was pushing the envelope, even for Cotter.

"By the way," Cotter continued. "Did Wojo call wondering where we were?"

"You bet he did. That son-of-a-bitch was mad, Sim. I'm serious. He wanted to know where you were, and Rick Roi, he wanted to know where Roi was, too. He threatened to come down here, Sim. I told him if he did and he intended to get anywhere talking like an asshole he'd wind up in fucking de-tox. That guy used language even I never heard, and I was in the fucking Marines, God dammit! Judge Twomey's clerk called too. He wanted to know when you expected to charge Rick Roi. I think Twomey thinks he's gonna get some politico mileage out of this one. I suppose he'd love to know you lost him."

"McHue, don't even think about going there. You have to work with me."

"I don't have to ruin my career covering your ass, Cotter," He was serious and Cotter knew it. "You're headed for some serious disciplinary action if this thing blows up in your face, friend. Do you recognize the word felony? That's what they call it when someone interferes with an investigation. It's called obstruction, Cotter, and I'm not going there."

"Pull yourself together, Reg. It isn't the end of the world."

McHue didn't say anything.

"Reg, I appreciate your help."

McHue still didn't respond. "Talk to you later, buddy," Cotter said, and signed off.

Cotter hung up the cell phone, got out of the car and rejoined Rick Roi on the stoop. The two men entered the house through the side door.

They walked through the living room and the front hall into the large, brightly lit kitchen. This was the main room in the house. It was the heart and soul room, the room to which everyone naturally migrated, day and night. The original red brick fireplace and hearth were the focal points of the room. A large cast-iron wood stove sat on the hearth in front of the fireplace.

When the men entered the kitchen, Janie was at the stove wearing an apron and looking awfully cute, Cotter thought. She ran over to him and they embraced. "This is Rick Roi," Cotter said to Janie. "This is my wife, Janie," he said to Roi. Janie and Roi shook hands.

"So you're the mystery man," Janie said. Roi didn't respond. Cotter immediately took Roi by the elbow and turned him around. He didn't want Roi to develop any degree of familiarity with his wife.

"Let me take you upstairs where you'll be staying," Cotter said. He turned to Janie before walking out of the kitchen and the two made eye contact. Janie gave Cotter a supportive nod.

The men walked out of the kitchen, back through the front hall into the living room and up the stairs that led to a large, open hallway on the second floor. To the right was a long hallway that led to a door that opened up to a very large room that extended over the garage, part of the barn, the tractor shed and the wood shed. It was enormous.

"This is where you'll be staying." Cotter opened the door and the two men walked in. In front of them was the huge room. Its plaster walls had many layers of wallpaper, the most recent a terribly faded and water-stained floral design on a beige background that looked more like soot than the rice paper it was intended to represent. It had been applied sometime around 1950. Uncomfortable wooden benches lined each wall with enough seating for close to two hundred people.

"What's this?" Roi asked.

"It's the old dance hall from the days when this place was run as an inn," Cotter said. Roi gazed at its breadth and starkness.

Cotter pointed to a small area in the corner of the great hall that had been prepared for Roi. It had a cot, a small table, a nightstand and lamp, a TV, another table with a microwave, an old black, rotary-dial telephone, and a clock radio. "This is where you'll stay," Cotter said. "There's only one bathroom, downstairs. Janie will make your meals, but I want you to eat up here. You don't have the run of the house. I want you to stay up here. Janie will get you whatever you need. Use the phone. Dial nine and the phones ring in the rest of the house. Janie will answer. You can go down to take a shit or a piss, but that's it. If you get restless, too bad. Think of this as your jail cell for the next few days. It may not look like much but it's a hell of a lot better than the cells at the Williston Barracks." Cotter looked at Roi. "You understand, Rick?"

"I do," the younger man replied.

"Good. Come down for dinner in a half hour. Tonight's an exception. You'll eat with us. If you want a shower before you get out of here, take it tonight. It'll be your last chance."

Roi put his pack on the cot and looked around. Cotter walked out of the room and headed downstairs to the kitchen. Janie had her back to Cotter when he grabbed her.

"Mmm, that smells great." Cotter wrapped his long arms around her waist from behind. He ran his right hand under her shirt and up her abdomen and pressed his palm against her chest, in between her breasts. She wasn't wearing a bra. She clasped her hands behind his back. Her nipples were enlarged. She wanted him to touch her. He knew it, and he didn't. That drove her wild. She spun around and pressed her lower abdomen against him.

"Not now," Cotter said, as he removed his hand.

Janie pressed herself harder against him.

Their first kiss was awkward, Cotter thought. The second kiss, however, was truly remarkable. Janie's tongue was like a serpent. Cotter reached into Janie's pants and pressed his palms against her buttocks forcing her crotch into his. He began to swell. They kissed again.

Cotter pushed her away. "I wanted to pick up some wine for tonight, but I couldn't stop for obvious reasons."

"That's O.K.," Janie said. "We're not going to need any wine tonight. Besides, wine will only dull your memory and I'm going to give you something to remember tonight, sailor." She kissed him again.

Cotter put his hands on her shoulders and pushed her gently away so he could talk to her. "I have some pills." He took a small vial out of his pocket and gave them to her. "I want you to put one in Roi's food, one per meal, three per day. They'll defuse him, take the edge off his nerves, make him want to sleep, mostly. Start with tonight's dinner."

"Are you worried about him?" Janie asked, nervously. "Because if you are..."

"Janie, I'm not worried about the guy, believe me. I just thought he'd go stir crazy in that room and I'd feel more comfortable knowing his senses were dulled."

Janie looked at him but didn't say anything. "Now don't get his food and yours mixed up. These are pretty potent, and with your small body weight they'll knock you out. O.K.?"

Cotter didn't notice that Roi was standing in the coat room listening to him tell Janie about the pills. Roi waited a few seconds before taking several loud steps into the kitchen.

Little was said at the table during dinner. The atmosphere was heavy and there was no room for conversation. Roi ate sparingly. Janie and Cotter tried to make small talk, but their minds were on each others' bodies. Roi wanted to speak but he couldn't say the things he wanted to say.

Roi finally excused himself and started for the living

room and the stairs.

"I'll go with you," Cotter said. The two men walked upstairs without speaking. Roi walked into the dance hall followed by Cotter.

"Can I shower?" Roi asked.

"Now's as good a time as any. Let's go downstairs. I'll give you a towel."

Roi took his boots off and grabbed some clean clothing from his backpack. The two men went back downstairs and into the bathroom. Cotter gave Roi a towel and closed the bathroom door behind him as he walked out.

The kitchen table was still full of dirty dishes and Cotter started to help Janie clear it off when he heard the water running in the shower. He stopped what he was doing and went upstairs to his bedroom where he grabbed a blanket from the hope chest. He took the blanket down the hallway to the dance hall. He saw the boots on the floor at the foot of Roi's cot and noted how Roi had placed them. Then he bent over and picked one up. He couldn't hear the water running from the dance hall. He hoped Roi didn't take a fireman's shower. He looked toward the hallway. "The stairs will give him away," he muttered.

The boot had a thick, black rubber sole. Cotter took an awl from his pocket and bored a small hole, about three sixteenths of an inch in diameter, into the side of the sole. From his other pocket he took a small chip that sent a homing signal to a receiver in his car. He inserted the tiny device into the hole. It went in easily. He filled the hole with a black, butyl-based caulk that would look like part of the sole when it cured.

Cotter didn't waste any time. He put the boot back as close to where it was originally situated as he could, dropped the blanket on the cot and left the dance hall, closing the door behind him. He started walking towards the stairs when Roi appeared coming off the top step.

Roi stopped when he saw Cotter and looked past Cotter towards the dance hall door. Cotter caught Roi's suspicious glance and was impressed at how protective people became of their space, no matter how modest, even when that space was in someone else's house.

Cotter walked past him, then stopped. "I put a blanket on your cot. I'll come see you in the morning before I leave." The two men stood at the top of the stairs. "Remember what I told you on the ferry. How you act during the next few days will determine your fate."

Roi nodded and walked toward the dance hall door. "By the way," Cotter said. Roi stopped and turned around. "The latch on the door only opens from the hallway." He paused again. "Go ahead, Rick." He motioned for Roi to enter the dance hall. "I'll latch it once you're inside."

Chapter Forty-Two

The Photograph

That evening Downey returned home from work about seven-thirty. When he entered the kitchen he smelled the unmistakable aroma of charcoal wafting into the house through the kitchen windows. It was wonderful. He walked through the kitchen and out onto the deck.

Leah was on her way back into the kitchen. They met face to face.

Leah's smile beamed when she saw her husband. She leaned into him and gave him a kiss.

"Hi," she said. Her smile was captivating. It forced a broad smile on Downey's face. "I thought I'd surprise you, first barbecue of the year. We're having grilled shrimp and vegetable kababs, zucchini, onions, green peppers, red peppers." She thought for a moment. "And broccoli. I'm not sure about the broccoli." She laughed. "Carolyn said she barbecued broccoli last weekend and Paul loved it." She paused. "Tommy's having hot dogs."

She took Downey by the hand and led him back into the house. "I have to make the salad." She started for the sink. Suddenly she turned around. "Oh, I almost forgot. There's an envelope on the table. It was taped to the door when I got back with Tommy."

Downey walked over to the table and picked up the envelope. He turned it over. The only writing on it was his name. It was underlined. He tore open the envelope and reached inside.

Leah watched from the sink.

Downey pulled a black and white photograph out of the envelope.

"What is it, Thomas?"

Downey didn't answer. He stared at the photograph.

"What's the matter?"

Downey didn't answer.

Leah walked over to Downey and looked at the photograph.

"Wow." Downey handed her the photo. He pursed his lips and exhaled. "Phew! That's a great picture." He forced a smile. "It's my class from elementary school. Nineteen sixty-four." He paused again. "That's amazing. I was ten."

Leah stared at the photograph. She pointed to her husband who was standing in the back row. "There you..." A startled look came over her face as she looked at her husband. "What's the matter, Thomas?"

"Nothing," Downey snapped. "Nothing. It's just that, I haven't seen a picture from school like this in years. It kind of took me by surprise." He paused. "That's amazing. It's like a whole different world." He nodded toward the photo. "Fourth grade." He paused again. "Mrs. Kasden's class. That's pretty amazing."

Leah looked at the photograph. "Where's your name? There. Thomas Downey." She stared at the picture. "Who was your best friend?" She looked at her husband, then back at the photograph. "You were so cute, Thomas."

Downey didn't hear a word. He was wondering who had left the envelope.

"Let's see," Leah said playfully. "How about this boy?" She pointed to the boy standing next to Downey in the back row. "Let's see..." Her eyes ran down the photograph. "Brian Fischer." She looked up at Downey.

Downey nodded toward the picture. "We were friends." He hoped Leah wouldn't notice the tears forming in his eyes. "I have something in my eye." He turned away from Leah and headed for the bathroom. "Boy, that's uncomfortable."

Leah smiled as she stared at the photo. "Who do you think left it here?"

"I don't know," Downey yelled from the bathroom. He came back into the kitchen holding a tissue to his left eye. "Must've been a piece of dust."

"Seriously, Thomas. Who do you think it was?" She paused. "Maybe it was one of the kids in your class."

Downey lowered his hand. "It could have been a couple who were in the store yesterday. They said they bought a house recently in town and found a whole bunch of photographs and things in the attic. We talked for quite a while. I told them I went to the school in the sixties when it was two rooms. They probably dropped the photograph off to give me a kick." He smiled at Leah. "I guess it worked."

Leah shrugged her shoulders and called upstairs. "Tommy. Pigs in a blanket."

After dinner Downey went upstairs to take a shower. The smoke from the barbecue had mixed with the body oil that had accumulated on his skin during the day. The shower was steaming hot when he stepped in and it caused a chill to run up his spine. After a few seconds it began to soothe him. He stood with his back to the shower head. The water poured onto his shoulders, ran down between his shoulder blades to the small of his back and continued its course between the cheeks of his buttocks and down the back of his legs. Steam filled the shower stall. He turned around and the water hit him in the chest and he shuddered. After a few seconds he reached out and turned the shower knob slightly to increase the temperature, then turned around again and the water hit him in the small of his back. At first it was almost too hot to bear. He bent over and put his hands on his knees and held that position as the hot water softened the stiffness in his back muscles.

He thought about the photograph. He thought about Brian Fischer. Two outsiders. Two flatlanders. What crime, exactly, did they commit?

He stood straight up and turned around so the water hit him directly in the face. He put his hands together to protect his face, not from the water, but from the sadness.

Twenty minutes later Downey stood in front of his closet with a towel wrapped around his waist. He flicked the switch next to the closet door. "He knows," he said softly.

Chapter Forty-Three

Back At The Red Bird

Mad love. Passionate love. It's going to have to last until this thing is over, Cotter said to himself as he stepped into the shower early the next morning. He thought about Janie, her long arms and the shape of her breasts when she sat up in bed. Her body was his idea of the perfect female figure.

He was nervous about the next few days. Had he made a mistake, trusting Rick Roi? Would Janie be O.K.?

Unlike Downey, Cotter was not a man of details. He was a man of courage, a doer. Downey was a planner, a man who wouldn't go to battle if the odds weren't overwhelmingly in his favor. Downey was McClellan. Cotter was Ulysses S. Grant. Cotter would attack first, then consider the odds. Odds didn't get results, action did.

The sun was well above the horizon when Cotter got into his car for the drive back up north. It was six-thirty and he wanted to be back in Eden Falls by nine. He had a lot to do. Janie kissed him passionately before he walked out the side door. She stood in the open doorway in her nightgown and watched him as he got into his cruiser.

After buckling himself in and starting the engine, Cotter unlocked his glove compartment and removed a small device that looked like a lap-top computer. It had a screen and a keyboard, but not a typical PC keyboard. This was the receiving end of the monitoring device Cotter had inserted in Rick Roi's boot. Cotter had asked Pete Newell, the SIU's resident computer whiz, to program the screen with first and second floor plans of the Cotter house. This would enable Cotter to accurately follow Roi's movements. As long as Cotter was within range and Rick Roi wore his boots, Cotter would know where he was.

Cotter turned the device on and a small red dot blinked on and off in the dance hall etched on the screen. He smiled at the thought of Pete Newell's genius. He looked up and waved to Janie. A passerby would have guessed the scene was the typical American family: Dad going off to work, Mom waving good-bye at the door. Nobody would have noticed Rick Roi watching from one of the dance hall windows.

The drive back to Eden Falls took a little over two hours. Cotter was pulled over for speeding just south of White River Junction. He was stopped by a rookie trooper who didn't know he wasn't supposed to pull over fellow cops, even if this one was going close to one hundred miles per hour. Even after he realized he had pulled over an officer with a superior rank, the young trooper lectured Cotter about the use of his siren and his warning lights if he wanted to go that fast. "It's a matter of your personal safety and the safety of others, Sir," the eager young trooper said. Cotter listened politely and took off. Within a few minutes he had his cruiser back up to one hundred.

By White River Junction, Cotter's thoughts shifted from Janie to Sheriff Wojohowski. How did Wojo know where Rick Roi was? Why did Sheriff Lanphere contact Wojo and not the New York State Police? It didn't make any sense.

Given the storm that was about to greet him at the Williston Barracks, Cotter decided to head straight for the Red Bird. He was back in his room a few minutes after nine. His first call was to Reggie McHue. He used an alias to get past the dispatcher.

"Reg? Is that you?"

"It's me. Where are you?"

"At the Red Bird. Listen, Reg, I want you to check on

a sheriff over in New York State, Tripp's Corners. His name is August Lanphere. L. A. N. P. H. E. R. E. Find out as much as you can about him."

"Lanphere?"

"Yeah, why, you know him?"

"Sounds familiar, Sim...Lanphere. I can't place it but I'll look into it. I know I know that name from somewhere. What the hell are you up to, anyway?"

"I can't tell you. Believe me. Anyway, Reg, I might need your help. If I need backup at some point, I'll call in."

"You better reconsider, Sim. You're gonna get fucked. You've been warned about this sort of thing before."

"Reg, if you want out, I understand. Just let me know, because if you say you'll help me I have to be able to depend on you."

McHue paused. "This is the last God-damned time. I swear!"

"Right," Cotter replied.

"Hey, Simeon, your buddy, Wojohowski, called again looking for you. He's still hot about Roi, wants to know what's going on."

"Well, I think he's going to get a lot hotter before this thing is over. "If he calls again tell him I'm on my way over to his office."

"Judge Twomey called again, too," McHue added. "He wants to know when the D.A's gonna arraign Roi."

"Tell him you haven't spoken to me and don't expect to for a couple of days," Cotter said. "I need to put him off. The last thing I need's an over-zealous, psychotic hanging judge breathing down my back."

McHue chuckled. "What about Rick Roi?" he finally asked in a much more serious tone.

"He didn't do it," Cotter said. "Don't ask me how I know, just take my word for it. He didn't do it."

"Do you know where he is?"

"I don't think he's too far away. He's not gonna go too

far, he has too much to lose. He'll show up."

"You're lying to me, Cotter. You're pulling something here. Where is he, really?" McHue waited for Cotter to answer but he didn't. "Sim?"

"That's the way it is, Reg. I'm sorry. You'll know everything you need to know in a few days. I promise."

"You're a fucking asshole, Cotter!" There was an extended pause. "Good luck, buddy," McHue added. "I'll be here."

"Hey, Reg," Cotter said before hanging up. "Before I let you go I want to ask you something. How is it that Wojohowski found Rick Roi and we couldn't? And how come the New York State Police didn't find him? He was right under their noses!"

"I don't know, Sim. That's a very good question. I don't see how he could have unless he knew where Roi was all along."

Cotter hadn't considered that. "It's possible. But it just doesn't compute. I haven't seen anything to suggest that. Besides, why would he tell us where he is now? That doesn't make sense either."

"Maybe Wojohowski's smarter than you think, and maybe he knows you, Cotter. Maybe he figured you'd pull a stunt like this and he set you up. What do you think of that?"

Cotter didn't answer. "Good bye, Reg," he finally said.

By eleven-thirty, Cotter was in the parking lot of the Eden Falls Town Hall. He got out of his car and walked down the steps and into the glass foyer that separated the conference room from the sheriff's office. Wojo had just come through the door from his office into the foyer and the two men almost collided.

Wojo stopped suddenly and looked straight into Cotter's face. "What the...Where the hell have you been? Where's Rick?"

"Come inside, Sheriff," Cotter said. "We need to talk."

"Damn straight we do!" Wojo about-faced and went

back into his office. He told Cain to get out and walked behind his desk and sat down. "Now, State Police Detective Cotter, what the hell is going on? Where's Rick Roi?"

"I went to Tripp's Corners to get Rick because I know he didn't kill anybody. Taking off like he did after his stepfather was shot was a stupid thing to do, but it hasn't altered my opinion."

Wojo looked puzzled, at first. "Smart man," he said. "But where is he?"

"I can't tell you that. All I can tell you is he's safe and nobody can touch him until we can prove he's not involved. If he's found, the SIU, the DA and Judge Twomey will become a lynch mob. Twomey's called my office several times asking why Rick hasn't been arraigned yet. The press will get involved and Rick will be tried and convicted before he goes to trial." Cotter leaned forward and put his hands on the edge of Wojo's desk. "Personally, I don't wish Rick Roi any harm but I'm not doing this for him. I need him out of the way so I can concentrate on the person I believe killed Rick's stepfather, and the others." He paused again. "You get what I'm trying to say here, Sheriff?"

Wojo smiled again. "Let me get this straight. You've got Rick Roi, but you're not going to turn him in?"

"That's right."

Wojo's smile grew larger. He leaned forward and got up out of his chair. "That's pretty good, coming from one of you state boys." He turned his back on Cotter and walked over to the window behind his desk. "Where's he now?"

"I can't tell you, Sheriff, and don't ask me again, because you'll get the same answer."

Wojo stared out the window for a few seconds, then he turned around to face Cotter. "If you're convinced Rick didn't do it, who did?"

Cotter looked pensive. "I'm leaning toward your deputy. Deputy Cain. From what I can see, he's the likely candidate. My only problem is, it's just gut instinct. There really isn't anything concrete to go on, just instinct. That's why I need Rick out of the way, so I can concentrate my efforts on Cain. When I get something on him, which I hope to do in the next couple of days, Rick will come back."

Wojo liked what he was hearing. "I'll go along with that, Detective. For once, one of you state boys actually knows what he's doing."

"You'll help me, if I need you, won't you, Sheriff?"

"You can bet on it, Detective."

Chapter Forty-Four

A Visitor

That evening a set of headlamps pierced the curtain in Cotter's room at the Red Bird. Cotter was sitting on the edge of his bed eating leftover eggplant from a Tupperware tub and reading a very intimate note Janie had slipped into the bag of goodies she had packed for her husband. He looked up at the curtain when he saw the bright light go out and heard the car door slam. As the man's footsteps got louder Cotter knew they were coming towards his room.

Suddenly the footsteps stopped. There was a weak rap on the door. Cotter put the container of food on the bed and opened the door. It was Doctor Jessup.

"Aren't you going to ask me in?" Jessup said.

Cotter didn't realize he was staring at Jessup, who was still outside. Jessup was the last person in the world Cotter had expected to see that evening, especially at his room at the Red Bird at nine o'clock at night.

"Yes, I'm sorry," Cotter said. "Please come into my very humble home away from home, and the local office of the Vermont State Police."

Cotter took the chair out from under a small table in the corner and asked Doctor Jessup to sit down. It was the only chair in the room. The doctor obliged and said thank you. Cotter looked at his container of food and started to offer some to Dr. Jessup. Jessup saw what was coming and was gracious enough to take Cotter off the hook. He lifted both hands and turned his palms toward Cotter and the Tupperware tub full of eggplant.

"No, thanks," Dr. Jessup said. "I know what it's like living away from home, son. It must be difficult for you." He looked around the room. "Especially at the Red Bird."

Cotter laughed. He knew the doctor was telling him to relax. It was obvious Dr. Jessup hadn't come for food and Cotter didn't have to make excuses for the Red Bird. The two men looked at each other for a minute. Cotter knew there was only one reason Jessup would have come to see him, especially at his motel room at night. Jessup wanted to tell him something, something that was eating at him inside. Cotter hoped it would be good.

"I'm here because I've heard you believe Deputy Cain may be involved in the murders," Dr. Jessup said.

For the second time in less than five minutes Cotter was taken completely by surprise. It was true, supposedly, but the only person to whom Cotter talked about Deputy Cain was Sheriff Wojohowski. Cotter didn't ask Jessup how he knew about Cain. He knew Jessup would only refuse to tell him or just lie about it, so why bother.

"That's partially correct, Dr. Jessup. Cain is one of several suspects."

Dr. Jessup was having trouble breathing. It was a chronic problem brought on by years of cigarette smoking. He breathed two or three times between sentences.

"I want to tell you something, Detective Cotter," Jessup said, after regaining his breath. "You're probably under the impression Deputy Cain was one of the boys involved in the hanging behind the school, years ago."

Dr. Jessup looked up at Cotter, who was sitting on the side of the bed facing him. "You're probably of the opinion that Deputy Cain, for some reason, killed the other three because of their involvement in the hanging."

Cotter didn't respond. His blank stare disguised the curiosity that suddenly engulfed him. He tried his best to wait, patiently, as Jessup got up the emotional fortitude and physical strength to continue.

Dr. Jessup was sad, remorseful. His voice cracked. He lowered his head and tilted it, slowly, from side to side as he spoke. "Cain didn't kill anybody." He paused to catch his breath. "Cain was not involved in the hanging."

Cotter hadn't noticed Jessup's shortness of breath during his visit to the doctor's house. Nor did he realize how old Jessup looked.

The doctor looked up at Cotter and continued slowly. "Later that night another boy came to see me with his mother. She was in tears. The front of the boy's shirt was covered with blood and his mother had blood on her blouse and skirt. The boy's mouth was full of cotton." He stopped and took several deep breaths. "I examined the boy and found his tongue had been sliced across the top, laterally, about an inch in from the tip. It was sliced like a piece of meat, but not all the way through. I did my best to sew it back together. The boy was lucky the knife was so sharp. It was a very clean slice. I must have used thirty-five stitches to close the wound." Jessup paused and looked down as he pictured the procedure all over again, stitch by stitch, the boy lying on the examination table, crying, his hands gripped around his mother's hands.

Cotter waited for Dr. Jessup to continue. Jessup was getting more upset as he spoke. He stopped to take several deep breaths. He kept his head down, fighting back the tears.

"I couldn't knock the boy out because I needed him to be alert, to move his tongue around so I could sew it. It was very painful for him. I felt very sorry for that boy."

"Dr. Jessup," Cotter said finally, in a gentle voice.

Jessup looked up. "Yes, excuse me. I'm an embarrassment. I'm sorry." He tried to compose himself. "I haven't relived that experience for thirty-two years. It's amazing how strong our minds are, to be able to block something like that out of our consciousness for so long."

Cotter waited for the doctor to continue.

"The boy in my office that night, was Deputy Cain. That's why he doesn't talk. Apparently I didn't do a very good job attatching the nerves. The wound healed, but he has no feeling or control of the tip of his tongue." Jessup looked at Cotter. "He can't form letters or even controlled sounds. That's why he doesn't speak. Otherwise, for all intents and purposes, the procedure was successful, by 1960's standards. At least I was able to save his tongue, for whatever that's worth. Today, we would have attached the nerves so he'd have use of his whole tongue, but, back then...," Jessup looked at Cotter. He was beginning to ramble and he knew it.

Cotter didn't move a muscle.

"He's not, slow either," Dr. Jessup added. "In fact, he's as bright as any of us, except he's never learned how to use his brain. Sheriff Wojohowski treats him like an idiot, so that's how he acts." Jessup coughed to clear his throat. "Cain was at the hanging but he wasn't involved. He watched the hanging while hiding in some bushes. When the older boys ran off, Cain cut the other boy down, the boy who was taken to Dr. Hughes. Cain saved that boy's life. That boy never knew it...to this day, I don't believe he ever found out." Jessup paused again. "Unfortunately, the oldest boy found out about Cain later that day. To keep Cain from talking, the boy tried to cut out his tongue. To my knowledge, Cain's never told anyone."

Cotter was speechless. He was trying to put this new piece of information together with what he had learned from Mrs. Hughes during his second visit to Manchester. Amazingly, it all fit, like a jigsaw puzzle.

"So you see, Detective, if you arrest Cain for the three murders you'll be arresting the wrong man. I can assure you." He paused. "At least consider what I have just told you."

Cotter got off the bed and walked toward the bathroom door. It was the only place to walk. He turned to Jessup and spoke. "I want to thank you for coming to see me like this, Dr. Jessup. I know how hard it must be for you, how hard it must have been for you all these years."

Jessup looked down in his lap, again.

"You knew this thing would someday come to resolution, didn't you?" Cotter asked. It wasn't a question that required an answer. "I'm glad you've decided to help that happen, sir."

Dr. Jessup got up and said, "Well, I must go home. I'm not feeling very well tonight and I'm very tired."

"Can I drive you home, Dr. Jessup?"

"No, no thank you." Jessup looked at Cotter. "Good luck," he said, and put out his hand. Cotter took it and thanked him. Dr. Jessup turned to open the door when Cotter cleared his throat and touched the older man gently on the arm. Jessup turned back toward Cotter.

"Dr. Jessup, perhaps you could save me a trip to the town hall tomorrow, sir. Do you happen to know the name of Fanny Roi's first husband?"

Jessup looked at Cotter. "Lanphere, I think. I believe his first name was August."

"Thank you, Doctor, you've been a big help." He reached around the doctor and opened the door for him. The two men exchanged good nights.

The next morning Cotter left the Red Bird before dawn. He headed west on Route 14, toward an appointment that he believed would determine the fate of his investigation and whether he would receive accolades for his work, or spend the rest of his career driving a state police cruiser up and down Route 89 on the midnight to-dawn-shift, including Saturdays, Sundays and holidays.

Chapter Forty-Five

The Blue Belt

Wojo told Cain he was going out but he didn't say where. He was in a surly mood. Cain watched him as he walked through the outer glass door and up the concrete steps to the parking lot.

Thomas Downey rarely ate lunch at the store. He'd nibble on things all day, a banana, a slice of homemade bread, an orange or an apple. He'd drink three or four cups of coffee, too, but he never took time to sit down for a half-hour, inaccessible and totally relaxed. Today was no different. He was standing near the front of the store eating a banana and thinking about a new display when he saw the sheriff's cruiser pull up. He chewed slowly at first as he watched Wojo get out of the car and head for the front door. When he realized how obtuse he must look, staring at Wojo through the front window with a mouth full of banana, he turned away and swallowed his food.

There were several customers in the store. Burt was waiting on one, the other was just browsing. Downey walked back toward the front desk. He heard the door chimes ring and turned to greet whoever had just walked in. He acted surprised when he saw it was Wojo but he didn't say anything until Wojo was near the counter.

"So, Sheriff, how did the hiking boots work out?"

Wojo had forgotten about the boots and was momentarily caught off guard. "Ah, fine, fine," he said.

"I'm glad." Downey looked at Wojo. Wojo made him nervous. Where was Detective Cotter?

"Like to look at a few things, if you don't mind," Wojo said. "I need a new belt. I thought you might have something a little better than Wal-Mart."

"We do, indeed, Sheriff. You can start right behind you." Downey pointed to a rack of brightly colored nylon knit belts. "Those are extremely durable but they're really intended for serious backpacking and climbing," Downey pointed out. "Leather belts are over by the other leather products." Downey pointed to the opposite side of the store.

Wojo looked in the direction Downey pointed and quickly surveyed the rest of the store. Burt and his customer were in the camping section looking at sleeping bags. The other customer had left the store.

"Show me, would you please," Wojo said.

"Of course." Downey walked out from behind the counter.

"Hear about Deputy Cain?" Wojo asked matter-of-factly.

"Deputy Cain?"

"Son of a bitch," Wojo said laughing. "After all these years nobody had any idea." He took a dark blue, size forty-four belt off the rack. "Son of a bitch."

"What about him?" Downey asked.

Wojo looked up. "What?" he said. He attempted to read the label on the belt. "How do they get this leather so blue? I never seen a blue cow. Huh!" He looked at Downey and laughed.

"Deputy Cain," Downey said. "What about him?"

Wojo put the blue belt back on the rack and picked off another one. "Turns out that little son of a bitch must've been the last boy involved in that Fischer hanging." He looked at Downey. "Yeah, it looks like they're gonna arrest him for the murders of Bessette and Roi, and Douglas. Figure he killed 'em because one of 'em was about to talk. Christ, you think you know someone. I never would've figured it." He shook his head. "That dumb son-of-a-bitch. Huh!"

"How sure are they?" Downey asked.

"Pretty sure, I guess. Guess Mae Bessette broke down and told Cotter everything. Came forward and said her husband told her who the others were. Course Cain's the only one left now. Cotter said she went on and on about some mask. Guess Cain wore a mask. That's why no one knew it was him except the other three boys. What a crazy son of a bitch." Wojo looked at Downey and smiled. "Guess he must be the one."

Downey reached for the blue belt Wojo just put back on the rack and straightened it out so it hung like the others in its row.

"Trouble is," Wojo continued, "he'll probably get off with just a slap on the wrist, if they can convict him at all. Been so long. Can't see how they'll make it stick now."

Downey's head was spinning with confusion. It couldn't have been Cain. But why not?

Wojo laughed and reached for another belt.

Downey suffered inside. The one in the mask. After all this time he said to himself. He watched Wojo pick through the rack. Cain. He knew he didn't have much time, if Cain's arrest was iminent.

Wojo put the other belts back on the rack and took the blue one off again. "I guess I'll take this one," he said. "It'll go with my new blue sheriff's jacket." He laughed. Downey took the belt and brought it over to the register to ring it up. Burt was at the register finishing up another sale.

Downey was relieved to see Burt. His mind was consumed with thoughts of Deputy Cain. He was already contemplating how he was going to get him before the authorities arrested him.

"Thank you for your patronage, Sheriff," Downey said. "Burt will ring that up for you. I have some things to do."

I'll bet, Wojo thought.

Burt rang up the blue belt and put it in a bag for Wojo.

"Thanks, Sheriff," Burt said.

"Yup," Wojo replied, looking towards the rear of the store where Downey had disappeared. He looked back at Burt. "Anytime," he said, and walked out.

Chapter Forty-Six

The Fourth

The only thing Downey knew about Deputy Cain was that he lived off Route 14, across the road from the Douglas Farm. He knew the driveway that led up to his house served just one home, and no one else used it besides Cain. Downey had been up there once, by mistake, when he first opened the store. He was looking for another house in the area that had received a package that was supposed to have been delivered to his store. Rather than wait for the shipper to pick it up and redeliver it, Downey decided to get it himself. He got lost and wound up at Cain's house.

Downey remembered the place but in insufficient detail to properly plan his strategy. He knew the Cain driveway started opposite the Douglas farm and he thought the distance from Route 14 to the tree line was about a quarter of a mile. He remembered the driveway continuing through the woods for another two hundred yards or so, then turning sharply toward the left where it ran for another several hundred feet to the end. The driveway didn't go all the way to the house. A large outcropping of ledge on the right side of the driveway prevented that.

The more Downey thought about his only visit to Deputy Cain's house, the more details started to come back to him. The house sat on the level area above the ledge. He could picture it clearly. A wood stairway led up the ledge, about thirty feet to a platform at the top. Everything from groceries to firewood had to be carried up the stairs.

This would be an ideal place for what Downey had to do. He considered a number of scenarios during the rest of the afternoon. He covered all three elements of the incursion: the way in, the actual event, and the way out. He would have to deal with other things as well, a weapon, an alibi and Leah.

Once again, Leah would prove to be Downey's biggest concern. Not only would he need an excuse for not coming home that evening, but it would have to be tighter than for most people. Worse, he thought, he would have to face Leah after it was over. That would be the most difficult thing of all. She would read him, not his words, but his movements, his expressions, his mood. It was a miracle she hadn't caught on about the others. But would his luck continue? Could he continue the masquerade?

Downey's Outfitters was supposed to close at six. Downey told Burt he planned to stay awhile and he'd lock up when he left. Then he called Leah.

"Hi," Downey said.

"Hi, Honey," Leah said. "Wait, Tommy wants to talk with you."

"Hi Daddy," Tommy said. "Mommy got hot dogs for dinner. She's gonna make chickens in the basket...what?" Downey could hear Tommy talking to Leah. "Pigs in the basket," Tommy said giggling. "What?...pigs in the blanket, I mean.

"Tommy, I have to work late tonight, ask Mommy if we can have pigs in the blanket on another night."

"Hi," Leah said. "You have to work tonight?"

"Yeah, I want to get a head start on inventory by going through all the stuff in the basement. I was down there today and it's really gotten out of hand. There's a lot of old inventory we should get rid of. We can have a giant sidewalk sale."

"Why tonight?" Leah asked. "Can't you do it tomorrow night? Tommy was looking forward to dinner tonight. Did you hear him? Chickens in the basket?"

"I'd like to get it over with," Downey said. "You know me. Until I do, I'm not going to be in a social mood anyway. I'd really like to get it done. It's going to take a few days, anyway."

"Are you going to pull an all-nighter?" Leah asked. "I missed you last night. You fell asleep early."

Downey didn't respond. The subject was getting too intimate for the telephone, especially for Downey.

"Are you blushing, Thomas?" Leah teased.

"No, I'm not blushing. So it's O.K. with you, right? Tell Tommy we'll do it tomorrow or over the weekend. Tell him we'll rent *Willie Wonka and the Chocolate Factory* and we'll eat pigs in the blanket in the den while we watch the movie. He'll love that."

"What about dinner?"

"I'll grab something at Toot's and put it in the microwave. I'll be fine. O.K.?"

"Do I have a choice?" Leah replied.

"Come on, don't be like that." There was a pause on the other end. "Leah?"

"Go ahead, I'm fine. Really, Thomas, it's all right. I'll see you when you get home. Just don't be too late. Promise?"

"I promise." The two hung up.

With that resolved, Downey shifted his attention to a weapon. He wished he hadn't gotten rid of the rifle. That would have been perfect. Instead he would have to use the pistol he kept at the store.

The gun would be untraceable, even if they found it, Downey thought. He was sure of that. There was nothing to tie him to the weapon. The only problem was, it was a pistol and it would require that he get close enough to Cain to fire a killing shot. There was a possibility Cain might discover him before he could ready himself and fire. Cain would probably be armed. It made him extremely uncomfortable. He wished he had more time, and a better weapon.

The plan. This was Downey's forte. The plan. Details.

Proper planning would ensure his success. But this plan would be different than the others. This plan could only provide a basis from which he would have to make decisions and adjustments as he proceeded. Still, there had to be a framework, considerations for various contingencies based on their odds of occurring.

Downey sat behind the counter, alone. He pictured the driveway to Cain's house and ran through the stages of his assault. He would arrive shortly after eight and park behind the dairy barn at the Douglas Farm. The place was all boarded up and no one would see his car. He would be there before sunset so he wouldn't have to use his headlights when he pulled into the yard. Then he would wait until just before dark before crossing the road. It was supposed to be a clear night and there was a three-quarter moon, so there would be ample moonlight for him to move around without the aid of a flashlight once he left the car. That was critical. The timing had to be just right. The beam of a flashlight would be seen from the road and by Cain, if he happened to be outside or looking out of a window.

Downey would cross the road and move across the field toward the tree line without using the driveway. With no cover on the portion of the drive that traversed the field, Downey could easily be spotted by someone driving up to Cain's house, even if he dove for the ground. He would stay forty to fifty feet off the driveway. If he had to, he could dive for cover in the tall grass. That would be sufficient to reduce the odds of someone who wouldn't expect him to be there seeing him. At the tree line he would move over to the driveway. The cut in the trees for the driveway would allow enough light through the canopy for Downey to see. The woods were much darker.

What bothered Downey was his fuzzy memory of the configuration of the interior of the house. He also couldn't picture the lines of sight from the house to the ledge, the wooden platform at the top of the ledge and the driveway. These were critical.

Downey would make the ledge and hide. There he would wait until it was as dark as it would get, about nine o'clock, before moving up to the house. He would look through the windows on each side of the house to determine if Cain was alone. If not, Downey would abort. But Cain had a reputation as a loner, and Downey expected him to be by himself. Once that was established, Downey would use his cell phone to call Cain. He would disguise his voice and say he was a state trooper calling for Sheriff Wojohowski who needed Cain right away at the site of a traffic accident. Downey would wait for Cain by the front door and shoot him the moment he came out.

It was a dangerous plan because there were so many assumptions, Downey thought. It assumed Cain would be home. It assumed he'd be alone. It assumed he had a phone and he'd pick it up, after all, he was a mute, and it assumed he'd fall for the fake call about an accident. And it assumed Downey would be able to hike in and out of the Cain property, to the house and back, surprise and shoot Deputy Cain on his front porch at point-blank range, without leaving a trace.

Downey thought about Deputy Cain. Like many others, he had always assumed Cain was slow. But did anybody really know for sure? He was counting on Cain's reputation as a man of below average intelligence. His plan was based on the odds that Cain was more likely to react to circumstances than to evaluate them and execute a calculated response. There was also a chance Cain would be gun-shy. Certainly he must be nervous with the other three dead. But he wore a mask, and he probably believed he would escape revenge by virtue of his anonymity during the hanging incident. Even so, he was likely to be on edge. This was a major concern. Downey would have to be at his best, relaxed, true to his aim, senses tuned, like the predator he had become, efficient, deadly, undaunted and free of remorse, totally free of remorse.

At seven-thirty Downey left the store and drove out of

town along Route 14 toward the Douglas Farm. He was early. He pulled into the yard in front of the Douglas House at seven forty. There were no cars coming in either direction when he pulled off Route 14.

He drove around the milking parlor and parked his car so it would be out of the sight of cars coming from either direction on Route 14. There he waited for nearly forty-five minutes until the sun went down. The sky was clear and jet black and Downey could see every star from horizon to horizon. He remembered driving with his father once on Route 89, late at night in the middle of the winter, returning from a visit to a great aunt in New Hampshire who'd just had a stroke. He remembered how black it was that night, and how he had looked down into the villages in the valleys, seeing all the lights and knowing there was a person connected to each light. He wondered who they were and what they were doing and if they were as fortunate as he. He wondered how many worlds like Earth existed among all those stars. Downey thought that people who lived in cities never saw a sight like this, because of the indirect light from the buildings and bridges and street lights and homes. He gazed upward for the longest time. He wished he were on one of those worlds far away, where he wouldn't have to do what he was going to do.

At eight twenty-five he moved across the road and began hiking up the field toward the tree line. A few cars passed in both directions along Route 14, but Downey could hear them coming before they were in view and he had plenty of time to drop to the ground, out of sight. At the tree line he moved over to the driveway and continued toward the house along the edge of the drive.

When he got to the bend that swung dramatically to the left his body froze. He had heard a branch crack. It wasn't his imagination. It was loud and it was distinct and it was a person.

Is it Cain, he wondered? It didn't matter. He silently lowered his body to the ground and slid himself into the ditch on the side of the driveway, careful not to give away his presence. He tried to figure out all the possible sources of the sound. Someone had stepped on a twig and broken it. He knew that animals who move about the forest at night don't give away their presence by stepping on a twig. It had to be a person.

Downey's heart pounded. He considered his options and decided he had to abort. But this would not be easy. He'd have to retreat without exposing himself. He couldn't go through the woods, especially at night. There was no way he could avoid snapping unseen twigs under his boots in the dark, alerting every living thing in a hundred-yard radius to his presence and his exact location. But if he retreated along the driveway, there was a strong chance he'd be spotted. Unfortunately there was no other way out. It had to be one or the other. Downey looked back down the driveway in the direction of Route 14. He knew the driveway was his only option.

Downey hadn't heard another noise since the twig snapped and he didn't know where the other person was. This was untenable. The first thing he had learned in counter-intelligence school was to know the identity, location and strength of your adversary. Downey failed on all three counts. He looked up the driveway but saw nothing, no silhouettes, no shadows of human figures in the moonlight. Was the person walking up the driveway toward Cain's house just ahead of Downey, or was he coming down the driveway toward Route 14? Could it have been Cain, himself, taking a walk?

Downey decided to wait.

After lying silently in the ditch next to the driveway for more than a half-hour, Downey decided to make a move. Slowly, and without making a sound, he extricated himself from the ditch and crouched by the edge of the gravel drive. He was on the side of the driveway that was shadowed from the moonlight by a canopy of large maple trees. That was no accident. Taking one step at a time he began walking backwards, slowly down the driveway, his eyes and ears focused in front of him. It took him twice as long to work his way back toward the tree line as it had moving toward the house in the other direction. He stopped every ten or fifteen feet to listen for sounds, the tell-tale sounds of someone following him. He heard nothing. At the tree line he moved well away from the road and sat in the field in the shadows of the trees at the edge of the woods. He listened for the sounds of twigs breaking under a man's foot or the sound of a dead branch being snapped away from the trunk. There was nothing but silence. He looked toward the driveway to see if someone was following him. Again there was nothing. He wondered if what he had heard was really the sound of another man, or his imagination running away with him.

It wasn't my imagination, he insisted. He thought about Leah. It was late and she'd be wondering about him.

After sitting at the edge of the woods for more than thirty minutes without seeing or hearing anything unusual, Downey decided it was safe to move across the field toward Route 14. He crossed the road and walked quickly across the yard in front of the Douglas house and behind the milking parlor where he opened the door to his car and got in. He started the engine and drove around the milking parlor and out onto Route 14 without turning on the headlights. He continued down Route 14 back towards the center of town, slowly navigating by the reflection of the moonlight off the double yellow line. A mile or so down the road he turned on his lights.

Downey felt awful. This was a worst-case scenario. But it was real and there was nothing he could do about it. Worse, he would have to go through the whole routine with Leah again tomorrow night. It might be his last chance. If whoever was out there tonight was out there again tomorrow night, it might also mean Downey would never get another shot at Cain. This was the worst feeling of all. Everything he had done, the others he had killed, would be for naught if he couldn't get Cain, for he was the one who mattered most, the boy in the mask, the boy who had laughed as he strung him up, the boy who had kicked him the hardest when he lay on the ground, who had mocked him, who had taunted him and left him for dead, the boy who had appeared in his nightmares for so many years, the boy in the mask, the boy who had nearly robbed him of life.

Cain. He had to get him.

Chapter Forty-Seven

Help From an Unlikely Source

Detective Cotter's cruiser was sitting in Downey's driveway with the headlights off when Downey returned from his aborted mission. Cotter was sitting in the driver's seat. At first, Downey debated pulling into his own driveway. But he knew whatever Cotter had on him would have to be faced at some point. Downey was prepared for anything.

As the headlights from Downey's car illuminated the inside of Cotter's cruiser, Downey saw Cotter's silhouette. He could feel his pulse increase as he pulled into his driveway and stopped abreast of the cruiser. Downey looked over at Cotter. Cotter looked back at Downey and signaled him to turn off his headlights and the car's motor and join him in the front seat of the cruiser. Downey understood and complied.

The two men sat in the cruiser staring at each other. Cotter was calm and showed it. Downey's palms were wet with perspiration. Instead of being relieved that he was able to retreat from Cain's house without incident, Downey was horribly disappointed. Worse, he was sitting in the front seat of a state police cruiser parked in his driveway at ten p.m., with the detective working on the murders he'd already committed. He looked at Cotter and wondered how much he knew. He had to know something. Otherwise he wouldn't be here. Downey thought of the loaded pistol in his jacket pocket.

Cotter's voice broke the spell. "Good evening, Mr. Downey."

Downey looked at Cotter, but he didn't respond. This was Cotter's show, Downey thought. Let him speak.

The windshield began to fog up and Cotter turned away from Downey to roll the driver's-side window down a crack. He looked back at Downey. "There's a rather delicate matter I'd like to discuss with you, Mr. Downey, if you don't mind."

Downey didn't respond.

Cotter took that as an invitation to continue. "When I was seven years old I overheard my parents talking about a hanging that took place in Eden Falls the previous day. A young boy was hung." He paused. "By a group of high school boys." He paused again. He knew he had to move very slowly. "During the next few days I overheard other kids talking about it and I must have overheard news reports on the TV and radio. It had a very profound impact on my life. It wasn't fear. It was the image of that young boy hanging there, the terror he must have felt...," Cotter stopped. There was a long pause. "I felt what that boy must have felt, inside. It haunted me, for a long time. I can't explain why. For a while after I learned about the hanging I was afraid to close my eyes. I hated going to bed at night. My mother had to lie down with me and when I awoke, if she wasn't there, I'd go into my parents' bedroom and crawl into bed with them."

Downey remained silent and expressionless. Cotter was visibly upset. He hadn't talked about his reaction to the hanging with anyone, including his parents, since he was a child. Even now, after so many years, it still had an effect on him. He looked out the driver's side window and tried to compose himself. After another lengthy pause he looked back at Downey and continued.

"There was another boy, Mr. Downey. No one knew about him except those involved, his family, and the doctor who treated him. Dr. Hughes."

Downey didn't stir.

"I'm not here to arrest you, Mr. Downey. I need your

help." He wanted that statement to sink in before continuing.

Downey still didn't react.

Downey's silence bothered Cotter. He needed Downey to say something or do something to let on what he was feeling. He finally asked Downey a question that required an answer. "May I call you Thomas?"

"Certainly," Downey replied, after a brief pause.

That was a start, Cotter thought. "Thomas, I was the one who made the noise you heard on Deputy Cain's driveway this evening. I knew you'd come for him. I knew you believed Cain was the fourth boy involved in the hanging."

Downey's eyes opened wide. "You?"

Cotter nodded his head.

Downey stared at Cotter. He wasn't sure how to react or if he should react at all. "You know, don't you?" Downey's eyes fixed on Cotter. "About me."

"I spoke with Mrs. Hughes, the widow of Dr. Hughes. She told me. I've known for a few days."

"What else do you know, Detective?"

"Please call me Sim. We're about to embark on a journey, together, Thomas, and *Detective* will get in the way. Don't you agree?"

"I'm not sure," Downey said.

"Fair enough. I know about the others. I know you took justice into your own hands after all these years. I'm O.K. with that, for now, depending on where we go from here. I also know who the fourth boy was and it wasn't Deputy Cain."

Downey considered the magnitude of what he was hearing. The worst part was the realization that he had come perilously close to killing an innocent man. Had he become so inured to murder that he would kill at the slightest urge? He had had no proof it was Cain, except Sheriff Wojohowski's word. Yet he was prepared to take the man's life. On Wojohowski's word, he said to himself.

At that moment Downey felt like the killer he had become. How could he be so callous and come home and expect Leah and little Tommy to love him? For the first time since he shot Adrian Bessette, Thomas Downey regretted what he had become, even if he felt his actions were justified.

"I knew once you found out I was going to arrest Deputy Cain you'd put two and two together and you'd come after him," Cotter continued. "So I was there tonight, to prevent you from making a mistake. I knew you wouldn't take a chance and go through with it if you thought you weren't alone."

Downey listened in disbelief.

"Thomas, I know you want to know who the fourth boy was, but I'm not going to tell you. Instead, I want you to help me trap him. Together we can get him to expose himself. There is no statute of limitations on murder. I want to try him for the murder of Brian Fischer. Nobody has to know about you. We can keep that our little secret. But I can't pull this off without you. You, unfortunately, are the bait."

"What is it you want me to do?" Downey asked.

"Thomas, there was a third person in the woods tonight. He was waiting for you. He didn't see me but I saw him."

Downey felt like a fool. So much for his attention to detail. All the careful planning and, while stealth was his objective, there were two people, not one, in the woods below Deputy Cain's house watching his every move. He was mortified. "Who was it?" he asked.

"I can't tell you that. All I can tell you is, it was the fourth boy involved in the hanging. My feeling is, he's watched you eliminate the others and he figured you'd take care of number four the same way."

"But why was he there? That doesn't make sense. He'd be exposing himself with nothing to gain. If I killed Deputy Cain, he'd be off the hook forever. Why follow me up there?"

"There is a reason and it will become apparent to you as things unfold. I can't tell you everything I know, right now, because it will affect your ability to help me put this guy away. I can't risk that. You have to work with me, Thomas."

"Go ahead," Downey said.

"We need to draw him out again tomorrow night, to Deputy Cain's house. You have to pretend you're coming for Cain again, same time, same M.O., just a different result. I want you to continue up the driveway to the stairs at the ledge. Are you familiar with Cain's house?"

"Not as familiar as I'd like to be."

"Well, if you climb the stairs up the ledge you'll come out in what amounts to the side yard. The front of the house faces the left. There's a porch in the front. Cain usually sits in a chair facing the TV in the front room. There are only three rooms downstairs. If you wanted to shoot Cain in the back of the neck you'd do it from a side window facing the ledge. Get yourself into position at that window and fire a couple of shots into the chair. That will draw our man out."

"What about Cain?" Downey asked.

"Don't worry about him. I'll take care of that. He won't be in the house. Once you draw our man out, I will appear and arrest him. I'll be with you the whole way. You don't have to worry."

Downey thought about what Cotter said. "I don't see anything wrong with that plan but I need to think about it."

"There's no time for that, Thomas. You have to trust me."

"I still need some time to think about..."

"No!" Cotter interrupted. "You don't. You have to decide now. If you help me, I'll take care of you, Thomas. I promise you won't serve any time for the others. Don't ask me how I'm going to do that but you have to trust me. If you don't help me, then you might as well kiss your wife and son goodbye because I'll take you in on the other murders and you'll probably do twenty-five to life. Your grandchildren will be your son's age when you get out. Is that what you really want?"

Downey knew he had no choice. He had little faith in the criminal justice system and he knew he might never get a shot at the fourth boy again. While it was a risky plan, Downey knew it might be the only way.

"I'm going to have to tell Leah I need to work late again tomorrow night," Downey said. "That might be a problem."

"Work it out, Thomas. Pretend you're going back for Deputy Cain."

Downey looked straight ahead.

"Repeat your moves exactly as you made them tonight," Cotter continued. "Be at the top of the driveway by the stairs at exactly nine o'clock. Not a minute before or later."

Downey nodded.

"Start climbing the stairs five minutes after you get there, but take a few minutes to look around. Do the things you would do on any covert mission. Don't let on that you have no fear. Pretend it was like tonight. Use extreme caution. We can't let our friend know you're setting him up."

Downey said he understood.

"I'll see you tomorrow night, my friend," Cotter said.

Downey started to get out of the car. He stopped with one leg out and turned back to Cotter. "This is it, isn't it, Detective?"

"This is it, Mr. Downey. After thirty-two years, this is it."

Chapter Forty-Eight

The Fourth, (A Second Time)

"Thomas, what's wrong?" Leah asked.

"Nothing's wrong."

"I know you, Thomas, there's something bothering you. I've sensed it for days." She paused. "Why didn't you wake me when you got in last night?"

"You looked so comfortable and you were really out like a light. You must've been tired, so I didn't want to wake you. And besides, take my word for it, there's nothing wrong. I just need to get this basement cleared out and get things organized here. We let it go much too long."

Leah was silent on the other end of the line.

"I told you yesterday it might take more than one night to do this."

"Do you want me to get a babysitter and come down to help you? That might be the only way I'll ever get to see you."

"No, thanks. I'd rather work on it myself. That way I'll know exactly what's down there. You and Tommy bear with me just one more night and tomorrow we'll rent Willie Wonka. We'll all watch together. O.K.?"

"I guess so," Leah sighed.

"I love you, Leah."

"I love you too, Thomas."

Downey knew Leah was close to realizing something was not right. She didn't suspect what was really happening to her husband, but she was at the point where she wanted to know and would find out soon enough. When Leah decided to get into Thomas's head, she did. He had no defense for her determination.

As sunset approached Downey locked the store and headed toward the Douglas Farm on Route 14. Everything was going according to plan. Downey stowed the car behind the milking parlor, made his way to the tree line on the far side of the field, and headed up the driveway toward the ledge at Cain's house. It was as light as the previous evening, the stars glimmering against the black sky, the moon lighting up the earth like a giant light bulb.

Downey did his best to act as if he were alone. He crouched when one would expect an intruder to crouch, he waited when one would be expected to wait. He took three hundred sixty-degree scans of the area when one would be expected to do that as well. He knew someone was watching him, and that went against his grain. He didn't like being the bait. He felt helpless, exposed, hardly in control of the variables that could bring him down. For a moment he regretted putting himself in this situation. He should have stood up to Detective Cotter and said no, or simply played dumb and denied everything. Yet deep down inside he knew he had to go through with it. He knew it might be the only chance he would get to see this thing through to the end, as he had promised himself he would do. Besides, if it weren't for Cotter he might be dead, or sitting in a jail cell for the rest of his life.

He moved forward until he was at the staircase that led up the ledge to the house. He crouched by the bottom step and looked around the driveway where it widened out into two parking areas. Cain's cruiser was parked about twenty feet from the steps. An old, rusted Ford pickup sat on blocks next to the cruiser. Downey remembered it from the time he had been there.

At two minutes to nine he started his ascent up the steps. He was as quiet as possible, although the steps seemed to echo every footstep across the driveway and into the woods beyond. He reached the top step and slowly crab-walked across the wooden platform that egressed onto the yard facing the side of Cain's house. He took in his surroundings and didn't see or hear anything. He wondered where the object of their setup was hiding. He also wondered where Cotter was hiding. He hoped Cotter was as prepared as he needed to be to intercept the fourth man before he could engage Downey. He touched his pistol.

Satisfied the coast was clear, Downey moved in a low crouch across the yard and stopped at the window through which he was supposed to fire the shots. He faced the wall of the house and slowly raised his body up to the window sill. Pretending he was satisfied the coast was clear, he raised his head over the sill and peered inside. He saw the chair in which Cain was supposed to be sitting while watching television. It was empty. He raised himself even higher and started to reach for the revolver to fire the shots into the back of the chair through the window. He was concentrating so hard on what he was doing that he didn't hear the footsteps and heavy breathing behind him.

Suddenly he felt a terrible pain in the back of his skull, and his senses went numb. He was in a suspended state, not unconscious, but severely stunned. He felt a man's arm encircle his throat and force him to the ground. He felt the rope being tied around his neck. Then he began to regain his senses.

He was on his knees and his head pounded with pain. He felt blood dripping down his collar and he knew he had suffered a terrible blow. He looked straight ahead and saw the ground under the porch and the side of the porch rail. Then, to his horror, he realized his neck was in a noose.

The man pulled on the rope and yanked Downey's head back.

Downey was instantly transposed thirty-two years back in time. At first he couldn't believe it was happening all over again. It was his nightmare coming true. How could this be? This wasn't supposed to happen! He began to panic and struggled to free himself but the harder he struggled the more his tormentor pulled on the rope around his neck and the more it hurt. Finally the man jerked him up and pushed him over to the edge of the porch. He threw the free end of the rope over a beam at the edge of the porch that was used to support a hammock years ago. The rope flipped over the beam and the man grabbed the free end. Downey watched in disbelief but he still couldn't see his tormentor, who stayed behind him, controlling him with his arm and the rope.

With a sickening groan the rope was pulled tight and pain shot through Downey's neck. He was snapped upright and his feet barely touched the ground. He tried to shout but nothing came out. He tried to catch his breath but nothing came in. Images of those he had shot to death raced through his mind and he pictured how each man had looked the moment the bullet struck, and he thought of how his face looked, bright red, exposing the pain in his lungs, and he wondered if somehow his victims could see him now, and if it was comforting to them. He thought of Leah and Tommy and his mind shot back and forth between Brian Fischer and Dr. Hughes and Cotter. Then his body was spun around like a top and he saw him. The man in a mask. The same mask he had seen thirty-two years ago.

"I'm going to finish what I started," the voice behind the mask said. "Nobody here to save you this time. I knew about your little plan with Detective Cotter. It wasn't hard to figure out what you boys were up to last night, sitting in his cruiser in your driveway. So I took care of your police buddy this afternoon so he wouldn't interfere. Detective Simeon Cotter is currently lying on the floor of his room at the Red Bird, two bullets in his heart. Very dead, no doubt."

Downey's eyes were focused on the mask. He was beginning to lose consciousness. His lungs burned and pleaded for oxygen. They would only hold out for a few more seconds. Then the man removed his mask.

"Wojo!" Cotter's voice rang out from the tree line beyond the porch about twenty feet away. "Let him down or I'll shoot." Cotter pointed a twelve-gauge shotgun at Wojohowski's head. Deputy Cain emerged from the woods next to Cotter, also pointing the barrel of a twelve-gauge at Wojo. Wojo hesitated. Cotter pumped a slug into the chamber. Wojo finally released the rope and Downey, barely conscious, fell to the ground. Cain rushed over and released the tension on the noose and pulled it off Downey's neck.

Wojo stood with his hands held out to the side, smiling. Cain reached for Wojo's gun and Wojo stepped back from Cain, preventing him from taking it.

"Give me an excuse, Sheriff," Cotter said. "I'm itching to fire this thing into your big, fat body to see how much shit flies out."

Wojo stopped smiling. Nobody had ever talked to him like that. Cain reached for the gun again and Wojo didn't resist. Cain took the gun and slipped it into his belt. Cotter was now upon them.

"Make sure Mr. Downey's all right," Cotter said to Cain. Cotter kept the shotgun trained on Wojo's face. Wojo didn't move. Cain helped Downey stand up. Downey massaged his throat and tried to swallow.

"You're supposed to be dead," Wojo said to Cotter. "Guess I didn't shoot you good enough," he snickered. "Next time I'll finish you off before I leave."

"There won't be a next time, Wojo. You're through, as a sheriff, and as a murderer."

"You think you're gonna make any of this stick, asshole? You think a grand jury's gonna take the word of a mute and a god-damned murderer? Fucking aye! You'll be lucky to get an indictment, let alone a conviction."

Cotter looked at Wojo and shook his head. "I knew you'd come for me. You saw me here last night and you knew you had to get rid of me to get Downey. You figured you'd hang Downey, go arrest Deputy Cain and charge him with all four murders, and say he killed me because I was on to his scheme." He stared at Wojo. "You're so fucking ignorant."

Wojo shot a wad of spit in Cotter's direction.

"You had me." Cotter shook his head. "But you're so fucking stupid. You don't execute someone by shooting them in the chest, especially if they're wearing a bullet-proof vest. You're supposed to shoot them in the head. Even Mr. Downey, here, knows that. But, that's just my good fortune, I guess. No what I mean, Wojo?"

Downey looked at Deputy Cain who was glaring at Wojo.

Wojo's face was bright crimson. Cotter imagined how many escape scenarios must be passing through his head. But there was no chance. Cotter was steady and his twelve gauge was pointed directly at Wojo's face.

Cain pulled Wojo's hands behind his back and cuffed them together. Wojo was mortified. "You little shit, you fucking little mute piece of shit," he said to Cain. "I'll kill you, you fucking piece of shit."

"And now, Sheriff Stanley T. Wojohowski," Cotter said, "you are going to be introduced to justice, Simeon Cotter style."

"You're gonna take me in, Cotter? Go ahead. I'll be out before you know it."

"Take you in?" Cotter looked at Cain and Downey, then back at Wojo. "Who said anything about taking you in? I have no intention of taking you in. I said I intended to see that justice was served, Sheriff. I never said anything about arresting you."

Wojo looked confused. Then Cain grabbed the rope and slipped the noose over Wojo's head. Wojo shook his head violently back and forth to shake the rope. His hat flew off. Cain slapped Wojo with a wicked back-hand across the face. Wojo was stunned. Blood trickled from his nose.

Wojo was enraged. "You're out of your fucking mind,

Cotter. You'll never get away with this. You're out of your fucking mind."

"I don't think I'll have any problem getting away with it." Cotter turned toward Cain. "Do you, Deputy Cain?"

Cain smiled at Wojo. It was the first time since 1965 that Wojo had seen Cain smile.

Cotter turned toward Downey. "I don't think Mr. Downey, here, will say anything to anybody either, Sheriff. For obvious reasons."

Wojo began to struggle again. Cain hit him in the mouth with the butt end of his shotgun. Wojo staggered backward against the house. Blood flowed freely from his mouth.

Cain threw the free end of the rope over the beam and grabbed it as it dangled on the other side. He pulled hard to take up the slack. Wojo's head jerked upward toward the beam.

Downey's head ached but he was alert. He watched Cain intently, sensing what was about to happen. He knew Deputy Cain was incapable of lifting Wojo off the ground by himself. He grabbed the free end of the rope with Cain. Together the two men gave the rope a mighty pull, lifting the fuming but helpless Wojohowski off the ground. Wojo struggled but his gyrations only made the pain in his throat worse. His Adam's apple was crushed. He tried holding his breath but the pressure from his lungs made his chest feel like it would explode.

Wojohowski's face looked like it was about to explode. All three men stared at Wojo. His eyes bugged out of his head like the eyes of a dead fish lying in the bilge of a boat. He dangled from the rope, straining it to its limit, the beam struggling to stay up under the weight of its enormous load. It was the consummate insult, his mute deputy sheriff, a flatlander, and a God-damned college-educated, fucking state trooper watching his demise. Rage was the last emotion he would feel. Sheriff Stanley T. Wojohowski, eighth-generation Vermonter, father born here, grandfather born here... was dead.

Thomas Downey, Deputy Cain and Detective Cotter stood silently and watched. Each man contemplated his own satisfaction knowing Wojo had gotten exactly what he deserved. Each man felt redeemed from his private hell, if for only a moment. Each man knew justice, true justice, had been served. Each man knew, no matter how satisfying the sight before them, justice would not ease the pain.

Chapter Forty-Nine

Suicide

Detective Cotter picked up a copy of the *Burlington Free Press* the next day as he checked out of the Red Bird. There was a large headline about Sheriff Wojohowski's death, followed by a lengthy account of the previous night's activities. Cotter sat in the driver's seat of his cruiser and read the article with great interest.

Eden Falls Sheriff Commits Suicide
Officials say death linked to recent murders

Eden Falls, Vermont:

Vermont State Police received a major break in the investigation of the murders of three prominent Eden Falls residents last night with the discovery of the body of Sheriff Stanley T. Wojohowski. Police have tentatively ruled Wojohowski's death a suicide. According to police, Sheriff Wojohowski hanged himself after attempting to turn himself in to Sheriff's Deputy Dennis Cain. Police believe Wojohowski was responsible for the string of murders that has plagued this small, rural community for the past several months.

Wojohowski's body was found hanging from a beam on the porch of his deputy's residence just off Route 14 by the interstate. Detective Reginald McHue, of the Vermont State Police Special Investigations Unit, told reporters it looked like Wojohowski attempted to surrender to Cain three days after the murder of Vesticate

Douglas, the third victim. Police speculate Wojohowski must have become despondent when he realized Cain wasn't home, and took his own life.

McHue said Wojohowski, a long-time resident of Eden Falls, was the primary suspect in the killings of Adrian Bessette, Peter Roi and Douglas, all successful local businessmen. All three victims were boyhood friends of Wojohowski. The three men were partners in a three million-dollar real estate deal off Route 14 in Eden Falls. Wojohowski was also a partner. McHue said his unit was tipped off to Wojohowski's involvement when the sheriff failed to disclose his business relationship with the victims earlier in the investigation.

Wojohowski's body was discovered a few minutes after eleven by Deputy Cain. He was pronounced dead at the scene by Chittenden County Medical Examiner Donald Smith. Police plan to close the investigation as soon as the official cause of death is determined.

"As far as we're concerned, it's over," McHue said. "The people of Eden Falls can go to sleep again without worrying. We were very fortunate."

Wojohowski had been sheriff of Eden Falls since 1979, taking over for his father when the older Wojohowski retired the same year. His father had been sheriff since 1961.

Cotter finished the article and flipped to Wojohowski's obituary in the local news section. It told about the sheriff's many fine accomplishments and how much he would be missed. The article singled out Fanny Roi from among those who were left behind. *He will be missed most of all by his long-time special friend Fanny Roi and her son, Rick Roi.* Cotter read that sentence again. He thought it was odd, but he wasn't sure why. Why single out Fanny and Rick Roi, he wondered.

He folded up the paper, started his motor and pulled out of the Red Bird parking lot for the last time. That he no longer had to live in that little room at the Red Bird was reason enough to feel elated. He headed west on Route 14 into Eden Falls Center to see Thomas Downey. When he arrived at the store he noticed it looked dark inside. He parked his cruiser and walked up to the front door. It was locked. A sign on the door said; *Closed for a special family holiday*. Cotter smiled. He walked back to his cruiser and headed for Downey's house.

Downey and Leah were home when Cotter rang the bell by the side door. Leah invited him in. She knew who Cotter was even though she had never met him. "Come in," she said. "Thomas has been waiting for you." She put out her hand and led Cotter to the family room off the kitchen. Downey was sitting on the couch with copies of the *Free Press*, the *Rutland Herald* and *The Boston Globe*. He stood up when he saw Cotter.

"Detective," Downey said.

"We're back to formalities again, Mr. Downey?"

"I'm sorry, Simeon," Downey said. He looked at Leah and introduced her to Cotter. She looked up at his towering six-four frame and shook his hand.

"I'm very pleased to meet you," she said.

Cotter knew from her gaze that Downey had told her everything.

"I have to pick up Tommy," she said. "Anyway, I'm sure you two need some time alone. Good-bye, Detective Cotter. I hope to see you again."

The two men watched as Leah left the room.

"You've seen today's paper?" Downey asked.

"Yes," said Cotter.

"Do you think it's going to fly?"

"I'm sure of it. It's over, Thomas. You can relax now. It's over. Nothing else is going to happen. It's our secret, and Deputy Cain's."

"I owe him my life," Downey said.

"I would say you do. But I don't think he's looking for gratitude. I think he's looking for respect. And dignity. Those things are harder to find."

Downey sat down. "How did you know it was Wojo?"

"I suspected him ever since he told me there were only

three boys involved in the hanging. His father was the sheriff. He had to know there were four. He was playing with me. Dr. Jessup confirmed there were four boys. The bit about the deed to the land next to the Douglas farm also gave him away. When he showed me a copy of the deed, he had whited-out his own name. I saw the original that same day at the town hall. That pretty much clinched it. Mrs. Hughes confirmed my suspicions. She also told me about you. Otherwise I'd still be lost."

"Yes, well..." Downey paused.

"I'm sorry I couldn't tell you who the fourth boy was, Thomas. Now you understand why. I couldn't take the chance you'd go after him on your own. You would have lost, and Wojo would have gotten away with your murder as well as Brian Fischer's. That was unacceptable." Cotter's tone became almost fatherly. "Thomas, about the three murders, you mustn't feel guilty about what you did. Those men deserved to die. They..."

"Three?" Downey interrupted. "I only killed Bessette and Roi." He looked confused. "I didn't kill Vesticate Douglas. I thought you knew that."

Cotter wasn't sure if had heard correctly. "You what? What do you mean you didn't kill Douglas?"

"I didn't kill Vesticate Douglas. I thought you knew that."

Cotter looked very confused. His world which was so neatly framed a moment ago was unravelling. "If you didn't, who did?"

"I don't know. I assumed you knew all along. I guess I assumed it was Sheriff Wojohowski."

"It wasn't Wojohowski," Cotter snapped. He looked very disturbed. His thoughts ran wild. This isn't the way it was supposed to end. All the killings were supposed to be accounted for, and justice meted out to those responsible. He racked his brain for possibilities. Then his face took on an awful expression, a look one gets with the realization something terrible has just happened. His throat went dry. He jumped up. "I need your phone." He reached for the phone on the table next to the couch without waiting for an answer from Downey.

"Reg. Sim. Don't say a word, just listen to me. I want you to go to Tripp's Corners, New York and find Sheriff Lanphere. I want you to go yourself, don't send anyone else. I want you to find him and ask him who Rick Roi's real father is. I don't care if you have to beat it out of him. Don't take no for an answer. Tell him if he doesn't tell you, you're gonna get a warrant for his arrest and he's gonna be charged with obstruction, hiding a fugitive and anything else you can think of."

"What the..."

"Reg, don't ask me why or say another word. Just do it! I'll be in my car, so call me as soon as you find out. Got it?" He hung up without waiting for McHue to respond. He turned to Downey. "I have to get to my house as fast as I can."

"I want to go," Downey said.

"Don't be ridiculous," Cotter snapped. "This is my battle, not yours."

"Wrong, Detective, this is our battle and I'm going with you. I can help you. I'm not totally bereft in matters like this."

Cotter was across the kitchen and half-way out the mudroom door when he told Downey to hurry if he was coming. The two men jumped into Cotter's cruiser, sped out of the driveway and headed for the interstate.

Chapter Fifty

What Price Justice?

Cotter hit the on-ramp to Interstate 89 at Moretown and headed south. He pushed his cruiser well over one hundred miles per hour. They reached White River Junction in less than an hour and turned onto Interstate 91 heading south. By noon they were outside of Brattleboro and the homing device Cotter had placed in Rick Roi's shoe was in range. Cotter took the receiver out of the glove compartment and turned it on. The little dot blinked.

To Cotter's horror, the dot was not where it was supposed to be. The dot was supposed to be in the center of the screen indicating Roi was in the dance hall. It wasn't. Instead, the blinking light was on the extreme right hand side of the screen indicating Roi was in Cotter's bedroom. Cotter was horrified. He shot off the interstate at the exit for Route 9, west, and headed toward Wilmington at close to seventy miles per hour, a dangerous speed for this two-lane secondary road. Cotter didn't care. He put on his flashing red lights and passed several cars by crossing the double yellow line.

Within fifteen minutes Cotter and Downey covered the twenty miles from the interstate to the intersection of Route 9 and Route 112, the road that ran due south into Halifax and the road the Cotters lived on. Cotter turned his cruiser down Route 112 and continued at an extremely high rate of speed. He shut off his flashing lights just outside of Wilmington. When he was within a mile of his house he slowed down and pulled to the side of the road. He needed a plan. But first, he dialed Reggie McHue's number in Williston on his cell phone.

"Sim, I was just about to call you," McHue said. "Are you ready for this? First of all, that Sheriff Lanphere's a sick piece of work. I had to threaten him like you said, Sim. There's something wrong with that guy."

"Cut the bullshit, Reg. What did you find out?"

"Rick Roi's real father was your old buddy, Stanley T. Wojohowski."

"Shit," Cotter said, and hung up without saying anything else to McHue.

"What's the matter?" Downey asked.

"It's my fault," Cotter said. "I deserve everything that's coming to me but Janie's gonna take the brunt of it if I don't do something fast. I have to get her out of this."

"What's the matter?" Downey asked again.

Cotter looked at Downey. "I should have known. How stupid could I be. It makes so much sense. Fuck!" He slammed the heel of his fist against the steering wheel.

"What's the matter?" Downey asked a third time.

"Rick Roi is Stanley Wojohowski's son." Cotter looked toward the road. "He killed Vesticate Douglas. And he's at my house right now, right down that road, with Janie. If he knows what happened to his father, Janie's in great danger."

"Why would he kill Douglas?"

"If you were arrested the whole thing comes back. The hanging, the coverup, Wojo, his father. The only remaining link to Wojo was Vesticate Douglas. He had to die." Cotter paused. "And he knew it."

"What are you going to do?"

"I'm going to get Janie out of there and I'm going to kill Rick Roi, and I'm going to put an end to this matter once and for all."

"Do you have some strategy in mind?" Downey calmly asked. "Or are you going in there hell bent and probably get yourself and your wife killed?"

Cotter looked at Downey. "Yeah, I do. Like I said, I'm gonna get Janie out of there and I'm gonna kill Rick Roi."

"Let me help you," Downey insisted. "We still have time. Please let me help you. I'm quite skilled at this. I'm well-trained."

Cotter looked at Downey and remembered what he was told at the Pentagon. Cotter decided to take Downey up on his offer. "Well?"

Chapter Fifty-One

The Plan

"We have time," Downey said. "He has nothing to gain by harming Janie before you get there. If he intends to do anything to her, he's gonna save it until after he subdues you. If he was going to hurt her to fulfill some psychopathic desire, he would have done it already. But he's not that type, Simeon."

Cotter didn't want to believe him but he knew he was right. Still, his emotions were getting the better of him and he wanted to rush the house, guns ablaze, storm in and save his wife.

Downey read his new friend's mind. "It doesn't work that way. Use your head. I mean it. Let's take a little bit of time and put together a plan of attack. Beat him with your mind, not your guns."

Downey asked Cotter to brief him on the layout of the house and property. Cotter reached into the glove box and removed a piece of paper on which he sketched a floor plan of the house and explained all the details about the building's hidden entrances, trap doors and secret passageways.

Downey watched intently as Cotter drew everything out. He asked Cotter about the lines of sight and the distances between the house, the barn and the road. He was especially intrigued by the homing device.

Unfortunately, it looked like Roi was still in Cotter's bedroom and this made Cotter crazy. He felt like bagging Downey and his calm approach.

"You have to maintain your cool, Detective, if you want to succeed. If you go off half-cocked, like you are right now, you'll reduce your chances of success and increase the chances something will happen to you, and your wife. Trust me."

Cotter looked through the windshield down Route 112 toward his house. Downey wasn't even sure if Cotter had heard him. He knew what it was like to contemplate what Cotter was about to do. He knew what was going through his friend's mind.

"Let's go over what we know and what we can reasonably assume," Downey said. "One: We know Roi has free movement around the house and the outdoors. Two: We can assume he's secured the house. He doesn't want anybody sneaking in and catching him by surprise. Three: He doesn't know about the homing device. Four: Given all the publicity, we must assume he knows about Wojohowski. Five: We have to assume he expects you to come for him soon. That means he's probably holding your wife as a hostage. He'll be waiting for you. If he gets an advantage over you, he'll kill you." Downey paused. "Did he have access to a phone?"

Cotter turned around and looked at Downey. "Obviously, if he has access to the whole house."

"Then we have to assume he's had contact with others. He may not even be alone."

Cotter didn't reply. He looked at the screen on the receiver. It looked like Roi was moving inside the house. "Look at this." He tilted the screen towards Downey. "Watch this. He's going from the bedroom to the stairs, down the stairs...he's going into the wood shed. Look. There! He's in the wood shed. I've been watching him since we've been sitting here. He's moved from the bedroom to the wood shed and back several times since we've been here."

The two men watched as the blinker stayed in the wood shed for several minutes, then moved back upstairs to Cotter's bedroom. It stayed there for less than a minute, then moved down into the kitchen. Cotter narrated Roi's movement to Downey.

"This is great," Downey said. "My guess is your wife's either in the bedroom or the wood shed, based on his movements. Can you tell when he's in the bathroom?"

"Yes," said Cotter.

"Unfortunately we can't pin down with any certainty whether your wife is in the wood shed or the bedroom," Downey said. "There's logic to both locations. Personally, I don't understand why he'd be going in and out of your bedroom if your wife wasn't there. My guess is she's in your bedroom."

"The computer's in our bedroom," Cotter said. "He could be using the internet to buy airline tickets or something like that. That would explain why he keeps going back there." Cotter paused. "I believe Janie's in the wood shed. That makes more sense. Other than Janie, he'd have no reason to go out there." Cotter looked at Downey.

"Fine," said Downey. "Let's assume that. Can you get into the wood shed without going into the house?"

"There's a back door to the wood shed, but I'm sure Roi locked it from the inside. He's not stupid. There's a way into the basement through a stone in the foundation. From the basement you can get to any room in the house without being seen. I can get into the wood shed through a trap door under the pig stalls. I'll wait until Roi goes back upstairs before coming up into the shed. Janie can go back down the same way. When Roi comes back for Janie I'll have a little surprise for him."

"That's risky," Downey said. "You don't know how long he's going to stay upstairs. You may have only a minute or two. Maybe you should wait till he goes to the bathroom. If he goes into the bathroom, you'll have more time, especially if he has to take a shit."

"I'm going now," Cotter said, without looking at Downey. He took a .357 magnum pistol out of his holster and looked at Downey. "I want you to stay here, Thomas. This is my fight, not yours. You and I are square and I want to keep it that way. Roi's gonna be armed because he's probably been in my gun cabinet. I don't want to have to tell your wife and kid you got it trying to help me."

Downey looked at Cotter. "Good luck."

Cotter opened the door to the cruiser, grabbed the receiver, and got out. It took him ten minutes to get to the house. He worked his way around the hay field toward the dirt road that ran past the barn from the main road. He approached the house from the dirt road using the barn to shield him from the view from the kitchen and bedroom windows where Roi was likely to be, but he still had to cross fifty feet of open lawn to get to the house itself. If Roi happened to look out a window at that time, he'd be forewarned.

The blip on the screen began to move from the bedroom to the kitchen. Cotter looked around the corner of the barn trying to get a glimpse of Roi through one of the kitchen windows. He couldn't see him. Suddenly the blinking light moved into the living room and back up the stairs. Cotter broke from the barn and sprinted across the lawn to the house. He dove for the ground about five feet from the kitchen window and rolled to a stop up against the foundation.

The Green River followed Route 112 from southern Vermont into Colrain, Massachusetts. Opposite the Cotters' house it was down a long, gradual embankment. It was possible to follow the embankment along the road until you were abreast of the Cotters' front door, without being seen. This was not the route Cotter had chosen. He had gone through the woods behind their property. But Downey chose the river bank. He was directly opposite the front of the house in a little more than ten minutes. He sat behind the guardrail next to Route 112 and watched the house.

Cotter looked at the stones in the foundation immediately in front of him and tried several to see which one was loose. The stones were part of the original foundation.

Someone had loosened one stone so a man could slip in and out of the basement without detection. It was also a convenient way to move cases of whiskey in and out of the house without the local constable or other interested parties catching on. The loosened stone had been chiseled into a shape that allowed one to spin it out of the way and back into place quickly, without help. Cotter and Janie had tried all the stones when they read the history of the house before making an offer, and found not one, but several stones that had been arranged as secret entrances to the basement. One was where Cotter lay by the foundation wall. Another allowed access to the crawl space under the wood shed from the basement, and a third opened up to the crawl space under the room beneath the dance hall.

Cotter tried several stones until one rotated inward, opening a hole in the foundation large enough for a man to fit through. Without hesitation he went into the hole, feet first, and dropped into the basement.

The only source of light was a small window along the back wall. It was more than sufficient to light up most of the basement. Cotter moved quickly along the dirt floor to the far corner near the staircase. Now, at last, he felt the advantage had truly swung in his favor. He could access the entire house without Roi knowing he was there.

Cotter looked at the digital screen. Roi was in the bathroom. Cotter could hear him flush the toilet and walk into the kitchen. Roi's heavy shoes betrayed every step. The blinker moved through the kitchen and into the living room right above Cotter's head. Roi jogged up the stairs to the second floor. Every step creaked as it accepted his weight. The blinker moved into the bedroom. Cotter began to feel the stones near the top of the foundation wall that abutted the wood shed and found one that was loose. He slid it to the side, then pushed it easily into the crawl space under the wood shed. With a little jump, he hoisted himself through the hole into the crawl space. He left the stone where it was as the hole was the only source of light.

The position of the blinker indicated Roi was still in the bedroom. Cotter crawled along the dirt floor on his belly. He was certain the trap door to the shed was under the stall that Janie had prepared for some piglets she was going to raise. He checked the screen and saw that Roi was still in the bedroom. He rolled over and lay on his back. His hands reached the underside of the floor boards. His heart pounded as he thought of Janie.

He pushed up against the trap door. Nothing happened. He pushed harder. It didn't move. Something was wrong. He and Janie had played with the door before they put the hay down for the pigs. They had opened it easily and had tried to imagine what it was like to be a part of this house's charismatic history. But it wouldn't move. It felt like it had been nailed shut.

Cotter was confused. This was his golden opportunity. He was so close to Janie he felt like exploding through the floor and grabbing her up in his arms. He tried to figure out what was wrong. Perhaps he and Downey were wrong. Maybe Janie was in the bedroom after all. But that wouldn't explain why the trap door wouldn't open.

Time seemed to stand still. Cotter was in a state of suspended reality. It was like a nightmare in which he would never see Janie again.

Cotter rolled back onto his belly and crawled back to the opening in the foundation wall. He would use the secret chase behind the staircase to move up to the second floor. From there he would climb onto the dance hall ceiling and over the rafters into the eaves over the chicken coop. That would put him up against the knee-wall in the dance hall. From there he would remove a hidden panel under the bench along the rear wall of the dance hall. This would give him access to the rooms on the second floor. If Roi had secured the door from the dance hall to the main house, as Cotter suspected, he would have to use another concealed panel that led into the third bedroom. Once he was in that room, he would have access to the main hallway and the bedroom he and Janie used, the room where he now believed Roi had Janie stashed as a hostage. Thank God for prohibition, Cotter thought.

Halfway through the hole in the foundation wall he heard loud footsteps, then the unmistakable sound of a person coming down the stairs. "Roi," Cotter said softly.

Roi hit the bottom step and opened the door to the shed. He was no more than a few feet from Cotter, the two men separated from each other by three-quarter-inch thick wooden floor-boards. Dust fell on Cotter as Roi walked into the shed. He moved directly to the stall that had the trap door. That explained it. Janie was in there. She must have been lying on the trap door.

"Pretty soon, Mrs. Cotter," a voice said. It was Rick Roi. "Your husband will be here pretty soon, I hope. That way we can get this over as quickly as possible. I want your husband to see you like this. I wonder what he'd do if he knew I could see every part of you. I bet he has fun with you, running his hand up your leg to your pussy. I bet you get off on that, too."

Janie tried to answer but her words were slurred. She was drugged. Somehow Roi had gotten to Janie and the pills Cotter had intended for Roi's consumption. If Roi slipped Janie the same dose that Cotter had intended for him, then Janie would be out of it.

Janie tried to talk again. She sounded like Cotter imagined Deputy Cain would sound if he tried to speak. Nothing came out but a string of disconnected sounds and a sickening groan.

Cotter couldn't stand it, but he had to remain cool. He tried to think. What would Downey do in this situation? Cotter asked himself. Screw Downey. What would Simeon Cotter do? That was a more germane question.

Cotter slid his body through the hole in the foundation back into the basement and moved silently up the staircase to the first floor. There was a door at the top of the stairs that opened to the living room about four feet from the door from the living room into the wood shed. He climbed the stairs slowly, keeping the creaks to a minimum. At the top of the stairs he listened for Roi. The blinker showed he was still in the shed.

Roi removed his pants and lay down next to Janie. He rolled her over on her back and looked at her naked body. He was hard as a rock and ready for her. He bent over and kissed her nipples. She tried to move away from him but she couldn't. Roi fondled her breasts and moved his hand down her abdomen to her crotch. He played with her hair as he prepared to enter her. He spread her legs and ran his hand up and down her thigh. He thought of Cotter as he inserted himself into Janie.

Suddenly the door to the shed burst open. Cotter rushed in with both hands on his .357. He pointed it at Roi. Before Roi could react Cotter heard footsteps running across the second floor hall and down the stairs. He spun around toward the door to the living room. To his amazement, Fanny Roi came through the wood shed door pointing a revolver at him.

He had no choice. Cotter unloaded three shots into Fanny Roi's chest. She flew backwards into the living room but not before she got off a round of her own. The bullet struck Cotter in the thigh and took a large chunk of flesh and bone with it as it exited his leg. Cotter went down instantly, losing his gun as he hit the floor.

Rick Roi jumped off Janie and stood up. He was unarmed but he grabbed a pitchfork leaning against the inside of the stall. He was enraged. The man who had hanged his father and just shot his mother was lying helpless on the wood shed floor just a few feet from where he stood. Roi moved toward Cotter and raised the pitch fork above his head. Then he had a change of heart. He looked at Janie and back at Cotter. Cotter was still conscious but he was immobilized. Roi walked back over to Janie and put the pitch fork down.

"I'll put you out of your misery in a few minutes, you fucking bastard," Roi said to Cotter. "But first I want you to see something." He grabbed Janie by the feet and pulled her limp, naked body into the middle of the shed where she was in full view of Cotter.

Cotter watched in horror.

Janie lay on her back no more than a few feet from Cotter. Roi straddled her chest and dropped to his knees. He reached for her head and grabbed her by the ears. He pulled her head towards his crotch, which was ready. He pressed himself against Janie's lips until they parted, then forced himself inside her mouth. He groaned and looked back at Cotter. Cotter watched every move but was frozen to the ground. He was going into shock. Roi continued his act while looking back at Cotter. When he finished, he let go of Janie's ears and her head fell back and hit the wood shed floor, making an awful thud.

Roi got up and picked up the pitch fork and moved toward Cotter. He began to raise it above his head when the trap door flew open. Downey poked his head up through the opening. His hands followed, wrapped around the handle of a pistol. "I thought I'd find you here," Downey said, and fired two shots into Rick Roi's face. Roi collapsed and fell onto Cotter. Blood oozed from his wounds and mixed with Cotter's blood on the wood shed floor. Roi was dead.

Downey rushed over to Cotter, pushed Roi off him, and realized his wound was not life threatening. He took off his belt and wrapped it around Cotter's upper thigh to stop the bleeding. He stood up and moved over to Janie. She looked awful. He stepped over Fanny Roi and went into the house to get a blanket, came back out to the wood shed and placed it over her.

Justice, he said to himself. He shook his head.

Chapter Fifty-Two

A New Life

Janie stood by Cotter's bed. She held his hand. The doctor had just told her Cotter could go home from the hospital that afternoon. Janie looked a hundred percent better than she had two days ago. Her hair was beautifully groomed and her skin glowed like a school girl's. She smiled at Cotter.

"How do you feel about coming home?" she asked him.

"Are you kidding?" Then he thought about what had happened in the wood shed. He pressed her hand in his own and looked at her soft blue eyes. He didn't know how much she remembered.

"Are you all right, honey?" she asked him.

"I'm all right", Cotter said. "How about you?"

"I'm fine, except for a mild concussion and this nasty bump on my head." She reached back and felt the spot. "He must have hit me at some point. Otherwise, I guess I was pretty lucky, huh. He could have messed me up pretty bad. In a way I feel sorry for him. He could have had his way with me, Simeon, but he didn't. He never touched me." She leaned over and kissed him. "I guess we're both pretty lucky."

Cotter smiled and said nothing. He knew he'd have to tell her what had happened at some point, but this was not the time.

"By the way," Janie said. "I have three messages for you. Reggie McHue wanted me to tell you they found a pickup truck behind Sheriff Wojohowski's barn with a damaged right front fender." She paused. "And a Mrs. Jessup called and wanted you to know her husband passed away Sunday." She looked at Cotter. "Was he a friend of yours, Simeon?"

"Her husband was the family doctor in Eden Falls back in the sixties." Cotter shifted his head on the pillow. "He was a good man." He looked into Janie's eyes. "I'm sorry to hear that."

"Mrs. Jessup also wanted me to tell you one of the last things her husband said was to be sure to thank Detective Cotter for him." Janie put the paper down and looked at Cotter. "What did you do for him, Sim?"

Cotter looked away. He seemed distant. "I'm not sure."

"There's another one, Sim." Janie took out another piece of paper. "Thomas Downey called to see how you were doing. He said he didn't wait for you to come out of surgery because he wanted to see his wife and son. He said you'd understand." She smiled. "Then he made sure I'd give you his exact words. He said you wouldn't want him to hang around anymore." She paused, leaned over and kissed Cotter lightly on the lips, then leaned back and sat straight up as before. "I wonder what he meant by that, Sim?"

"Beats me," Cotter said.

Coming soon

The Borschenschaft

by Richard Mindell

Something is wrong on the campus of Mountain State University, Vermont's largest and most prestigious college. Tucked away in the state's sparsely populated northeast kingdom, Mountain State University is being plagued by a series of unexplained student disappearances and other disturbing events.

The school's administration and local police insist there is no foul play, but Detective Simeon Cotter, of the Vermont State Police Special Investigations Unit, believes otherwise. The intrepid Cotter turns the campus upside down until he realizes he's not looking for a single kidnapper, but members of a fraternity with a most unusual agenda.

In this second entry in the Detective Simeon Cotter series, Cotter finds himself up against people and forces he can't comprehend, that is, until he realizes that Mountain State University is a hall of mirrors and a campus of false identities, where young people go for a college education, and to die.

The Reginald vanFenwick Press
Stoughton, Mass